I0637282

# INTRODUCING THE SCARLET SCRAPPER

*Leonard Apa*

*Introducing the Scarlet Scrapper*

Text copyright © 2025 **Leonard Apa**

Edited by Rod Gilley

All rights reserved.

Published in North America and Europe by Running Wild Press.
Visit Running Wild Press at www.runningwildpublishing.com.
Educators, librarians, book clubs (as well as the eternally curious),
go to www.runningwildpublishing.com.

Paperback ISBN: 978-1-963869-23-1

*To Bill and Tom, the very first members of the Lil' Scrappers Club.*

# CONTENTS

# EPISODE 1

# RISE OF THE
# SCARLET SCRAPPER

# EPISODE ONE

## The Rise of the Scarlet Scrapper

From the episode "The Secret of the Safe" in
*The Adventures of the Scarlet Scrapper*
– October 11, 1943

**MOOSE:** We got'em Al, we got'em!

**BIG AL:** I see that Moose, now let's see who's under dat mask. You cover me while I pull it up.

**F/X:** FOOTSTEPS

**BIG AL:** I'll just lean over like this and grab the bottom of the mask.
**F/X:** CLANG OF METAL FOLLOWED BY A PIPE ROLLING AWAY

**MOOSE:** What was that?

**BIG AL:** We should check it out!

**KID:** HEY! What are you doing to the Scarlet Scrapper?

**BIG AL:** Just a kid. Go get'em while I find out who's under da mask. Wait a minute, the Scrapper, he's gone.

**MOOSE:** Quit squirming, kid. Where'd the Scrapper go, Al?

**F/X:** LOUD CRACK OF WOOD FOLLOWED BY TWO THUDS

**KID:** Oof.

**SCRAPPER:** Looking for me? Now you drop that pistol and I'll take it easy on you. Your friend here will have a headache for the first few days of imprisonment, but you can still go quietly.

**BIG AL:** Forget it. You won't take me alive!

**SCRAPPER:** I beg to differ.

**F/X:** PUNCH

**SCRAPPER:** This is for spreading your filthy un-American lies!

**F/X:** PUNCH

**SCRAPPER:** This is for trying to sabotage the war effort on the home front!

**F/X:** PUNCH, PUNCH

**SCRAPPER:** And this is for being a treasonous swine!

**F/X:** PUNCH; THUD

**SCRAPPER:** If you know what's good for you, you'll stay down. I guess you don't know what's good for you!

**F/X:** PUNCH

**KID:** Wow! That was great Scrapper! Say, Scrapper why you looking at me like that. (Pause) Gee, Scrapper don't be sore with me. I just wanted to help.

**SCRAPPER:** Kid, I couldn't be sore with you if I tried. You saved my life and my secret. If those two had learned my identity, I would no longer be an effective agent of justice and all that is good. My war on the home front would have ended. Now, help me tie them up and we'll go call the cops.

**KID:** You bet, Scrapper.

**SCRAPPER:** There, that should hold them, and now let me just put my mark on them, so the police know they are not just ordinary crooks, but troublemakers working to unbalance the goals of our fine country.

**KID:** Your mark looks like two fists.

**SCRAPPER:** That's right, kid. It's so everyone knows that I will continue to fight for truth, justice and all that is good, because I'm the Scarlet Scrapper.

*End of Excerpt*

# 1

Thomas Malloy leapt down the steps of the stoop and nearly fell flat on his rear as he slipped on the ice coating the sidewalk. Managing to right himself, he headed toward the docks. He loved visiting the docks, especially when it gave him an excuse to be late for school. His father worked as a longshoreman and had forgotten his lunch pail. So, mom had asked Thomas to drop it off before going to school. Thomas felt energized. It was his favorite day of the week because just after dinner he could sit and listen to the best show ever. He would join his hero in *The Adventures of the Scarlet Scrapper*.

The Scarlet Scrapper was the greatest hero of all time. No one could come close. Sure, there were characters like Superman, and Batman, and they were swell, but they weren't real like the Scrapper. Johnny from school said the Scrapper was based on a real guy out there. Just a normal guy doing what's right. Johnny said that every adventure was a true telling of one of the Scarlet Scrapper's many missions and that was why they didn't reveal his true identity on the show. Thomas often fantasized about seeing the Scrapper in action right there on the street, or in some alley, and he wanted nothing more than to join in.

Images of him and his hero rushed through his head. What grand adventure would the Scrapper be on tonight?

Rushing down the street, Thomas's breath came out in a cloud. He and his friends sometimes made it a game to stand on the corner and pretend to smoke cigarettes mimicking the older kids. Thomas had tried a real one once, but decided pretend would be good enough.

He stepped through the open gate and waved at the watchman.

"Hiya Mr. Donovan, have you seen my pop?"

"Tommy, shouldn't you be in school."

"Yeah, dad forgot his lunch, then I'm off." Thomas held up the lunch pail. Mr. Donovan nodded like that had settled it.

"I think I saw Terry go over by warehouse nine."

"Thanks, Mr. Donovan."

"Go learn something, that way you won't be no bum like the rest of us."

"Sure thing, sir."

Warehouse nine was the last warehouse on the left. Thomas shivered as the wind whipped in from the water creating a moaning noise as it went between the planks on the dock. The warmth of his classroom began to feel like the better option, so Thomas moved faster. Grabbing the metal latch of the door, Thomas found it locked. He turned around and looked at the mostly empty pier.

A group of men gathered at one of the other warehouses and looked his way. Thomas didn't know if they were staring at him, or someone else. *Maybe they know where dad is.* Thomas started in their direction, but he heard raised voices from behind. Then the metal sheets of the warehouse wall vibrated with a clang. Thomas started to walk in that direction.

"No kid," someone yelled, but Thomas ignored them.

He made his way around the side of the warehouse. His dad stood against the wall with three men surrounding him. One man shifted back and forth on the balls of his feet. The man rubbed at his hands and blew into them, he looked like he wanted to be anywhere else in the world but there. Thomas was beginning to feel the same way.

He opened his mouth to call out but froze when the man standing in front of his father threw a punch into his stomach.

For a moment, the world froze, and Thomas felt the lunch pail fall from his grasp. The clatter of the metal pail echoed on the concrete. There was a strange whine in the air, and it took Thomas only a second to realize that it was coming from his own throat. The men, including his father, turned to look at him.

The men stood as frozen as the world seemed to be a moment ago. Thomas's father rushed toward him and grabbed his hand with a rough yank.

"Y-your lunch," Thomas said stupidly.

"Forget it." He yanked Thomas's arm harder and pulled him away from the scene, leaving the lunch pail where it had fallen.

Thomas looked back expecting to see the three men coming after them, but they just stood and watched. His eyes fell onto the pail, and for some reason it seemed really important that he didn't leave it behind. Thomas broke free of his father's grasp and ran back. He snatched the pail just as his father grabbed his arm again and lugged him away. They were silent until they were halfway back to the dock's entrance.

"What's going on? Why- why did he hit you?"

"It's nothing, kiddo, just a little misunderstandin'. Ain't nothing to worry about." His father tugged harder and quickened his pace. Thomas had a hard time keeping up.

"Where are we going?" Thomas asked.

"You're going to school."

Terry Malloy towed his son the rest of the way to the schoolhouse. Thomas climbed the steps and turned back to his father before entering the building.

The worry that had invaded his mind and welled up in him the entire silent walk to the school, was about to flow over.

"Dad," Thomas began.

His father held up a hand to stop him.

"Thomas, everything will be fine. It will be all right. I promise. Go learn to be a better man than your old man."

A warm smile spread across Terry Malloy's face, and all the worry Thomas had felt, the eruption of fear, melted away. His father had never lied to him. It would be okay. Thomas waved to his father, turned, and went into the school.

# 2

When the drink was placed on the bar, Frank Hodge looked away like the brown liquid had nothing to do with him. He watched the hustle going on behind him through the mirror of the smoky bar. The usual couple danced slowly while the jukebox played some upbeat jive that didn't go with their swaying. A rough looking gentleman sat at his corner table smoking a large cigar and sipping a gin and tonic while dealing out a hand of solitaire. A couple, two newbies Hodge had never seen before, sat in a booth, and watched with a horrified fascination as some old timer came in and left a trail of his clothing on the way to his usual booth. When he sat, he had only his pants, boots, and long johns on. Alice, the haggard waitress, was already headed over with Harold's drink. She picked up Harold's hat, scarf, sweater, and gloves on her way back to the bar.

And still, Hodge ignored his drink. He waited. Patient. Aloof. He didn't need the drink. It was just something he liked. Hell, he hadn't even ordered one, it was just brought to him by Sam. Hodge ran the back of his hand over his mouth. Still looking in the mirror, he shifted his gaze from the action behind him to his own face. Handsome, yes, but the lines at the corner of his eyes were growing more prominent. The eyes themselves were losing that sense of charming mischief they had in his youth, only to be replaced with a pinch of bitterness, and a dash of cynicism. He wore a trim pencil mustache that he worked hard to keep neat. Hodge's brown hair was slicked back with a side part. A strand had come free of its brothers and fallen in a comma above Hodge's left eyebrow. He ran a hand through his hair and glanced at the drink. Hodge bit his lower lip and started reaching for the whiskey, but he let his hand drop instead.

Sam, the young bartender, looked up from wiping the bar at the opposite end from where Hodge sat.

"Everything alright with your drink, Mr. Hodge?"

"Sure thing, Sammy boy. Just taking in the scenery." Hodge smiled.

He reached for the glass and took a sip. He wanted to swallow it all down, but just a sip for now.

Sam nodded and went back to work on the bar. Hodge rolled the glass between his hands. He took another sip, and another. The drink was gone. He ran his finger through the ring of condensation where his glass had been.

Sam grabbed the bottle of whiskey from behind the bar and headed over. He poured Hodge another drink without asking. With this one, Hodge didn't play his game. He took the glass in his hand and swallowed it down in one gulp. Sam was ready to pour again.

"Good show for us tonight, Mr. Hodge?"

"Aren't they always?" Hodge made a raspberry noise with his tongue, and Sam went away smiling.

Hodge downed his drink and stood up from the bar. He tossed money down, including a generous tip for Sam, and grabbed his coat and hat from the rack near the door.

Outside the winter air bit into the exposed skin on his face and hands. It was not a good day to forget to wear his gloves. Hodge shoved his fists deep into the pockets of his long coat and hurried down the road. He was already late, and could already hear Jimmy pacing the floor, looking at his pocket watch and asking where Hodge had been. Hodge could already see Jimmy's look of disappointment. Not anger. No, with Jimmy it was never anger.

Hodge walked the two blocks to the station. He stood outside it and looked at the raised letters spelling out 'Radio'. Taking in a deep breath through his nose, he let it out slowly and stepped inside. Removing his hat, Hodge walked down the hallway, his footsteps echoing in the otherwise empty hall. A door at the end of the corridor opened and Jimmy stuck his plump head out. He rushed down the hall toward Hodge.

"Where have you been?" Jimmy sniffed the air. "Never mind, I don't want to know."

And there it was, that look of disappointment, the slight shake of the head.

"I'm not that late, Jimmy." Hodge tried not to let the look affect him, but it always did.

"Well, you're not exactly on time either," Jimmy, always the diplomat, said. He ushered Hodge down the hall and into the small studio space.

The other actors were already waiting. Bob Bradly leaned back in a chair with a foot resting on their worktable. Billy Bradly, Bob's younger brother, stood rigid straight with a cigarette hanging from the corner of his mouth. The sound men waited in their corner with various props including multiple blank firing guns, door frames complete with doors, plastic tubs of different types of gravel and a variety of men's and women's shoes.

"What are you all waiting around for?" Hodge asked. "Are we going to do this thing?"

He picked up the paper clipped script from the table and looked over the opening page. He got the script yesterday but hadn't read a word of it. He didn't need to. It was mostly drivel anyway. Hodge stepped up to the microphone and waited. Bob and Billy took their places on the opposite side of the table from him. Jake Thompson, the show's narrator and announcer took up his mic in the corner of the room. Jake nodded and the show's theme music came over the speakers.

Jake went through the commercial for their sponsor, Noble's Sweet Puff Cereal, and then introduced the show.

They picked up where the last episode left off. A cliffhanger where the thug, played by Bob Bradly had just gotten the drop on the Scarlet Scrapper.

The theme music faded, and Dolores, the shows organ player played a slow threatening melody.

"Any last words, Scrapper?" Bob read his line in a gruff voice.

"You can't win. Justice and America will always prevail." Hodge had to control the disgust in his voice.

"Not this time, it won't. I've got my gun pointed square at your head. Prepare to die, Scrapper."

From behind Hodge there was a click, but no bang. Hodge shot a look behind him. The sound men were fiddling with the revolver.

Hodge shook his head in disgust. He snapped his fingers on the dead side of the RCA 44BX to get their attention. When they looked up at him, Hodge mimicked a punch. The effects boys scrambled.

"You should have bought American." Hodge improvised just in time for the boys to roll up a newspaper and hit it with a stick. The result, for the audience listening at home, would be that the Scarlet Scrapper had just slugged the thug holding the gun.

The rest of the show went on without a hitch, and Hodge longed for another drink. His plan for the evening was to get blotto and nothing was going to stop him.

"That was a great show guys." Jimmy wore his usual look of relief and excitement at the end of the show.

"Was it?" Hodge turned to the head sound man.

"Sorry, Frankie, you know these guns are temperamental."

"Well, it's not like you have half a dozen sitting there in front of you," Hodge shot back.

"Script called for a revolver; we use a revolver. Good save though."

"Someone has to carry this garbage." Hodge shook his head in frustration. "I'm going home."

He left the room without another word.

Jimmy caught up to him in the hallway, but Hodge didn't stop until he reached the outer door. Handing Jimmy his hat, Hodge pulled his coat on. He grabbed the hat back from Jimmy and waited. Jimmy said nothing.

"What is it, Jimmy? I don't think you chased me out here

just to help with my coat."

"Why don't you come to dinner tonight? I'll call Betty, tell her to set an extra plate. The kids would love to see you. Aggie has been asking." Jimmy used the nickname Hodge gave his youngest daughter. Hodge did not fall for the ploy.

"No can do. I have plans for the evening."

"Oh yeah? What are you getting up to?"

"Just relaxing with an old friend named Jack."

A worried look crossed Jimmy's face. "Are you okay?"

"This again?" Hodge didn't want to be annoyed with Jimmy. He tried to be patient, but sometimes his old friend's mothering just rubbed him the wrong way.

"Frank, I smell it on you. It used to be sometimes you'd come in with a little buzz, but now it's all over you all the time."

"What are you, my mother?"

"I thought I was your friend."

Guilt rushed through him. Jimmy was his oldest friend. Hell, at this point Jimmy was Hodge's only friend. But Hodge didn't relent, he had a plan to get drunk, and the guilt and bitterness would only make that goal so much easier to achieve.

"You just keep writing the crap that puts bread on all of our tables, and booze in my glass. I'll keep reading it."

Hodge winked and gave Jimmy's cheeks two quick pats and stepped back out into the bitter cold.

"Good night, pally." Hodge called over his shoulder just as the door erased Jimmy from view.

# 3

Thomas stared at the old beat-up radio, but his eyes didn't see the chips and scratches, or the cracked tuning screen of the secondhand machine. With the neighboring building taking up the view of the windows, the dim yellow light of the tuning screen was all the light the small parlor got. What he did see was an entire world unfolding in front of him as the newest episode in *The Adventures of the Scarlet Scrapper* aired. The image of his father and those goons had haunted him all day. His father had reassured him, told him it was just a misunderstanding, no big deal, but Thomas kept seeing that big fist hit his father in the stomach. Then, his father's look of surprise and pain. Throughout the school day that's the only image his mind would conjure up. If there was ever a moment for the Scrapper to appear it had been then. Now, as the Scarlet Scrapper's adventure was beginning, his mind finally relented. Now he could see the concrete walls of the warehouse, could hear the water lapping against the docks. He could smell the oil and rust of old machinery.

Most of all he saw the Scarlet Scrapper. Thomas imagined every kick, every punch, and every action done all for the greater good, done in service of the United States. The Scarlet Scrapper helped fight the war on the home front. He worked to make sure that everyone here at home was safe. He fought greedy politicians, racketeers, everyday crooks, anyone who looked to profit from the war, and even foreign spies. The Scrapper fought all injustices while our boys were overseas. And Thomas imagined himself fighting side by side with him.

From behind him, threatening to pull him from his fantasy, his parents argued. That really wasn't anything new in the Malloy house. His parents always fought over something, usually money they didn't have. Thomas tried his best to ignore the arguing, but bits and pieces kept cutting through his adventure.

His mother was yelling, "You can't be stupid here. Terry,

you can't be going up against Ready Eddie, he's too powerful. He'll…"

"But I've got to do something, it isn't right what he's doing down at the docks. He-He's strangling us down there. Making it so we can't live, can't survive."

"No. No one can…"

"Nah Evie, you listen to me, I'm going to speak to that reporter. He'll help us to…"

Thomas fought to stay with the Scrapper, but the raised voices made it difficult to follow, and the argument and the episode were blending into one. Thomas had begged his father for a radio of his own, but they couldn't afford one. Thomas had thought about stealing one, and even came up with a plan to pull off the caper. He knew he could get away with it, but he also knew that he would get in trouble with his father afterward, and even worse, he would feel terrible about taking something that wasn't his.

Resigned to sitting in the living room and trying to get the most out of the episode he could, Thomas raised the volume on the radio and concentrated harder on the show.

The show's closing music came up, and then the announcer.

"Say, Lil' Scrappers, have you ever wanted to meet the Scarlet Scrapper himself? Well, remember that after Friday night's show, the Scrapper will be hanging around our studios to meet with all his fans. So, grab your folks and head on over to the studio for this special event. Photo opportunities will be available."

"Mom! Did you hear that?" Thomas stood up from the rug. "Mom! I can meet the Scrapper. The real Scarlet Scrapper."

He headed toward the lighted doorway of the kitchen, when the apartment's door burst in with a crash and wooden splinters rained down around him. Thomas froze as two masked men with guns rushed the apartment. From the kitchen, his father darkened the doorway and behind his father stood his mother still holding the dish towel from drying the dinner dishes.

"What the hell!" Thomas's father shouted. It was more an exclamation than a question.

"You were warned." The taller of the two men aimed his gun at Terry Malloy and fired a shot.

Thomas watched his father's head snap back with an explosion of scarlet. An intense ringing clouded Thomas' ears.

Evie Malloy screamed, but Thomas could hardly hear it through the ringing in his ears. He took a step back. His mother looked from the gunmen to the darkness of the living room. Her eyes were searching, then they locked onto Thomas.

"Go!"

Thomas took another step back.

"What the fuck are you doing?" the second gunman asked. "We were just supposed to send a message."

"This will be a message for any asshole who gets bright ideas. Ready Eddie won't go down for nobody. Now do the lady and let's get out of here."

"Wh-what?"

"You heard me. Do her."

"Get out!" Evie Malloy yelled.

"Who's she talking to?" The second gunman looked into the darkness of the living room.

The taller man raised his gun again and shot. Evie stood staring toward Thomas. A spreading red blossom stained her white blouse.

*Go*. Evie mouthed, but no sound came out. Thomas took a step backward. And another.

His back bumped against something solid. He reached out, grasping at the wall, grasping for something to hold him, tether him to now. Something that would hold him up.

"So, remember kids, if you have ever wanted to meet the

Scarlet Scrapper be sure to stop by." The announcer said again, or did he imagine it? Thomas didn't know.

His hand pressed against the cold glass of the window, and still in a daze, he lifted the window in its frame. He had to get out of there. He had to go. But how could he leave her? He turned back. His mother was on her knees. Their eyes locked and his mother's mouth was open in pain, in panic, in fear. It moved again, and again she mouthed that one syllable.

*Go.*

Thomas went.

"What is she staring at?"

"There! He's going through the window."

Thomas climbed up the fire escape, his bare feet clanging on the freezing metal. The skin going numb almost at once. He continued to climb as his hands and arms grew numb too.

On the roof, Thomas ran between the pigeon coops to the edge of the building. Metal continued to clang as one or both of the gunmen chased after him. Thomas looked to the next building. He backed up a few steps and peeked over his shoulder. A black blur made its way onto the roof. Thomas knew he had two choices: he could stay there, or he could jump. The blur moved fast, and Thomas had to make up his mind faster. He looked at the roof of the opposite building. He turned toward the fast-approaching gunman and started walking toward him. Thomas sucked in a deep breath and let it out slowly. The gunman, the shorter of the two men, stuck his hand out to grab at Thomas. Just before his fingers would have clasped the shoulder of his shirt, Thomas spun on his heel and ran toward the edge of the roof.

Snow crunched with each step, and gravel on the rooftop bit into his feet. When he reached the edge, Thomas put everything he could into his jump.

He flew through the air, his legs kicking the whole time as if they could propel him farther, faster. For just a second, Thomas thought he was flying, but then the fall began, and Thomas' stomach moved into his throat.

On impact, Thomas rolled a short way and gasped for breath as the wind had been knocked out of him. He got to his knees panting. Looking over toward the roof he had just leapt from, he saw the gunman staring.

Thomas winced as he climbed to his feet. Every muscle in his body felt strained. His skin, scraped and already bruising, ached, and stung. Every step Thomas took caused shooting, burning pain, and left bloody footprints on the crushed-up seashells and snow that littered the rooftop.

Thomas flipped the gunman the bird and limped away as fast as he could.

# 4

Light from the open curtains carved through his eyelids burrowing deep into his brain, stabbing, pounding, and chiseling away at his sanity. Hodge rolled onto his back with some relief from the sunlight streaming in, but there was a pulse at his temples.

He felt a warm presence next to him and then heard a soft moan. Running a hand over the scratchy stubble of his cheeks, he searched his foggy mind for the memories to make a connection to whom it was who lay next to him. The throb in his head persisted and no memory came to mind. He looked over at the woman. Her bare shoulder peeked out from under the silk sheet. Hodge could make out the shape of her body as the sheet hugged at her hip. Her blonde hair fanned out on the pillow, the waves straightening. He leaned over her and got a good look at her face. She was attractive, mighty attractive, but Hodge could not place who she was. He looked at his surroundings. At least he was home. Home with a stranger in bed, sure, but it wasn't the first time.

When he felt safe to move, Hodge threw his legs over the side of the bed, and the woman moaned again. A flash of something came to him. A smile from across a bar. A flick of blonde hair. That blonde hair had made him think of Grace, so he invited this woman home. Apparently, she had accepted. Naked, he stood up and stretched the kinks out of his back and neck. The taste of booze and cigarettes lingered in his mouth and threatened a revolt from his stomach. He never wanted to know what an ashtray tasted like, but he was sure what he tasted in his mouth was headed in the right direction.

"Where are you going?" the woman asked.

Her voice was breathy, sleepy. Hodge looked at her. The sheet had fallen away from her breasts, exposing her to him. While Hodge knew that last night, they had both been exposed, he still felt a sort of shame wash over him, and he looked away.

"Need the bathroom, Gracie."

"Wha? Who's Gracie?"

Hodge didn't reply, and the woman in his bed didn't seem to mind. She rolled away from him, and the sound of her soft snores filled the room.

In the bathroom Hodge took a swig of Sanitas. The alcohol burned his throat and the sensitive skin on the inside of his cheeks. He gargled, swished, and spit it into the sink. He didn't dare brush yet; sticking a toothbrush down his throat would definitely tip the scales of the battle raging in his stomach. Hodge did dare two aspirin in hopes of calming the storm within his head.

In the mirror a stranger stared back at him with red rimmed eyes. He looked at his toned muscles, the scar that ran up and down most of the left side of his torso. For a second, just one second, he let his mind wander through the nightmare that had caused the scar; that had caused so much trouble in his life. Many mornings, Hodge still woke up in a sweat, his heart racing, his head throbbing, and flames dancing in the recesses of his mind. The sound of explosions, gun fire, and screaming were never far behind. That was where the hooch came in. He drank to forget. He drank because at this point, he needed it more than he liked to admit.

Hodge forced the thoughts away. The war was over. At least for him it was. Yet everywhere he looked it still taunted him. The posters everywhere: *Defend Your Country*; *Buy War Bonds*; *Victory Begins at Home*; *When you ride ALONE you ride with Hitler.* Hell, even in his own show, the Scarlet Scrapper was always pushing American propaganda. Hodge felt he was as patriotic as it came, but he did his time. He fought for his country, and how was he repaid? Months in a convalescent home and then an inability to get hired at even the most menial of jobs. And any job he did manage to find, he found it difficult to focus on or care about. If it wasn't the job, it was the boss. Usually, some sniveling brat who wore his authority on his sleeve.

Then there was Grace, who stayed by his side until she couldn't stand him any longer; until the mood swings, and the drinking became unbearable for her.

A knock at the door broke him free of his thoughts. An aching in his hands made him look down. He was gripping the edge of the vanity top so tight that his fingers had gone white. Another knock at the door.

"Hey, Frankie, there is someone at the door knocking."

*At least she knows my name.* Hodge thought as he threw on the robe hanging behind the door. He shuffled past the blonde who was wearing nothing but his sheet and a sweet smile.

Tying the robe, he made his way to the front door. He peered through the peephole, let out a sigh of exasperation, but undid the chain and opened up. Hodge walked away from the door and toward the kitchen without greeting Jimmy. He knew Jimmy would follow. Hodge poured a glass of orange juice for himself and one for Jimmy. He slid one glass across the counter and Jimmy just barely caught it.

"What can I do for you? Am I late again?" Hodge lit his

first cigarette of the day.

"I just wanted to see if you were okay. You seemed… bothered in the studio yesterday."

"That's because the show is crap, Jimmy."

"The show is a hit, and we're working on some good stories."

From the bathroom the toilet flushed, and Jimmy turned a shade of red. Hodge couldn't help but smile. Jimmy and his wife never did approve of his ways since Grace left, but Hodge had to get his kicks somehow.

"I-I'm sorry, I didn't realize you had company."

"I don't."

Jimmy looked over his shoulder as the blonde, still wrapped in just the sheet, came their way. She took a sip from Hodge's orange juice glass and smiled at Jimmy with no shame.

"Hello," she said.

"G-good morning," Jimmy looked down at his hand and then up as if he were fighting off the embarrassment he felt.

The blonde put her head on Hodge's shoulder and the sheet slipped just a little. Jimmy turned a deeper shade of red, but he seemed to be having trouble keeping his gaze off the blonde.

"Anything else, Jimmy?"

"I was just checking blonde… on. Checking on. I was just checking on you. I wanted to make sure you'd be okay for the appearance tonight."

"Appearance?"

"Yeah. After the show tonight. We are trying to sell war bonds. Remember?"

"Sure, Jimmy, I remember. And I'm fine, pally." Hodge removed himself from the blonde and placed a hand on Jimmy's shoulder. He escorted him to the door.

"Who's the girl?" Jimmy asked.

"I have no idea." Hodge opened the door, shoved Jimmy out and as the door swung closed said, "See you later, pally."

He managed to get the woman out of his apartment without ever learning her name. Hodge assumed that he had known it at the beginning of their acquaintance, but had soon forgotten, or the whiskey had erased the memory of it. It didn't matter anyway because there would always be another bird pecking at him. When she was gone, he took a shower and came out feeling like a new man. While dressing, his thoughts went back to Grace. Hodge knew he was being sentimental. He and Grace never really worked together.

Their marriage was of the whirlwind assortment. Hodge was about to be deployed. He and Jimmy were out at a party and there she was across the room. She was the most beautiful woman in the joint. Hodge, always a bold type, went up to her and struck up a conversation. He couldn't remember what they talked about now, but he remembered the feelings. He remembered how things felt at ease, things felt natural, right in the world. All his problems seemed to melt away. His nerves about going overseas vanished, if just for a little while. They had spent the night together just talking. The next day, they were at city hall and that night they made love as husband and wife. One week later, Hodge was off to war.

When he returned it was never the same.

Hodge had trouble finding work, but found the bottle more and more. Grace had become distant. Whatever spark they shared had extinguished leaving her cold toward him. Whenever he saw the pink rubbery skin on his left side, he thought about the massacre that brought him back to Grace, and he would drink.

They lasted only a few months. Frank had gone out to look for work, but his job hunting had turned to a desperate climb into a bottle. When he had come home late one night, Grace was gone.

He rode the elevator down to the lobby and stepped out into the brisk city air. The bustle of the city struck Hodge as he pulled on his leather gloves. There was a lot of traffic but no taxis in sight, so Hodge was resigned to hoofing it.

The bitter cold morning was enough to numb the pounding in his head and help him see things a little clearer. He knew that he was being sentimental over his time with Grace, but he couldn't help feeling that if they had been together at any other time in their lives, they would have made it. They could have been happy. Hell, even now, maybe it was so.

"Hey mistah, want a paper?" A kid shoved the paper in his face.

Hodge glanced at the headlines. *Russians Liquidate Last Stalingrad Pocket*. That was all he needed, more war. He pushed the paper away and kept walking without a word to the newsboy. The cold that helped to sober him up was now causing some discomfort, so Hodge kept his eyes open for a cab. After walking another block, he hailed one.

The cab pulled over. Hodge climbed in and gave the cabbie Grace's address, and they sped off down the street.

The entire ride to the apartment Hodge wondered what he would say to her. He wondered why he felt he had to see her. He knew it was not a good idea, especially after the last time he had drank too much and went for a visit. But this time would be different. This time he had enough time to come to his senses, to know what he was doing. The blonde that morning was a wake-up call. All the blondes, and he did tend to lean that way, were telling him something. None of them were Grace, but Hodge felt sure they were leading him back to her.

The car came to a stop, and Hodge paid the cab driver his fare. He still didn't know what he would say to Grace when he saw her. Probably that he loved her, but even in his vulnerable state, where nothing seemed right in the world, he knew that wasn't really true. Did he ever love Grace? He wasn't sure. He knew that he had wanted her, and even needed her before he left for the war and especially when he came back. He just didn't know how to handle it. Any of it. He couldn't get a grip on life back at home.

He couldn't rectify what he saw over there, what he felt, with being home again. How could he have survived when so many others hadn't? How could he be called a hero when he failed so many? How could he earn medals, protect his country, and then be discarded, shoved aside when he stepped foot on its ground again?

As Hodge approached the door, a doorman stepped out and smiled as he opened his mouth to greet him. But the doorman stopped. His pleasant, kind eyes looked angry and worried all at once as recognition hit him.

"No," Cliff the doorman said.

Hodge tried on his most charming smile, the one that got women all weak in the knees, and men happy to be in his company. He looked at Cliff for a moment, just silence and that smile.

"Hiya, Cliff."

"No," Cliff repeated.

"I just need to see Gracie." Hodge amped up the wattage of that smile.

"No sir. It ain't gonna happen." He paused and shook his head. "Not after last time."

"It won't be like last time. I just need to see her. I'm not soaked."

"Your eyes say otherwise. She won't see you, and I won't let you in."

"Just a little hungover, but perfectly sober. Scouts honor." Hodge held up his left hand in a three-finger salute.

"You're using the wrong hand. I don't think you were ever a scout. And the answer is no."

"Alright, you got me, but Cliff, help a fella out, I just need to see her. The least you can do is call up, can't you?"

Cliff looked him up and down before letting out a resigned breath. He walked inside and Hodge followed him. Cliff glared back at him, and Hodge stopped where he was. Cliff kept walking and picked up a phone at a small desk. Cliff looked his way as if to make sure that Hodge wasn't trying to sneak past. Then he hung up the phone and came back over.

"Sorry, Mr. Hodge, but she won't see you."

"Thanks anyway, fella. You were always one of the good ones."

Hodge stepped back out into the cold. He knew Grace wouldn't have received him well anyway and once he sobered up, he knew she wasn't the answer he was truly seeking.

# 5

Thomas climbed through the window of the abandoned Kenzie apartment two floors down from his own. His friend Pat and his family had to scatter because Pat's dad was behind on the rent and couldn't pay. Thomas had no idea where they went, and he missed his pal, but he was glad they were gone, otherwise those two men might have gotten him like they did his parents. The apartment had no heat, but it was still warmer inside, away from the wind. He was lucky enough to find an old torn sweater and gloves left behind in the family's rush to leave, but he had no winter coat, or shoes. In the bedroom that Pat used to share with his three brothers, Thomas huddled in the corner near the window. *What am I supposed to do now? Where can I go?*

Thomas was sure it wouldn't be safe to go back to his own home, those men would be long gone by now, but he just couldn't go into that space ever again. He looked around the small room and settled on the blackened doorway. His father stepped into the dead space and Thomas, lost in excitement, started to stand, but then his father's head snapped back again, and there was the eruption of blood. Thomas shook his head and his father disappeared. He couldn't go back home. His parents were still there, and he couldn't face that. Not after… His body shuddered. Hot tears sprang from his eyes and rolled down his cheeks. His chest felt like he was burning from the inside while something sat on top of him cutting off his breath.

Thomas, alone, cold, heartbroken, and scared, cried until he fell asleep.

Sunlight drifted into the room. Thomas blinked his eyes. His body betrayed him as he tried to jump to his feet. His muscles cramped, like he had a full body charlie horse. *Where am I? No one is around. I'm not home…* His groggy mind caught up. He wasn't at home because he no longer had a home. He was orphaned, and his parents were probably still lying where their bodies had fallen. Thomas closed his eyes trying to fight the tears that wanted to fall. In the darkness of his closed eyes, he saw a flash of light and his father's head snapped back. Then a second flash and his mother's white blouse blossomed a red flower that should not have been there. She told him to go, and he did. Now his parents were dead, and he was alone. He had no one. Nowhere to go.

Thomas knew he couldn't stay at the old Kenzie place. Now that it was light out, he checked around the apartment hoping to find something else he could use. Some shoes, some new socks, heavier clothes, anything, but the place was wiped clean.

He headed out the same window he had entered through and climbed down the fire escape. He dropped the five feet from the last step, pain shot up his right leg when he landed. Thomas fell down onto the dirty alleyway, the stench of garbage assaulting his nose. Climbing slowly back to his feet, he realized that he couldn't put pressure on his bad leg. He limped to the mouth of the alley and looked around. Thomas knew he had to go to the police but was half tempted to go to school for some sense of normalcy. He just wanted to pretend that nothing had happened, that his parents were okay. His dad was off to work down by the docks, and his mom was home doing whatever she did during the day. And when he got back from school, they would be okay. Thomas looked up at his apartment building. He could see the apartment's front window from the street. He knew that they were in there. He knew they were not okay.

Before he could become overcome with grief, he started to limp in the direction of the police station. The pain was no longer just in his ankle, there was a pain in his foot too, like it was being torn open bit by bit. Thomas looked down at his feet and saw the red blood contrasting severely with the white snow that covered the sidewalk. He needed shoes fast.

A sort of hush cut through the busy sidewalk and Thomas noticed the crowd for the first time. People stared at him as they walked by, but nobody stopped to see if he was okay, to see if he needed anything. Thomas wouldn't know what to say to them if they had. Was any of it even real? Maybe he was just in his bed, and this was a horrific nightmare. But he took a step and felt the pain in his ankle and feet. He knew it was all too real. He kept his eyes down and began walking again, every step a torture of pain.

Before going far, a light hand fell on his shoulder. Thomas tensed.

"Are you alright?" The woman's voice was old, kind. Thomas turned to look at her. She was short and hunched with a feathered hat that had seen better days. The old woman held her purse clutched to her chest in one hand, the other still on Thomas. "Boy, I asked if you are alright."

Her gaze locked onto his bare feet, which were turning blue with the cold. Thomas couldn't even feel them anymore.

"I-I" Thomas's teeth began to chatter violently so that he had to force them to slow, then stop. When he had composed himself, he took a deep breath and tried again, "I am c-cold. Feet hurt. H-hungry."

The woman looked around the street and shook her head. "I don't know what can be done about your feet at the moment, but let's say we get you warmed up and you can tell me your story." She wrapped an arm around Thomas and led him to the curb.

They crossed the street to a little diner. It was a converted rail dining car that maintained much of its sleekness and interior. It was empty inside except for a waitress behind the counter and a cook in all white. The smell of coffee and food at once invigorated him and made him realize he wasn't just hungry, he was starving. The old woman led Thomas to a table and helped him into a seat.

The waitress came over.

"Would you be so kind as to get my young friend here a hot cocoa, please?" The woman looked at Thomas and said, "and I think a plate of eggs would do him good."

The waitress jotted down the order on a little notepad. She smiled at the old woman and then, for the first time looked at Thomas. She froze as she looked into his eyes, noted the oversized sweater, the gloves. Then she saw his feet.

"Oh, honey." The waitress bent and took one of Thomas's bare feet into her hands. "Let me see."

Thomas let her look. She made a tsking noise and shook her head. "I'll put your order in, and then I am going to clean you up." She made one last tsking noise, gave another shake of her head and stood to go put the order in.

"Thank you," the old woman said, and turned back to Thomas, "Now, let's start with your name."

Thomas said nothing.

"And what has happened to you?"

Thomas shook his head. He didn't want to talk about it. He didn't want to think about them. Their bodies in the cold. He didn't want to…

"I can't help you if you don't tell me what has happened."

"I–" But he couldn't say more. The words would not come. Thomas opened his mouth to speak again, but the waitress came back over. She carried a white rag and a bottle of something in her hand. In her other hand was a pair of boots.

"This is going to sting," she said and dabbed the cloth on his foot. Thomas, feet still numb, only felt the barest of stinging. "You can take these boots. They look to be about your size. My son uses them when he shovels the walk. Clearly, he hasn't done that in a few days."

The waitress continued to talk and talk, but Thomas's mind drifted. He thought how his mother would respond when he told her about the waitress cleaning his feet and giving him the boots. But then, all at once it hit him again. He could not tell his mother anything. Not now. Not later. Not ever.

A bell rang and the waitress turned to the door. There was no one there. She looked back at the counter and a plate of eggs, and a steaming mug sat there.

"I'm just about done here, and then I'll get your food." She pulled wrappings from her apron and wrapped each foot. Then put the boots on and tied them good. "How does that feel?"

Thomas nodded weakly. The waitress tousled his hair and left to get the steaming food.

When she had gone, the old woman started up again. "Won't you at least tell me your name?"

Some of the frozen stiffness had left his body. He could not think of any reason not to tell the woman his name, and she was being so kind. "Thomas Malloy."

"Now, Thomas, tell me what has happened." It wasn't a demand, but she was urging him to do so.

Before Thomas could answer the waitress was back and the big plate of eggs was in front of him. Thomas looked at the plate and then back to the old woman. Her smile warm, she gave a slight nod and Thomas grabbed the fork and began shoveling the eggs into his mouth.

About halfway through the plate, another bell rang and this

time a man stood in the doorway. He stomped his feet, kicking off snow. His body gave a deep shiver, and his nose and cheeks were a bright red as if he had been out in the cold a long time. The man rubbed his hands together to warm them. Thomas barely had to look at the man to realize who he was.

"Thomas? Are you okay? What's the matter? Is it your feet?"

"M-m-m-m..."

"What? What is it?"

Thomas stood up from the booth. Something crawled up from his stomach to his throat and tried to escape his mouth, choking him. He took a step back. And another. And he was back in his apartment escaping from the men who had murdered his parents. He took another step back. And another, until he hit the wall. But the wall moved... No, not a wall. It was another door. A sliver of cold air washed over him. Thomas pushed harder and a third bell drew everyone's attention to him. The red-faced man looked at Thomas, looked away, but then shot his gaze right back to the boy.

"You—"

But Thomas did not stay to hear anything further.

# 6

Hodge sat on his usual stool. He rolled the whiskey glass back and forth in his hands as he watched the activity in the bar behind him. Same old group doing the same old things. Hodge took a slow sip of his drink. He wanted to guzzle it down and slam his glass on the bar for another. He wanted to go behind the bar and drink from every bottle. He wanted to go home, play some Glenn Miller, and forget who he was for a while.

He placed the glass down and asked for his tab.

Sam gave it to him, and Hodge paid.

"Good show for us tonight, Mr. Hodge?" Sam asked.

Hodge snorted. "Aren't they always? Why don't you stop by and get your picture taken with the Scarlet Scrapper? You can hang it up right there beside your register."

"I may just do that." Sam took Hodge's glass and began to wipe the bar.

Hodge faced the barroom patrons and smiled his brightest. "Farewell my friends, I must cut our company short this evening. A hero's work is never done." He bowed and a couple, regulars, stopped dancing and clapped before they continued to cut a rug to the wrong music.

Hodge grabbed his coat and hat from the hook by the door. Just as he opened the door a woman walked by. He caught her scent in the crisp air. Something floral, powdery. She didn't look his way, but Hodge looked her up and down. And she was headed in the right direction. He placed his hat on his head and walked behind the woman.

Peeling his gaze away from the sway of her hips, Hodge looked at his watch. He was still early, so he had time to meet the young lady before being tortured with another bad script and a train of little brats who Jimmy called fans.

The woman rounded the same corner that Hodge needed to get to the studio, and he knew luck was on his side. He took the same turn only to be confronted, not by the lady's rear, but face to face. She stood with her hands on her hips, one eyebrow raised and a look of annoyance on her face. She looked him in the eyes, and for just a second something softened there. Hodge took that as a good sign.

"Something I can help you with mister?"

Looking into her eyes, something melted inside of him too. She was a knockout. Up until that moment Grace had been the

35

most beautiful woman he had ever seen, and everyone else was just a poor placeholder, but this woman was something else. A line from Shakespeare entered his mind, '*she doth teach the torches to burn bright.*' Hodge felt sure she could light up any room she entered.

She wore a blue Victory suit over a white blouse and a matching blue felt fedora. Her light brown hair hung down to her shoulders in loose curls. Her green eyes held a mischievous glint that Hodge had a tough time deciphering. *Is she being playful? Or is she just angry?*

Hodge smoothed out his mustache with his index finger and thumb. He employed his most charming smile, the one he only unleashed for the ladies.

"I was thinking dinner and dancing on Friday night." Hodge said.

"Oh, is that *all* you were thinking?"

"Darling, I couldn't think of anything better." He held out a hand. "I'm Frank."

"And forward too." She arched an eyebrow and let his hand hang there.

"I guess I am. So, what do you say to dinner?"

"Now, *let* me be frank. You're not just forward, you're also someone who likes to follow a lady down the street and leer at her inappropriately."

"I wouldn't call it leering as much as admiring. And the lady was going in my direction."

"Well, Frank, regarding your dinner invitation, I really must decline. I'm quite busy and I don't generally take a date with lascivious men." she said, and began to turn.

"Lascivious men? You must not go on many dates then, sister."

She turned back. Any hint of humor, or softness from the

beginning of their conversation vanished from her demeanor. Hodge watched as any trace of a chance diminished. He hid the disappointment he felt and just looked at her. It used to be that he could win them over with just his smile. Somewhere along the years his charm had begun to wane, and Hodge had an idea that it had something to do with the scar on his torso, or maybe the booze. He thought back to the other night in the bar as he examined his face in the mirror. His own humor and good nature had dwindled, and with it his smile became just an ordinary thing. Then there was Grace. He had succumbed to nostalgia, and it hit him hard.

She still hadn't said anything.

*after you* gesture.

The woman just stood there, that eyebrow raised again. "Maybe you should take the lead here, mister." she said dryly. She held her own arm out mockingly ushering him past.

Hodge laughed to hide his disappointment and began walking ahead of the woman. He crossed to the next block and heard her heels clicking the whole way. He opened the station door and heard her footsteps come to a stop as well.

Hodge looked at the woman. "I'm sorry lady, I don't take dates with lascivious women."

"I don't think you take dates with any other kind," she said and stepped forward. "Now if you'll excuse me." She tried to step past him.

"What, are you a fan?" Hodge blocked the doorway.

"Excuse me?"

"The appearance isn't until after the show. You should come back then." Hodge stepped inside the studio and did not hold the door. The woman pulled the door open, and Hodge was again accompanied by the clicks of her heels.

"Lady, give it a rest. I'm sorry if we got off to a lousy start, but enough. Do you really love the show that much? Because I don't, and I'm the star."

"Frank Hodge, I could kiss you." Jimmy grinned like the Cheshire cat.

"I don't think that would be appropriate in front of the lady." Hodge pointed over his shoulder.

Jimmy adjusted his glasses and looked at the woman like he was just now seeing her. "Who's this?"

"Some fan of the show. She followed me in here. I told her the appearance wasn't until later."

"I'm not a fan, I'm here for work."

"Work?" Both Hodge and Jimmy said.

"Yes. My name is Mary Allen. I'm a reporter with the New York Daily PM Edition."

Jimmy held out a hand to shake with Mary.

"No," Hodge said. "She doesn't shake hands."

Mary Allen, raising one corner of her mouth into a smirk, looked at Hodge and shook Jimmy's hand.

"Oh, Ms. Allen." Jimmy gripped her hand with both of his and pumped them up and down with excitement. "I'm Jimmy Childers. I spoke with your editor on the phone. It's good to have you with us tonight. And I see you already met the Scarlet Scrapper himself, Frank Hodge."

"Yes, Mr. Hodge and I did have the pleasure."

Hodge noted the lack of any pleasure in her voice. If Jimmy had noticed the tension between the two, he had chosen to ignore it, but Hodge figured Jimmy was in his own world that night. The Scarlet Scrapper was Jimmy's baby. He created the character, he got him on the radio, approved the stories, and even wrote or co-wrote the scripts. He was the one who took a chance on Hodge when no one else would. Hodge didn't know if he should strangle his old friend for that or kiss his feet. Up to that point he hadn't done either, but the night was young.

"Ms. Allen, do you mind if I give you the tour while I talk a little shop with Frank?"

"No, that would be fine. And, please, call me Mary."

Her gentle smile caused a flutter in Hodge's heart. For just a moment it seemed to stop beating. He cleared his throat and felt the presence of Jimmy's hand on his back, as if he was the one who needed the tour of the studio.

"We've come up with a story." Jimmy said. Hodge felt the excitement emanating from Jimmy in waves. Whatever the boys had come up with, Jimmy was proud. "You know, for the origin. The true identity of the Scarlet Scrapper."

"I'm sorry to interrupt, but his identity has never been revealed?" Mary asked from behind them.

"No, we thought it would add a layer of mystery for a while, and then we couldn't come up with something good enough." Jimmy shrugged, and then giggled like a schoolboy. "We've got it now. You ready?" They pushed through the door into the studio.

Hodge nodded and the three of them stood in a sort of triangle near the table where Hodge was about to perform the show. The sound effects boys were getting their station set up and the other actors sat relaxing and smoking. The other men in the room started looking at Mary, and Hodge felt a moment of possessive jealousy. Jimmy broke him out of it before he could think too much about the feeling.

"The Scrapper's real name is Ace Martin. He was just an average guy with a family, right? A family man, and ex-boxer, he works hard to provide for his family. Makes sure they are taken care of and happy." Jimmy paused to see if Hodge was following. Impatient, Hodge made a *go-ahead* gesture with his hand, although he already hated the name, and wasn't too fond of the story.

"So, one night Ace is leaving a carnival with his wife, Anne, and his son Wayne when they get held up. The mugger shoots and kills Anne and Wayne before Ace can sock him one. Even though the mugger gets arrested and placed on death row,

Ace isn't done yet. He makes a vow that what happened to him will never happen to anyone else and using the blood-soaked dress of his murdered wife, he becomes the Scarlet Scrapper."

Jimmy looked at them both like he was expecting a burst of applause. Like he wanted them to hoist him up on their shoulders and parade him around. Hodge let out an exasperated breath.

"What?" Jimmy said.

"That's it?" Hodge took a cigarette out of a silver case in his jacket pocket and lit it. "That's the story?"

"What's wrong with it?" Jimmy looked petulant.

"Why, it's Batman."

Both men turned to Mary.

"Huh?"

"Well, its Batman's story, but if the father survived instead of the son." Mary said. They both looked at her in surprise. Mary shrugged. "I have a kid nephew."

"No," Jimmy said in despair. "It's the secret origin of the Scarlet Scrapper." He pouted now. Hodge placed a consoling hand on Jimmy's shoulder. With his free hand he took a drag of his cigarette.

"Pally, you even named the Scrapper's kid Wayne. Hopefully, he doesn't make a living working as a butler for a guy named Alfred."

Mary laughed and Hodge grudgingly liked the sound of it. They looked at each other again, and Mary stopped laughing. Hodge was sure she didn't want him to think that she enjoyed any part of his company. Jimmy looked deep in thought. Then triumph overtook his face.

"Yeah, but…" He held up a finger as if he had a point. Jimmy removed his glasses and pinched the bridge of his nose. "Crap. We just stole Batman's story."

"You'll come up with something," Hodge said.

"Do you have any ideas, Frank?" Jimmy pleaded.

"As a matter of fact, I do." Hodge stubbed his cigarette out into an ash tray. "Don't make him a strange visitor from another planet. We steal enough from other characters as it is."

He wasn't sure where the energy came from, whether the script was a little better on that episode than usual, or that he was performing for an audience of one. The fact that that audience happened to be an attractive woman may have played a part in the matter too. Sure, he and Mary Allen had gotten off on the wrong foot, but Hodge was never one to give up, especially when a pretty bird was involved. He read his lines with gusto, throwing the spent script pages over his shoulder rather than letting them fall to the floor like they normally did.

"How could you betray your country to work with those who would bring us to our knees?" Hodge said with a mix of hero and venom.

"Ah, can it Scrapper. I'm doin what needs doin. You can't stop progress. These krauts will come over and make us a stronger country." Michael Freeman said. He was new to the show, but the kid was holding his own.

"Enough!" Bob Bradley stepped up to the microphone. "You are wrong Herr Scarlet Scrapper. We will make your country great. We will show the world how to evolve into superior beings. We will start with you, I think. Turn on the mind warper!" Bob did a passable German accent.

The sound effect boys did their magic and the sound of an electronic hum filled the air. Hodge waited a few seconds.

"No. I must escape. Must warn everyone. Must... obey. What is thy bidding master?" Hodge stepped away from the mic. Bob let out a loud maniacal laugh and stepped backward to cause the sound to fade. The theme music rose up and after a few seconds lowered under the voice of the narrator telling all those little kiddies out there to tune in next time for the exciting conclusion of 'The Case of the Mind Meld.'

"That was a great show, Frank." Jimmy said.

"You think so?"

"Yeah, I'd say one of our best. And I have some news."

"What? Is the Scarlet Scrapper going to know what evil lurks in the hearts of men? Because the Shadow already knows. And we already stole his look."

"Look, Frank, I'm sorry about the origin. We have been working really hard. We have been trying to find some proper motivation, but... We'll get it."

"Why do these heroes always need revenge to get them going? Why can't they just want to do the right thing?" Hodge took a cigarette from his silver case and lit it. "What's the news, pally?"

"The place is packed. Almost every seat is filled and they're all here to see you, the Scarlet Scrapper."

Hodge could tell Jimmy was truly excited, and he tried for his friend, but now that the show was over, he couldn't bring himself to feel that same excitement.

"That's great, pally."

# 7

At the end of the block Thomas was stopped by a man standing in front of him. With his eyes still down, he saw a pair of legs and polished shoes. As Thomas looked up, he saw another man approaching with his hands deep in his pockets, the man from the diner. He knew who they both were. He could tell that the taller man knew who he was too, as a smirk spread at the corner of his mouth. Despite the cold, a sweat broke out on Thomas' face.

He felt the same heat burning him from the inside as he felt the night before. The same weight in his stomach, only this time more severe. *Maybe, I should just give up, let them take me. I got no one now. I got nowhere to go. What's the point of fighting?* He looked at that smug smirk and the fire inside him changed. He was scared still, horrified even, but he would not make it easy for these men. They took everything he had ever known away, and he would fight.

"Gotcha!" the man said. But Thomas was already turning to run.

Wincing with every hard step, Thomas fought through the pain in his feet and ankle; he pushed harder. From behind someone shouted. A woman screamed and Thomas just kept running. He couldn't look back. If he did, Thomas knew that would be the end. He couldn't think of the pain, of his heartbeat pounding in his chest. He couldn't think of the strain on his lungs, the shortness of breath. He could only think of escape.

"Hey, that kid stole my wallet." someone shouted.

Suddenly, there were phantom hands grabbing at him from all angles. Thomas managed to evade the hands, but one held on so tight it tore his overlarge sweater and another pulled a chunk of his hair out.

Thomas managed to break free of the crowd despite his injuries. He knew that they had slowed him up and the two men would be on him. He didn't dare look back. Turning the next corner, Thomas nearly collided with a woman carrying bags of groceries from the market up the street, he shoved past her and kept going.

"Hey," the woman said too late to be about him.

He risked a look back and saw that one of the men lay tangled with the woman on the sidewalk. The other slowed for a moment but stayed in pursuit.

*Forget the pain*, Thomas thought, pumping his arms. This was it. This was his chance to get away. He was down to one

43

pursuer, and Thomas could hear his heavy, chasing footfalls. He picked up the pace a little bit more. The footsteps grew fainter. *Forget the pain.*

Thomas knew from the footsteps that he had a good lead on the men, but could he keep up this pace? Could he keep the lead? And for how long? Up ahead Thomas had a choice to make. Left or right. But which way would lead to his salvation? He pushed harder. *Forget the pain.*

*How far behind are they?* His lungs wanted to quit, his legs began to grow weak, like rubber. His heart felt ready to explode in his chest. *How far to go?*


Thomas fell forward, his cheeks and hands dragging on the icy sidewalk bringing fresh scratches and blood. He wasn't sure if he could stand up, if he could fight any longer. Every muscle screamed at him, but his feet and ankle screamed the loudest. He shook the daze from his head and expected to be grabbed at any second. He looked back and saw the two men rushing toward him, side by side, but they were no longer running. The shorter man held a hand on his stomach and hip, wincing with every step. The taller man was gasping, taking quick shallow breaths of the frigid air.

*Get up! Ignore the pain!* Thomas's mind screamed at his body. Watching the men get closer, he climbed to his feet. The effort, in reality mere seconds, took an eternity. The men got closer and closer. And Thomas got to his feet. He saw the two men were beaten. He stuck up his middle finger in defiance.

"Get the car!" the taller of the two men said.

The shorter one, still holding onto his side began to run in the opposite direction. The taller man smiled at Thomas; his breathing was already becoming more regular. Thomas turned and ran.

When he reached the street corner, Thomas made a left and began to cross. A truck was heading toward him. *There's my chance. My only chance.* He watched the tall man, still smiling as he now took his time to get to him. Thomas reached the truck as it slowed to a stop and climbed into the bed just as the truck began to roll again. The tall man stopped his chase and watched.

Thomas looked around the truck bed. He was surrounded by crates of fruits and vegetables. The smell of it was both sweet and nauseating. Sitting next to one of the crates, and Thomas, was a small stack of two by fours. Thomas grabbed an apple from one of the crates and took a big bite out of it. Juice dribbled down his chin, but Thomas didn't care, he was getting away.

Chewing the gritty meat of the apple, Thomas watched the scene behind him.

Down the end of the block a shiny black car screamed around the corner and came to a stop next to the tall man. He climbed into the car, and they shot forward after the truck.

# 8

"How long is this going on for?" Hodge asked.

"Probably a couple of hours. There are a lot of kids out there and they all want a picture with the Scarlet Scrapper," said Jimmy.

"And we couldn't get someone else to wear the costume?"

"Frank, they know your voice. They listen to *you* on the radio two times a week. They worry every time *you* are about to meet your demise."

"You mean every episode? And then I somehow just happen to make it out okay. How many times is this guy going to walk into a trap and figure a way out, or dumb luck his way out at the last moment?"

"It's what the audience wants."

"Well, the audience are idiots."

"Should I quote that?" Mary Allen walked up from her seat in the corner of the studio. Jimmy looked appalled.

Pushing his glasses up the bridge of his squat nose, Jimmy said, "Please don't, Miss Allen. Frank is just a little cranky since we didn't come up with an origin story."

What Jimmy didn't say is that Hodge had been a little cranky for most of his time on the show. Jimmy had a vision, and Hodge respected that, but that didn't mean the show's storylines couldn't have some variety. Still, Jimmy was Hodge's oldest friend, and he had taken a shot on Hodge when no one else would, so, Hodge sucked up his annoyance and instead turned the charm on.

"We've been trying to crack that nut for a while now. It's frustrating, is all." Hodge smiled.

He took Mary by the arm and escorted her to a chair. She looked shocked by the complete turnaround in Hodge's demeanor, bothered by his touch on her arm.

"I guess that's understandable," Mary said after clearing her throat.

She took a notepad and pencil from her purse and got comfortable in the chair. Hodge took a seat across from her, and Jimmy took one next to him. Hodge glanced at the open page of Mary's notebook.

"Say, are you sure you're a real reporter? What is all that nonsense you've got written there?" Hodge asked.

"I am a real reporter, Mr. Hodge, and this is called shorthand."

"Whatever you say, sister."

Hodge and Mary locked eyes. She was smirking, but that smirk turned into a smile, and Hodge felt like it was a smile just for him. His mood began an upward swing.

"Mr. Hodge, when did you first begin working in radio?" Mary had her pencil poised to write.

"Please, call me Frank," Hodge said. "This show, *The Adventures of the Scarlet Scrapper*, is my first work in radio. I did some acting when I was younger, and then went overseas. When I got back, Jimmy came to me with the opportunity."

Hodge left out all the lousy details: his marriage to Grace; their toxic time spent together; what he experienced overseas; the divorce; his unemployment, not from a lack of trying; his drinking.

"So, you were a soldier?" Mary asked.

Hodge nodded, but he didn't like the direction the interview was taking. He didn't want to talk about the war. He didn't want to talk about his nightmares, the friends he'd lost, the blood. Suddenly his collar was strangling him. It was too tight. Hodge ran a finger around his shirt collar to loosen it.

Mary opened her mouth to ask something, but she stopped. She watched him for a moment and when she asked her next question, Hodge knew it wasn't the one she had intended on asking. And he was grateful for that.

"Do you enjoy being the voice of a hero? Being someone that little boys and girls look up to? They dress like your character and role play the episodes. How does that make you feel?"

"To be honest, horrified that these little scamps put so much faith in me. I am not a hero, and certainly shouldn't be a role model. There are times when I feel like I would rather be doing anything else in the world. Then, other times when I actually have fun. The show gives me a sort of freedom."

"What do you mean, freedom?"

Mary watched him, waiting, but Hodge didn't quite know what he meant. The answer just slipped out.

"I guess, what I mean is, the Scarlet Scrapper is not just an escape for the audience. It's an escape for me. A time where I get to be someone else. Live a different life, despite the monotony of that life." Here, he shot a glance at Jimmy.

"And the appearance tonight, who came up with the idea to use the Scarlet Scrapper's platform to sell war bonds?"

Mary continued to mark up her paper with her dashes and loops. Hodge had no idea how anyone could read it.

"That was all Jimmy. The whole show, in fact, is Jimmy's baby."

Mary turned to Jimmy and Hodge felt that sense of jealousy again that her attention was not on him. He shook the feeling off, sat back and lit another cigarette.

"What made you decide to help the war effort in this way?"

Mary waited for Jimmy to reply, but in normal Jimmy fashion he stammered, like he was shocked anyone would talk to him.

Mary nodded. She asked a few more questions about the show, about the technical side of it, but Hodge stopped paying attention to the words. He got lost in her green eyes, in the shape of her mouth, and how it moved when she talked. The curve of her lips when she said something clever, the wrinkle of her nose when she laughed, held his attention completely. It was a face that Hodge would like to see more often.

Once she finished asking her questions, there was a brief awkward silence between the three of them. Hodge continued to watch Mary, and she turned her attention back to him, as if she was reevaluating the man on the street with the man in the studio. Jimmy mumbled something and walked away. Hodge didn't know what his friend had said, but he was thankful for the time alone with the reporter.

"Will you be staying for the appearance, Ms. Allen?" Hodge asked.

"I really should write and file the story."

Mary packed her notebook and pencil into her purse.

"You don't have the full story until you've seen the crowd. Until you feel the energy." Jimmy's voice over Hodge's shoulder caused him to jump. *When the heck did he come back?* It didn't matter, Hodge was going to let it lie and let Mary go, but Jimmy, brilliant, brilliant Jimmy came back with the perfect answer to keep her there. Hodge could have kissed him, if it weren't a wildly inappropriate thing to do in front of the woman he was hoping to get a date with.

Mary thought about it for a moment, and then nodded. "You're right." She took her notebook and pencil from her bag again.

"That's great to hear. Do you mind waiting here for a few minutes while I get this guy ready?" Jimmy asked.

"No, I don't mind. May I look around the studio?"

"Of course. Come on, Frankie, wait until you see what I've got for you."

"Sure thing, pally, but go on ahead, I would like to ask Ms. Allen something."

Jimmy looked confused for a moment, but he caught up, nodded nervously, and left the room.

Hodge could tell by Mary's body language she had heard what he said to Jimmy, but he couldn't read her response to it. *Is she happy to be alone with me? Is she still angry about earlier?*

"Don't think I haven't forgotten earlier." She said, but she said it with a smile.

This helped Hodge relax. He was not in a good place earlier when he followed her. He had just come from Grace's place, and then had a few drinks. He felt looser now, more like himself.

"I do apologize for my behavior. I would love to make it up to you."

"And just how are you going to do that?" Mary asked.

"Dinner?" Hodge paused a moment, then asked, "Dinner. Say, eight o'clock at the Rose Club?"

Mary thought about it briefly and nodded.

"Then it's a date," Hodge said.

"Don't be late, Frank."

"Mary, nothing could keep me away,"

Jimmy held the door open for Hodge. They stepped into the station's small kitchen. The room had a refrigerator, a sink, a table with four chairs around it, and an old sofa shoved tight into a back corner. On the wall opposite the couch was the door to the restroom. On the table was a deep hat box with a floral print that Jimmy had probably taken from his mother's basement. Hodge decided not to comment on it.

"What are we doing in here?"

Hodge and Jimmy were alone, and Hodge had a bad feeling about the grin Jimmy wore. The door behind them clicked shut and Jimmy's grin grew even wider.

"Frank, I want you to turn around."

"There better be someone there with a big bottle and a cigarette, otherwise I don't like surprises."

Jimmy motioned with his head for Hodge to turn. He did. Hanging from the door was a black suit.

"Well?" Jimmy took the suit from the door and held it out.

"It's a suit, Jimmy. What am I supposed to be impressed about?"

"It's the costume." Hodge showed no reaction, so Jimmy went on. "For the appearance."

"It's a suit."

"Right, like the intro says, a suit the black of midnight."

"And a mask the crimson of blood. Oh God."

Hodge looked toward the box on the table, his own face took on a mask the crimson of mortification. "No."

"Come on, Frank, you haven't even seen it yet."

50

"I don't need to see it. Why the hell is he wearing a suit, anyway? With a name like the Scarlet Scrapper, shouldn't he be wearing boxing gear or something? Like a fighter?"

"The Green Hornet doesn't dress like an insect. And the Shadow doesn't dress like... well, he does kind of come off as a shadow. Regardless, it's not just the suit."

Jimmy lifted the hat box from the table and held it out to Hodge. Hodge didn't move. Jimmy nodded his head in encouragement.

Lifting the lid off the box, Hodge set it aside. Hodge gripped a tear drop crown and took out a black fedora with a deep red band. He looked into the box again.

"No." Hodge tossed the hat onto the table and stepped back like it would bite him.

"Frank, you promised."

"No."

"Reach in there and take it out."

Jimmy's voice was hushed, like they were in the company of a holy relic.

"Frank." Jimmy held the box out to him.

Hodge, jaw clamped shut, reached into the box again. The fabric was soft and smooth. He took it out and held the red balaclava up and sighed.

"It's a mask."

"I see that. Thank you." Hodge reached his hand into the mask and wiggled his fingers through the eyeholes. "And you want me to wear this?"

"Of course, who else would wear it?"

Jimmy took the mask from Hodge and walked over to the mannequin head he had seen earlier. He stretched the fabric over the top, and then put the fedora on the head and tilted it just so. He held the mask up for Hodge to see. While Hodge wouldn't admit it, the mask with the fedora tilted just right did have a menacing look.

Despite the sinister look of the mask, Hodge didn't relent.

"How about anyone else in the world can wear that garbage. I'll look ridiculous."

"But they can't, Frank. Only you can wear it. Only you are the Scarlet Scrapper."

"I'm not wearing it. I won't be made a fool in front of all these people."

"We made a promise. Remember, this is to help the war effort."

Jimmy pulled the mask from the mannequin head and handed it to Hodge.

"Maybe you've forgotten, but I already made my contribution to the war effort. I have the scars to prove it. What have you done?"

Despite the anger he felt, Hodge regretted the words. Jimmy cowered back like Hodge had hit him, and, in a way, he knew he had.

Jimmy made himself taller.

"That's not fair, and you know it. That's…" his voice trailed off.

Hodge knew he had taken it too far even before the slap of hurt had hit Jimmy's face. He knew that Jimmy had tried to enlist on more than one occasion, but Jimmy was cursed with nearsightedness and was sent away each time. He had done more things on the home front than anyone else Hodge knew.

"I know. I'm sorry, pally. I just… no, there is no excuse."

Hodge patted Jimmy on the shoulder and pulled him into a sideways hug. Jimmy's body stiffened at first, but he relaxed and touched Hodge's arm.

"It's okay. I know you're not happy with the show. I know this is more of a chore than a good time. I'm trying to make things better, but if you could just help out sometimes. Help me make the show stronger, then I think we have something really special here."

If Hodge felt bad for the low blow about Jimmy before, he felt as low as the crud you wiped off your shoe now. Jimmy had faith in the show that Hodge had never even come close to having. Where Hodge saw poor writing, and clichéd storylines, Jimmy saw promise. Hodge did it for the money, and as the show became more popular, he was bringing in some good dough, but Jimmy did it because he loved it. He loved the character. He loved to make people happy. Hodge knew that Jimmy didn't want to just help the war effort with the appearance, he wanted the Scarlet Scrapper's fans to get a kick out of meeting their hero. He wanted to make people happy.

"I'll do what I can. You know, start pitching in more. I'm gonna go change."

Hodge grabbed the costume and went into the restroom.

# 9

The truck only took him four blocks before the driver realized that Thomas was hitching a ride. In the span of those four blocks, the two men had caught up in their own car and pulled to a stop a short distance from where the truck had pulled over. The driver, an old heavyset man with a large bald spot that gleamed in the sun, bent down to talk to Thomas face to face.

"Whatcha doin on me truck?" His brogue had mixed with his New York to create an accent all its own.

Before Thomas could answer, the two men got out of their car. The taller of the two stayed by the driver's door and caught Thomas's eye. With a squint in his eye, he shook his head. Thomas opened his mouth, but the man reached into his jacket pocket. Thomas looked at the truck driver, but the driver hadn't noticed.

The thug's meaning was clear. If Thomas uttered a word of warning, or tried to communicate the danger in any way, then the old man's blood would be on his hands.

The shorter man put on an '*aw golly*' face as he approached Thomas and the truck driver. Thomas was reminded of a mime he had seen in Central Park with his father. When the mime was stuck in its box he wore a similar expression; wonder and astonishment. Though the mime played the face better.

"You gottum. Thanks."

"He was on me truck." the old man said.

"Probably tryin-ta steal from you too. The little rascal. He stole my watch and my buddy's wallet."

The short man motioned to the man by the car. He still had a hand in his jacket.

The truck driver looked at Thomas. He looked at him from head to toe. Thomas wanted to protest, to scream and shout and cry. He wanted to tell this old man everything that had really happened. Thomas wanted to tell him about his parents, about being chased, about how hungry he was, how cold, tired, and alone he felt. He wanted to rage against these men. *They should pay for what they did to my parents.* But, he didn't want the truck driver to get hurt.

"Is that your game, then?" the truck driver asked, "You're as guilty as your face is red, aren't ya?"

The only thing Thomas felt guilty of was not helping his parents somehow; not being a hero like the Scarlet Scrapper would have been. But he felt his face flush deeper. He felt the burning in his belly, the pulsing in his head. Still, he said nothing.

"Or are ya?" He knelt down and placed a hand on Thomas's shoulder. "You tell me what happened?"

Thomas opened his mouth to speak but froze when he saw the thug grasp one of the two-by-fours from the bed of the truck. The hard wood swung like a baseball bat and, for just a second, the old man's face took the shape of Thomas' father's. His head snapped back and when his neck pushed it forward again it was the old man. Blood flowed free from a gash in his forehead into his eyes.

Thomas stared as the man fell to his knees and then down into the snowy street. Thomas began to cry. The old man groaned, but didn't get up. Blood spread in the white snow, and Thomas was reminded of the blooming flower of blood on his mother's white blouse.

"Why don't you just kill me?" Thomas' voice came out in a whisper.

"Look kid, just get in the car, alright." The two-by-four fell to the road and the shorter man reached into his coat and held his hand there. "It's freezing and we ain't got time."

Thomas continued to cry. He wanted to lay next to the old man in the road and never get up. It was cold. Freezing. His parents would be...

"Freezing. I never closed the window." Thomas said.

His legs felt weak, like they would topple. Thomas didn't care. He didn't care if he never moved again. He could just fall and freeze like the old man. Like his parents.

"What?"

"I- I never closed the window. They- They're probably freezing."

Thomas pictured the lifeless bodies of his parents. He's read the stories; he's listened to them on the radio. They would be cold and stiff, like they had been put in an ice box. And he didn't close the window when he left.

"Let's go," the taller man by the car said.

"Come on, kid."

Thomas found it hard to draw breath into his lungs.

"Just grab him. We gotta get out of here."

The shorter man grabbed Thomas by the arm and pulled. Thomas was yanked off his feet. He landed on the street and looked up at the man. But it was this man's fault. He and his friend.

"Move it," the man said.

Thomas got to his feet and stared the guy down. *You caused everything. You tore my world away, took the lives of my parents, took my life too. And the old man, why did you hurt him?* Thomas pictured his parents again. His breathing grew more rapid. His heart raced. These men stole away something that Thomas would never get back. He didn't know what that was exactly, but he felt the hurt. He felt the hole in him.

Thomas continued to look into the man's eyes and something cold and hard clicked into place.

The rest of the sentence ended in a whiny squeal as Thomas's foot rocketed into the man's groin. He fell to his knees and Thomas felt some satisfaction at the hurt and shock on his face. The squeal turned into a sort of phlegmy whistle and tapered out, but above that Thomas screamed a fierce war cry that seemed to echo off the nearby buildings. He reached down for the two-by-four and hit the man in the face. He fell next to the old man, and Thomas took off down the road.

They would not get him.

# 10

*And,* he thought, *I'd rather have those little brats climbing all over this than one of my own suits.* He could see them now with their pudgy cheeks, missing or cracked teeth, dirt smudged on their grimy little faces, chocolate smeared on their hands and cheeks. The parents probably weren't in much better shape than the kids.

Grudgingly, Hodge stripped down to his boxers and sleeveless undershirt. He looked at the mask. *Maybe*, he thought, *I should give all those little creeps a shock and go out just wearing the mask.*

Hodge smoothed his mustache with his thumb and index finger and began to dress. When the last button was secure, he added the jacket and stepped in front of the mirror. The suit wasn't actually half bad. Although the jacket's sleeves were a little short, and the chest a little tight, Jimmy had made a decent approximation of his size. The suit, poor as it was, still probably cost a pretty penny. The show couldn't afford such extravagance, which left Hodge to believe that Jimmy probably paid out of his own pocket.

The mannequin head still wore his mask and fedora. Hodge picked it up and looked into the blank white eyes, and those eyes stared right back at him. Mocking him.

"Frankie," Jimmy said knocking on the door. "You almost ready?"

"Yeah, yeah. Keep your shorts on."

Hodge could see Jimmy as clearly as if he were in the toilet with him. Jimmy's pudgy cheeks would be red, perspiration would be dripping down his face, and he would be looking at the face of his grandfather's pocket watch.

He looked at the mask again, the eyes still watched him, mocked him. Hodge removed the hat and pulled the mask from the mannequin head. *Why couldn't it be a domino mask, like the Lone Ranger, or a scarf covering the mouth and nose like the Shadow? This thing will likely suffocate me.*

The red fabric was tight over the cap of his head, his nose, his cheeks, but when it hit the mouth, the fabric tapered out slightly and Hodge found that he could actually breathe quite well. Still, the heat of his breath warmed his face, and the sour of the alcohol there assaulted him. The eye holes were just large enough to not obscure his vision. Hodge looked at himself in the mirror. He guessed there was a sort of menacing appearance to him, but he figured it could go one of two ways if he were really out there on the streets fighting crime: they would either be terrified of him and run, or he'd win because whatever criminal scum he was fighting would die laughing first.

"Frank?"

"I'm coming."

Jimmy pushed off the wall he leaned against. His face lit up, and Hodge debated turning around and getting back in his own suit. Maybe finding a rock to climb under. *How do I get myself into these situations?*

"Like an idiot? Like someone who escaped from the looney bin? Completely ridiculous?"

"No, no. You look amazing. You look absolutely amazing. It's just how I pictured the Scarlet Scrapper. You've got your black suit, and red mask. Wow. This really came together."

Jimmy was excited, giddy even. He was like a big kid who was meeting his hero, and that gave Hodge a vision of what his night would entail.

"Well, it's not how I pictured him, but what do I know. The Scrapper has always been your baby."

"Seriously, this is going to be great. Those kids are just going to eat you up."

"Yeah, pally, that's what I'm afraid of. That and the germs they carry."

"Behave tonight. It's just a couple of hours," Jimmy said.

"Alright, alright. Let's get this thing moving. I've got places to be."

Through the closed door, Hodge could hear the murmur of the crowd. Little voices raised to the maximum level to yell over one another. He could picture them already. The little boys with dirt-streaked faces, wearing jeans cuffed up at the bottom like hooligans. Some would wear shirts and ties. Then there'd be the little girls in pretty little dresses. They would have ribbons tied up in their hair and be just too shy to look him in the eyes. Standing nearby would be all those good mommies and daddies who agreed to take their little ones to see their favorite radio hero the Scarlet Scrapper. They probably regretted that decision now, though it was more than his own father would have done. Hodge would have gotten a good smack on the back of the head for even asking.

"Sure."

Hodge pulled the red mask up over his mouth and nose and lit a cigarette. Jimmy reached out for the door but stopped. He turned back to Hodge and placed a hand on his shoulder.

"Thanks for doing this. I know you'd rather be anywhere else right now."

"That's true," Hodge said. "But this means something big to you, and I wouldn't miss it, Jimmy."

Jimmy looked as shocked by hearing the words as Hodge felt by saying them. Jimmy opened his mouth, but closed it fast. Hodge was sure there were tears in his friend's eyes, but he made no note or notice of it. Instead, he took a puff on his cigarette.

"You should get in there, pally, the natives sound restless."

Jimmy wiped a stray tear, took a deep breath and opened the door. There was a momentary hush, but then an explosion of screams and cheers. The event had officially started. Hodge pressed his back up against the wall as the noise from the crowd inside lowered. There was a burst of electronic feedback, and then in place of the screaming cheers was Jimmy's amplified voice. Hodge took a drag of his cigarette and listened.

"Good evening, ladies, gentlemen, and Little Scrappers. I'm glad you all came out here for this very special occasion. Tonight, with great pleasure, I will be introducing you to a hero. A man who fights for truth. He fights for justice, and he fights for all that is good. You might have heard of him, the Scarlet Scrapper!" The crowd erupted in whistles and cheers. Jimmy continued, "But that's not the only reason we're here this evening. Our country needs you. Our country needs us all to work together. I don't expect you to go overseas and fight alongside our brave men on the warfront. No, but we are facing battles right here on the home front.

"As a nation, as a community, we need to do our part to save American lives overseas. If we all do our part, we can win this war. Now, to talk more about this, I am very proud and excited to bring up our guest of honor. Ladies and gentlemen, Little Scrappers, it is with great pleasure that tonight, I am introducing the Scarlet Scrapper!"

The applause was the loudest yet. Hodge stubbed out his cigarette and let the smoke drift lazily from his nostrils. With one hand he pulled down the mask while with the other he shoved the door open.

"It's him!"

"There he is."

"Look."

As all eyes and some grubby fingers were pointed his way, Hodge adopted a somber walk and didn't acknowledge the crowded room. By the time he reached the podium on the small stage the crowd's roar shrank down to a hush. He looked up and took in the crowd. The place was packed. *Maybe there is something to this whole Scrapper thing after all*, Hodge thought.

"Good evening, Little Scrappers, and big Scrappers." There was a polite laugh. Hodge continued, "We live in a country of freedom. We live in a country where we can speak our minds, choose our own path in life, and we live in a country where we are united as one. But that freedom comes at a price. With that in mind, that unity, I'd like to suggest that we all do our part to help our soldiers who are fighting to keep those freedoms. The front that unites us all is here, on our home soil. It is the only place that men, women, and children of all races can *unite* and fight to make a difference, to do their part." Hodge was on a roll now.

"But how? How can we help, Scrapper? You might ask.

Well, let me just tell you. Instead of birthday presents, why don't you ask for a war bond instead? You can work at a local victory garden, or start your own. Grow your own, can your own. You can find and recycle aluminum to help build the planes we need to win this war. If you can sew, why not knit some clothes for our boys? Socks, scarves, gloves, everything will help. Let's do our part here, to ensure that our good soldiers can do their part over there. The Scarlet Scrapper thanks you for coming."

Hodge looked over the entire crowd. He made sure to gaze up and down each row, to make sure that everyone in the audience felt his message was for them. He threw a wave out and stepped back from the podium. Jimmy took his place. He pushed his glasses up the bridge of his nose and waited for the crowd to settle.

"Thank you all for coming." There was a tremble in his voice. "The Scarlet Scrapper will return momentarily to take photos. Remember all photo proceeds also help the war effort. Please sit tight while we get the stage set up." Jimmy placed a hand on Hodge's shoulder and escorted him back through the door.

"How'd we do?" Hodge removed his hat and mask.

"Frank, that was fantastic, you were amazing."

"I agree."

Mary Allen stepped out of the door behind them. She looked at Jimmy but smiled at Hodge.

"Ah, Ms. Allen," Jimmy said. "Did you enjoy your evening with the Scarlet Scrapper?"

"Evening's not over yet, pally." Hodge said with a smirk.

Blushing, Mary cleared her throat and said, "I've got all I need here. I'm going to head back to the paper to write this up, but I'll see you at eight."

She touched Hodge's arm, and it was like an invigorating jolt of electricity.

"Rose Club. I'll see you there." Hodge said.

Mary turned a deeper shade of red before turning to Jimmy. "It was nice to have met you, Mr. Childers."

Mary shook his hand, gave Hodge one last meaningful glance, and left with her heels clicking the whole way. Both men watched her go. When she was out of sight, Jimmy spun to face Hodge.

"What just happened there?" He turned and looked over his shoulder at the empty hallway as if Mary were still walking away. "When she came in this afternoon, I felt tension between you two, but not the sexu... not the same kind I felt right now. Before it was hostile, like you would strangle each other. And now... what happened?"

Hodge shrugged. "I've no idea, pally. Anyway, we should get moving. I have a date tonight, and I have a feeling it will be the most important date of my life."

Once again, Hodge waited in the hallway with a cigarette dangling from his mouth. Jimmy said he would peak his head out when they were ready for him to take the stage. The noise from the room was kept at an enthused murmur as the little kiddies would be lining up to sit with the Scarlet Scrapper like he was Santa Clause. As seconds ticked into minutes, Hodge began to fidget. He wanted to freshen up some before meeting Mary at eight, and the way things were moving, he'd be lucky to make it there on time. 7:30 was the latest he'd stay. He didn't care how many of the little bastards were out there.

The door to the stage finally opened and Jimmy stuck his head out. Hodge could tell by the smile that Jimmy had another surprise up his sleeve. Hodge was terrified.

"You ready, Frank?"

"As I'll ever be."

Hodge put the cigarette out and pulled down his mask. He adjusted the fedora on his head and followed Jimmy.

"Wait until you see this." Jimmy spoke over his shoulder.

Hodge stepped through the door and first noticed that most of the seats in the room were empty. The children who had sat there now lined up against three of the walls in the room creating a sort of 'U'. His gaze moved next to the stage. The podium he and Jimmy had stood behind not fifteen minutes ago had been removed. The folding chairs that sat a little behind the podium were gone too. In their place, in the direct center of the stage was a tall structure covered by a sheet, of course the sheet was red. Two men in coveralls were removing the dolly from underneath it.

"Jimmy, what is this?"

In answer, Jimmy stepped up to the structure and grabbed the sheet. He looked at Hodge and winked. Jimmy pulled the sheet away to reveal a plush, crimson chair. No. Not a chair. A throne.

"What the hell is this?" Hodge said low, so only Jimmy could hear.

"It's a surprise for you. You know we've been playing with ideas for the Scrapper's origin, we've also come up with a sort of base of operations for him."

"Please don't tell me it's in a cave full of bats, or the North Pole."

"And this chair," Jimmy ignored him, "is where the Scrapper will unwind, or contemplate his mission. We're going to introduce it next week on the show."

"Why is it a throne?"

"It's not." Jimmy offered no further explanation. "You ready?"

Without waiting for an answer, Jimmy gave Hodge a shove toward the center of the stage, toward the chair. Hodge looked back at him and grimaced, but realized Jimmy couldn't see it behind the mask.

"The Scarlet Scrapper." Jimmy shouted over the noise and gestured to Hodge.

Youthful cheers and whistles erupted anew. From his high-backed throne, Hodge threw a wave to the little kiddies waiting in line. *At least they're already lined up*, Hodge thought, *that should make this thing run smoother.*

The relief that the event was organized wore off fast. It only took fifteen minutes of children swarming him, sitting on him, talking to him, and in one rather disgusting instance, sneezing on him, before Hodge thought he would lose his mind.

These little rats were what he made his living on, but that didn't mean he had to like them, and Hodge certainly did not. What surprised Hodge most, aside from how poorly some of these parents let their kids present themselves, was that the children thought he was a real hero. They believed he could do the things he did on the radio. Like any maniac would really be out there fighting crime in a red mask. They were so convinced that they thanked him for keeping the streets safer, for helping to keep the city safe from foreign threats. It made him feel dirty. Soiled. Hodge knew one thing for certain, he was no hero. He wanted to shout it, to scream at these kids for believing such drivel. He wanted to show them the harsh reality of the world and break them free of their ignorance.

Sure, then he could let them in on the secret that Santa Clause and the Easter Bunny were made up too. Hell, he could throw the Tooth Fairy in for good measure. What an encore that would make.

Had he ever been so young and gullible? He didn't think so, but then again, he never truly had the chance to be.

The line marched on. Children of various shapes, sizes and smells came and sat on his lap. Many of these children proudly bore their *Little Scrappers*

His knee still throbbed from some chocolate-stained fat kid who had come by earlier, at least Hodge hoped it was chocolate. His head pulsed and pounded from the noise and the constant blast of light from the photographer's flashbulbs. The line was growing thin now, but Hodge's patience had worn thin long ago. Fat kid aside, things had run smoothly, but now he was growing anxious for his date with Mary. Truth be told, it was the only thing that had gotten him through the night without being arrested for wringing the neck of one of these little twerps. *Why did they make children so... icky?* And Hodge thought he'd just about lose his mind if he had to see one more proudly displayed 'Little Scrappers' badge.

A scrawny kid stepped up to him. His hair looked like it hadn't seen a comb for ages, the stuffing was coming out of his coat, and his knees were patched with dark blue squares.

"Hiya Scrapper," the boy said. "Thanks for all you do."

*Again, with this?* Hodge thought. *Why don't they understand that the Scarlet Scrapper is not real? There is no masked avenger running around the streets of the city fighting crime. Never has been, never would be.*

"Sure thing, kid." Hodge replied.

His face was hot in the mask. It hadn't been so bad at first, but with the lights, the flashbulbs, the kids climbing all over him, and his own hot breath warming the material covering his face, it was getting to be too much. His lips were beginning to chafe from having to talk to the fans.

"It's Pete, sir." The kid said in an *aw shucks* manner.

"You're welcome, Pete."

"Say Scrapper, you want to see my Little Scrappers badge? It's one of my most cherished possessions."

Hodge fought the cringe that threatened him. "I'd love to see it."

Pete looked around, like he was handing off some top-secret information. He opened his coat to reveal the badge pinned to his chest next to a large tear in the armpit of his shirt.

65

"That's real nice. Don't you go flashing that around though. We wouldn't want those rabble rousers to come after you for defending truth and justice." Hodge said, but he thought, *this must be what hell feels like.*

Pete scurried off loudly relaying everything that happened while he sat on the Scarlet Scrapper's lap to his mother, who had stood there the whole time with him. The next kid was on Hodge's lap before Pete even got off the stage. That, Hodge didn't mind. He was done with this. Any enthusiasm he may have felt, and it was never very high to begin with, had waned and diminished thirty children ago. Now he just wanted it to end.

After five more children it did.

# 11

Thomas stopped running. He didn't know how he had lasted so long. His body ached as he heaved air into his lungs. All that vanished when he saw *him* standing there. In its place was a new sort of exhaustion. He had been so tense, so worked up, so drained, and then there stood his savior and Thomas felt like he was walking through a pool of thick mud. Now, the real pain began to settle into his feet, his legs, his arms. Still, he pushed on, pushed forward, because just across the street stood his hero. Next to a door in the alley, stood the Scarlet Scrapper.

Fresh tears ran down his cheeks, and as he approached the man in the crimson mask, his lip began to quiver.

He stood there in his midnight black suit. The red mask was pulled up over his mouth and nose and a cigarette dangled from his lips. The mask slid down the bridge of the Scrapper's nose, and he adjusted it.

"Hiya, kid," the Scarlet Scrapper said.

"I thought you'd be taller," said Thomas.

"Sorry to disappoint you. Did you need something, or did you just come by to tell me how much of a disappointment I am to you?"

"No, sir, it's not that, it's just…" Thomas looked back at the mouth of the alley expecting to see the men who had been chasing him. There was no one there.

"Well, spit it out, kid. What is it?"

Thomas opened his mouth to say more, but nothing came out. He hadn't spoken the words aloud yet. He knew that once he did, then it all would be real. His parents would really be dead. Men would really be chasing him. Once he spoke the words out loud, it would no longer be a nightmare, but a reality. Thomas looked up at the Scrapper as he caught his mask and shoved it higher up on his nose again.

"Well, what is it? You need an autograph or something?"

"I…"

"Speak up, kid, it's freezing out here, and I have to get back inside. Places to go and all that."

Thomas couldn't help it. He tried to be stronger. Tried not to act like a blubbering baby, but warm tears ran down his cheeks and his body shuddered.

"Christ, what'd I say? Where are your parents?"

This started Thomas crying even harder. His knees went weak, and he began to shake before his body was racked with convulsions. He wrapped his arms around the Scarlet Scrapper and hugged him tight.

"Kid, this doesn't seem appropriate. I asked you where your parents are."

"They…"

"What is it?"

"Dead. They killed 'em."

Thomas didn't let go. He wasn't sure he could. He had been

chased for nearly twenty-four hours. He was weak, hungry, and needed some warmth. If he let go now, he would sink to the ground and never get up again. Not ever.

"Say, quit the gag, kid. That isn't funny. Where are your folks?"

Thomas let go of his hero and took a step back. He shook his head.

"N-no gag, Scrapper. Men broke into our home and shot them. They- my ma and pop are prob-probably still there."

The Scarlet Scrapper took a handkerchief from his pocket and handed it to Thomas.

"Oh Jesus, kid, why the hell did you come to me? Why didn't you go straight to the cops?"

"You're the only one who can help me, Scrapper. You're the best around. These guys don't stand a chance against you."


"Come on!" Someone shouted from out in the street cutting off the Scrapper's words.

Thomas spun on his heel as the sound of pounding footsteps approached.

"Here he is. I found him! He's in the alley and he's with some sort of whackadoo in a mask."

"They're here Scrapper!"

# 12


Hodge, without thinking, stepped between the boy and the two men who had entered the alley. The damn mask slipped down his face again with the movement. Hodge realized he should have just torn the thing off when he left the studio for a smoke, but it was too late for that now. He didn't say a word, just looked the men up and down, sizing them up, and how they moved.

The newcomers were physical foils for each other. Where one man was tall, slender, and somehow pointy, reminding Hodge of a human toothpick, the other was short and squat. The shorter of the two was heavy in muscle, and had a face like a bull who had its snout smooshed in. Hodge could feel the kid gripping the jacket of his suit tight. If something of a more physical nature began, then Hodge knew the boy would be a hindrance to his movement. He hoped it wouldn't come down to a physical altercation.

The two men walked deeper into the alley toward them. The toothpick flipped a coin and caught it as if he had gone to the George Raft School of gangsters.

"We'll be taking the boy with us. We have... business to discuss. And, if you know what's good for you, you'll just go on inside and leave us be." The bull shaped man said.

"Now, what sort of business could two fine gentlemen like yourselves have with this young boy here?"

Hodge forced the boy's hands away from his jacket and took a step toward the man. He wanted to keep the kid at as much of a distance as possible.

"That business is none of your business. Now, unless you want to pay up, then shut up." The bull pulled a switchblade from his pocket and clicked the blade open.

"Gee, I don't think I can do that. See, my old man, he was kind of a louse, but he did manage to teach me some things. One of those things was not to take any crap from bullies. And that is all you two are. Just a couple of bullies."

Hodge took another step forward, putting more distance between the two men and the kid. He also got himself in range to throw a punch as he got into a fighter's stance, his fists blocking the lower half of his face. One of the other things his father had taught him was how to fight.

"See, that's where you're wrong, mister." The toothpick removed a gun from behind his back. "We ain't just bullies."

He pointed the gun at Hodge's face as if to prove his point.

Hodge had been around guns. He had faced gunfire in the war. But, he had never stared down the barrel of a gun before. Not this close. The black hole of the muzzle was like an endless pit waiting to swallow him up. He was scared. Horrified really. Hodge just hoped that his face didn't betray the numbing, cold feeling that coursed through his body. Then he remembered that he still wore the mask of the Scarlet Scrapper, and somehow that gave him some courage.

He felt a tug on his jacket from behind. Small hands wrapped in the fabric, tightening it to his skin. It was all Hodge needed. He wasn't a hero, but he would save this boy. He took a step backward. The muzzle of the gun moved to compensate. Hodge took another step back. He felt the kid moving with him.

"My friend and I are just going to step back inside now. There is a whole room full of people waiting for photographs. Can't let the fans down."

Hodge, with Thomas, took another step backward.

The shot was an explosion, the muzzle flashed brightly in the dark alley. Hodge winced expecting pain to spread like fire from wherever the bullet had gone. But he was not hurt.

"What are you, stupid?"

The bull, his words muffled and nearly lost below the ringing in Hodge's ears, slapped the toothpick's gun hand so the gun pointed toward the ground. The bull grabbed for the gun like he was reprimanding a child and taking away his toy. And, like a child, the toothpick pulled the gun back and cradled it against his chest.

"What?" the toothpick asked. "They was tryin'ta get away." His face sagged into a sort of petulant pout.

"Jesus Christ, Tony, I want you to shoot the lady last night, and nothing, but now we're on the street and you want to shoot? Christ."

From the building a screech of metal cut off the argument.

"Frank, you out here?" Jimmy peeked his head around the door.

Hodge stepped in front of Jimmy while still covering the boy.

"I'm here, Jimmy. Just me and some pals."

The gun disappeared behind the toothpick's back.

"Oh, I've been looking all over for you. Thought I heard some kind of ruckus." Jimmy looked from the two men, to Hodge, to the boy.

"Car backfired." The bull said and took a step forward.

"Yeah, we heard it out here. Scared the daylights out of us. Didn't it boys?" Hodge asked.

Jimmy looked at everyone in turn again. "Well, we're about to wrap up in here. Did you want me to walk back with you?"

"No, Jimmy. I'm just going to finish up out here, and I'll see you inside in a few minutes." Hodge said.

Something like suspicion crossed Jimmy's face.

"I'll be there in a few minutes, pally." Hodge smiled at his friend.

Jimmy nodded and his head disappeared back into the building. Hodge wished he could have somehow warned Jimmy, cried out for help, but if he had, he would put not only himself and the boy in danger, but Jimmy as well. He knew he couldn't take the risk.

Hodge turned back to the two men and the gun was already in the toothpick's hand again. He placed a hand on the kid's chest, hoping the boy would get the message to stay put. Hodge took a step toward the men. He held his hands up flat in front of his own chest and took another step forward.

"Okay, fellas, maybe we got off on the wrong foot." He took a step. "Let's see if we can figure all this out." Another step.

"Nothing to figure out, mister. The boy is coming with us, and that's that. Now, mind your business and hand the kid over."

Hodge nodded his head and took another step forward. The bull began talking, but Hodge ignored the words. His focus was on the gun. That was the only advantage these thugs had. Hodge had sized them up. He saw how they moved, how they carried themselves, what things they paid attention to. He could see that the bull could probably handle himself a little, but wouldn't last long, and the toothpick was more of a showboat, but no real skill. Their other disadvantage was they stood too close to each other. He could use that. Hodge had been taught to throw the first punch and end it hard and fast. If he could get the gun away, he would punch first, hard and fast.

The bull was still going on. Something about owing the kid nothing, and not worth the trouble.

"You know," Hodge cut him off. "You talk too much."

With the speed of a prize-fighter, Hodge leapt into action. He threw a quick one-two combo to stun the toothpick. With a twist of his body, he followed the combo with a left hook that sent the bull down to the pavement.

Back to the toothpick, Hodge tore the gun from his hand and tossed it somewhere into the alley. The toothpick's gaze followed the gun as it clattered and skittered across the concrete. He watched the gun, but he should have watched Hodge.

Hodge threw a hard right into toothpick's side. His body moved on instinct now. Bouncing on the balls of his feet, he danced back and forth, reacting to the slightest movement. With his fists held in a defensive posture, that hardly seemed necessary, Hodge was ready to defend his face or throw another punch.

The unexpected turn of events shocked the bull and toothpick into inaction. They stared as Hodge bounced around them throwing jabs. They continued to stare when he jumped in and threw another combo that started in toothpick's midsection, and ended with an uppercut that sent him falling backward.

The bull backed up and reached into his jacket. Hodge continued to dance around, his mind racing. He knew he would not get lucky again. This time when a gun was pulled, his time would be up. His feet skittered and skipped on the rough pavement. He wound a tight circle around the bull, who followed and faced Hodge every way he turned. The bull's hand came back out of his jacket. He held a knife.

A knife was not ideal, but it wasn't a gun either. That felt like a step in the right direction. Hodge removed his suit coat while still dancing. He wrapped it around his arm, hoping the thick material would catch the knife blade if it happened to come down. He hoped it wouldn't come to that.

The bull thrust the knife point toward Hodge and Hodge jumped back. The bull lunged again, but overextended the strike and began to lose balance. Hodge swung down hard on the back of the man's head and sent him back to the dirty concrete surface.

Hodge continued his dance. His gaze swept across the alley. The bull was down, moaning and rocking slightly. The knife next to his hand. Hodge kicked the knife away and found the toothpick on his knees. Rushing over, Hodge threw a severe left hook, putting all his weight into the twist of his body. The toothpick dropped with a splash into a puddle.

The kid appeared at his side, Hodge had forgotten about the boy, but surprised himself by pulling him close. Protecting him.

"We should get out of here, kid." Hodge grabbed the kid by the hand, and they ran from the alley.

More than a few people began to look their way, whether attracted by the noise of the fight, or the sudden emergence of a man in a red mask dragging a boy from a dark alley.

Hodge straightened the suit and tie and, instinctively, he removed his hat and ran his hand over his head to smooth his hair. The stupid mask of the Scarlet Scrapper still clung there. He pulled

73

the fabric from his face, the cool air soothing his damp, irritated skin, and shoved the mask in his pocket. He replaced the hat.

"Where are we going, Scrapper?"

"Where you should have gone to begin with. The cops."

# EPISODE 2

## CALL OF THE
## SCARLET SCRAPPER

# EPISODE TWO
## The Call of the Scarlet Scrapper

From the episode "And the Kid Makes Two" in
*The Adventures of the Scarlet Scrapper*
– October 11, 1943

**MOOSE:** We got'em Al, we got'em!

**BIG AL:** I see that Moose, now let's see who's under dat mask. You cover me while I pull it up.

**F/X:** FOOTSTEPS

**BIG AL:** I'll just lean over like this and grab the bottom of the mask.
**F/X:** CLANG OF METAL FOLLOWED BY A PIPE ROLLING AWAY

**MOOSE:** What was that?

**BIG AL:** We should check it out!

**KID:** HEY! What are you doing to the Scarlet Scrapper?

**BIG AL:** Just a kid. Go get'em while I find out who's under da mask. Wait a minute, the Scrapper, he's gone.

**MOOSE:** Quit squirming, kid. Where'd the Scrapper go, Al?

**F/X:** LOUD CRACK OF WOOD FOLLOWED BY TWO THUDS

**KID:** Oof.

**SCRAPPER:** Looking for me? Now you drop that pistol and I'll take it easy on you. Your friend here will have a headache for the first few days of imprisonment, but you can still go quietly.

**BIG AL:** Forget it. You won't take me alive!

**SCRAPPER:** I beg to differ.

**F/X:** PUNCH

**SCRAPPER:** This is for spreading your filthy un-American lies!

**F/X:** PUNCH

**SCRAPPER:** This is for trying to sabotage the war effort on the home front!

**F/X:** PUNCH, PUNCH

**SCRAPPER:** And this is for being a treasonous swine!

**F/X:** PUNCH; THUD

**SCRAPPER:** If you know what's good for you, you'll stay down. I guess you don't know what's good for you!

**F/X:** PUNCH

**KID:** Wow! That was great Scrapper! Say, Scrapper why you looking at me like that. (Pause) Gee, Scrapper don't be sore with me. I just wanted to help.

**SCRAPPER:** Kid, I couldn't be sore with you if I tried. You saved my life and my secret. If those two had learned my identity, I would no longer be an effective agent of justice and all that is good. My war on the home front would have ended. Now, help me tie them up and we'll go call the cops.

**KID:** You bet, Scrapper.

**SCRAPPER:** There, that should hold them, and now let me just put my mark on them, so the police know they are not just ordinary crooks, but troublemakers working to unbalance the goals of our fine country.

**KID:** Your mark looks like two fists.

**SCRAPPER:** That's right, kid. It's so everyone knows that I will continue to fight for truth, justice and all that is good, because I'm the Scarlet Scrapper.

*End of Excerpt*

# 1

"What's your name, kid?"

Hodge tugged at the boy's arm to keep him from falling behind. He saw the boy was limping, but he knew they had to move before those men caught up.

"Thomas," The kid said, a quiver in his voice.

Hodge looked over his shoulder. The two goons weren't on their tail yet. He stopped and turned to Thomas. The boy wore an overlarge, torn sweater, and boots that looked too big for his feet. The boots were black with dirt and whatever else he picked up from the street. Hodge also noted the splotches of something brownish red that he recognized as dried blood. The same dirt and blood that was all over Thomas's boots darkened his face as well. The kid's eyes were blood shot and shell shocked. Hodge didn't know if it was Thomas's blood or from someone else, but he had seen men in the war with a similar look. The kid needed help. But Hodge knew he wasn't the one who could help him.

He flagged down an approaching cab and started for it. Looking back at Thomas, and the kid's feet, Hodge picked the boy up from the sidewalk and carried him to the cab.

"You weigh more than you look."

"My dad said I was big boned." Thomas placed his head on Hodge's shoulder.

The cab driver chomped on the largest cigar that Hodge had ever seen. He didn't say a word, just looked through the rearview mirror awaiting instructions.

"Take us to the police station."

"Which one?" The cab driver looked impatient.

"Whichever is closest." Hodge moved Thomas to the seat next to him.

"You got it, Mack."

The cabbie's voice was as gruff as his look. He scribbled something on a clipboard, and they were off. The cab took the first left and Thomas fell into Hodge. The kid stayed pressed up against him, his head falling onto Hodge's arm.

Hodge was about to ask Thomas to shift over, but the boy's eyes closed, and Hodge let it ride.

The desk sergeant eyed them suspiciously when they stepped through the door. The sergeant's eyes furrowed together like he was deep in thought. His eyebrows like two large, fuzzy caterpillars locked in battle. Hodge wrapped an arm around Thomas's shoulder and escorted him to the desk. The sergeant looked between Hodge and Thomas. His gaze swept over the boy, lingered on the blood speckled face and torn shirt. But he settled on Hodge.

"You boys look like you've seen some action."

"I'll say." Hodge looked down at Thomas. The boy's stare was vacant, it was like he wasn't there at all. "We need to speak to someone. The boy says his parents were murdered, and then two men attacked us before we came here."

"What's your name?"

"Frank Hodge."

"Relationship to the boy?"

"None. I just met him."

"And his parents were murdered you say?"

"That's what the kid says. I just met him." Hodge repeated.

"Name?"

"Is this some kind of joke? My name is Frank Hodge."

"The boy's name."

The desk sergeant spoke as if he were talking to a small child.

"Thomas… Hey kid, what's your last name?" Hodge asked.

Thomas didn't say anything but stared straight ahead.

"Thomas, what is your last name?" Hodge asked again.

When the kid still said nothing, Hodge gave him a gentle nudge.

"Malloy." The answer was automatic. No feeling or emotion.

When Hodge looked back to the desk sergeant, he caught the tail end of a strange look that crossed the officer's face. *The police know what to do with the kid, he'll be safe now.*

"Is there someone here we can speak with? I'd just as soon be done with this business." Hodge said.

"Yeah. It's late so it may take a while, but I'll make a call. You two go sit over there." The desk sergeant pointed to a row of chairs against a wall. "The boy looks like he could use a rest."

"Thank you, officer."

"Sergeant Henry."

"Thank you, sergeant."

The chairs were worn out. The wall they sat in front of had stains of crude circles from the oil of the various heads of people who had sat there over the years. Hodge eyed the stains with disgust. He could use the seat, and knew the boy needed it even more. He sat Thomas down and took the chair next to him. Hodge leaned forward so that his elbows rested on his knees. Sergeant Henry watched them as they settled in. He picked up a phone and began to dial. Then they waited.

And waited.

Every uniform that walked by perked Hodge up, but they were all false alarms. The most they got was a cursory glance from the police in the station, but no one stopped to see how they were doing, or if they needed help. The first twenty minutes went by like this. Hodge, when his mind wasn't off in the distance, would occasionally catch Sergeant Henry, with his caterpillar eyebrows, watching them. The sergeant would issue a neutral smile and begin to shift papers around on his desk. The phone rang, and the sergeant snatched it quickly. After greeting the caller with the precinct number, he spun on his chair to face the other way. Hodge couldn't hear his words, but he hoped that the call was to let them know someone would be there soon.

Hodge glanced over at Thomas. The boy had been sitting so still that Hodge had almost forgotten he was there, why they were there. Thomas looked straight ahead, his eyes at half mast, but not really closed, and something was lacking in his gaze. Hodge wished he knew how to comfort the boy. Wished he knew something he could say to make it better, but then Thomas had just lost his family in a horrific way, and Hodge knew he was not qualified to help with that. Hodge suffered his own demons; had his own scars he couldn't deal with. How was he supposed to comfort a little boy?

Ten more minutes passed, and another ten after that. After forty minutes sitting, and shifting his weight in the chairs, Hodge understood how those stains ended up on the wall as his head fell back and rested there.

Another five minutes crawled by, and the desk sergeant stood up as a younger officer walked his way. Hodge lifted his head from the wall and watched. Sergeant Henry whispered something in the young officer's ear, and they both looked toward Hodge and Thomas. The younger officer nodded like he understood, and Sergeant Henry disappeared from sight.

Hodge stood up, about to walk over to the new officer at the desk, but Sergeant Henry came back into view and waved him over. Hodge looked back at Thomas, who showed no expression, or interest in what was going on, so he left him sitting.

"What's happening?" Hodge asked.

"We're going." Sergeant Henry replied.

He held up a small pair of two-tone shoes and nodded toward Thomas. The shoes were beat up, but they would help protect Thomas's feet. "These should fit him better than the ones he has on."

Hodge took the shoes absently. "Going where? I'm not sure the kid is up to travelling."

"Mr. Hodge, I was told to bring you in, so, I'm bringing you in." Sergeant Henry headed toward the door.

Heading back to Thomas, Hodge pulled off the old, oversized shoes and replaced them with the ones provided by Sergeant Henry. Thomas winced as the shoe touched the raw skin of the foot. Hodge felt some relief that the boy could feel anything at all. He put the other shoe on and tied them. "We have to go now."

Thomas walked with a limp as they stepped out of the station. Sergeant Henry waited for them at the bottom of the stairway. He had a lit cigarette in his mouth, and his hands on his hips. His right hand resting just above the butt of his pistol. When Hodge and Thomas reached him, the man with the dueling caterpillar eyebrows turned and walked toward a squad car without a word. The car, like a two-door tank, was black with the word *Police NY* stenciled in white on the hood. On the door, also stenciled in white, was the car's precinct number.

"Let's go," Sergeant Henry said as he climbed into the driver's side door.

Hodge opened the passenger door and let Thomas climb in first.

A funny feeling washed over Hodge. *Something doesn't feel right. Where are we going? The sergeant never answered. Who wanted us brought in? And where?*

"Well, get in." Henry said.

Hodge looked at the precinct building, at the squad car,

and the man in the uniform. If this was some sort of trick, then someone had gone a long way to pull it. He looked into the questioning eyes of the sergeant and climbed into the car. As soon as the door closed the sergeant took off.

# 2

The car headed east toward the water. Aside from a radio transmission here and there, they sat in silence. Sergeant Henry kept his eyes straight on the road, and his hands firmly on the wheel. The buildings surrounding them grew more derelict. Not run down where they should be condemned, but certainly not the posh surroundings Hodge felt used to. Even the air smelled different as they crossed the tracks, like they were entering a new world. A world where Hodge wasn't quite sure of the rules. This worried him, but he trusted the police, this sort of thing was their job, after all. And the kid was more of a concern at the moment.

Thomas sat next to him, still nearly catatonic. Hodge couldn't begin to guess what was running through the kid's head. Hodge patted the kid's hand in an attempt to comfort him, but Thomas just flinched and continued to stare. And that was it, Hodge was out of tricks meant to comfort.

"Where exactly is it you're taking us, Sergeant?" Hodge asked.

There was no response at all. Sergeant Henry drove on as if he hadn't heard Hodge's question.

"I expect an answer, sir. I am a tax paying citizen, and a decorated soldier. I have rights. We came to you for help, and I demand to know where this car is going."

To his own ears, Hodge thought his voice sounded shrill, desperate, but he hoped that it came off as commanding and in charge.

Sergeant Henry, eyes still on the road, smirked, "Easy soldier. The boss told me to bring you in, and that's what I'm doing." Henry removed a cigarette from his pocket and lit it. The car continued toward the pier. "Just a quick stop first."

Hodge sat back and watched the road. He was still on edge. He still didn't like it, but he assumed it was because of the night he was having. First those rotten kids at the appearance, and then Thomas and the fight in the alley. It was all too much, and Hodge needed a drink. Desperately. That's when Mary Allen popped in his head. He looked at his watch. It was well after eight. She would have gone home by now, probably hating him. She probably wouldn't talk to him, let him explain what happened. It all sounded like something out of the show anyway. Hodge knew he couldn't think about that now. He would get Thomas settled, and then figure it out from there. He rested his head on the back of the seat.

Train cars sat on unused tracks for what seemed like miles. Above it all, crane arms reached for the sky like the skeletons of some long dead race of giants. Up ahead there were three buildings that docked trade ships when they were not in use. The buildings were set together creating a crude U shape. The building at the center had the words GATES of NY SHIPPING in large, mostly faded letters. The cruiser continued toward the buildings and slowed to a stop.

Three patrol cars sat parked in a way as if to mimic the large U of the buildings. Three uniformed officers leaned against the patrol car at the center. The officers were younger than the sergeant, and stronger looking. This did nothing to appease Hodge's sense that something was wrong.

"Why are we here?" Hodge asked. "Who are these men?"

Sergeant Henry stepped out of the car without a word. He started to close the door, but stuck his head back in. "Wait here."

The sergeant straightened up and headed over to the younger officers.

"I'm not sure what's happening, kid. I figured he was taking us to a different precinct. Someplace closer to where you live. Is this near where you live? Kid?" Hodge looked at Thomas, but Thomas stared forward. "I need you with me, Thomas. Do you live around here?"

There was still no response from the boy.

"Damn it, Thomas, I know you're hurt. I know you feel lost, but I need some kind of response. Something's not right here, and I need to know what to do. Why would he take us here? Who are these other fellas? Do. You. Live. Around. Here?"

"Close by." His voice was low, and the chill in the tone sent a shiver through Hodge that had nothing to do with the cold outside.

"I don't like this. We need to get out of here. I'm going to scoot onto the other side of you, kid. We're taking this car."

Hodge looked at the ignition, but there was no key. He looked back through the windshield; the police officers were still talking. He drummed his fingers on the dashboard.

"Okay, no key means new plan. I'm going to go out there and talk to them. You stay here."

Thomas didn't respond. Hodge climbed out of the car. When he slammed the door, Sergeant Henry turned his way.

Hodge stepped in front of the car so that the hood was at his rear.

"I told you to stay in the car." Sergeant Henry said.

"The kid is cold, any chance you could toss me the keys so we can put the heat on?"

Sergeant Henry started back in Hodge's direction and the three other officers began to fan out and head over as well. Hodge did not like where this was headed.

"I told you to stay in the car. For a soldier, you don't listen and that is bad for you. See, Mr. Salazar just wants the Malloy kid, he said we can do what we want with you. He may have implied that we get rid of you. I didn't want to do it that way. The boys do. But, I figure we could talk some sense into you. From what you tell me, you don't know this kid. You just met him tonight, and that means you don't owe him nothing. So, I say we come to a sort of compromise. An understanding."

"What sort of compromise are you talking about?"

Hodge looked over his shoulder at the boy, then back at Sergeant Henry and the other officers.

"Walk away. Go on and get out of here. Forget everything that has happened tonight and just get on with your life. Easiest way out for you."

"And the boy?"

"The boy is not your concern. Boss needs him."

"What for?"

"Not your place, or mine to ask questions. I just do as I'm told, for a hefty price."

Sergeant Henry looked at the men surrounding him with a big grin. His officers joined in Henry's amusement, but Hodge felt torn up inside.

He looked over his shoulder at the kid again. *His name is Thomas. Thomas Malloy, who had just suffered the greatest loss a child could go through. His name is Thomas Malloy. And he can't defend himself. Can't fight back. I can't leave him all alone.*

"Well, what do you say? Are you going to make the smart choice here?"

"I…"

Hodge took a step back and bumped into the hood of the car. He closed his eyes and took in a deep breath. He felt his body begin to tighten; his mind came into focus. Before he knew it, his body knew his decision. He wouldn't abandon the kid.

"I need an answer. It's cold out and I should be home with the wife. These boys have families waiting as well. You going to make the smart choice?"

Hodge laughed, more to himself, than anything. "I've never

been known to make the smart choice, Sergeant."

Hodge had a terrible feeling of familiarity with the scene unfolding in front of him. It was like one of the horrible episodes of his radio show was coming to life around him. The poorly scripted dialogue of the corrupt goons, the inescapable situation. In this case four men with guns and billy-clubs against one unarmed man and a boy. The only weapon Hodge had at his disposal was the mask. Unlike the Scarlet Scrapper, Hodge would have no coincidental fix. No random act of God, no distractions to give him the edge he needed to beat the bad guys.

He didn't know what he was thinking, or maybe that was the problem, he wasn't thinking. Hodge reached into the pocket of his jacket and pulled out the red balaclava mask. He looked at it before pulling it over his head. With the mask concealing his face, somehow, he felt stronger, braver, more confident.

Hodge stepped forward.

The four cops stared at him. They looked between one another in confusion. One of the younger men laughed, and then they all laughed. Hodge got into a boxer's stance.

"Hey, I know who that is. That's the Scarlet Scrapper. With a suit the black of night, and a mask the scarlet of blood, it's the Scarlet Scrapper." The officer said this last bit in a deep, mysterious voice. He laughed, reached into his pocket, and took out a piece of Dubble Bubble. His friends looked at him, and the young officer tossed the gum into his mouth and shrugged. "What? My kids listen to the show. It's not that bad."

"It's the crimson of blood," Hodge corrected. "And you and your children have terrible taste."

"Enough of this," Sergeant Henry said. "Rourke, O'Malley grab his arms. Dodd, you get ready to club him."

Rourke, the gum chewer started over with the tallest of the bunch. The third officer, Dodd, pulled out his wooden baton and smacked his hand a couple of times before following Rourke and O'Malley.

Hodge felt his body loosen. The built-up tension released, and he chose the man in the lead, Rourke, to focus on. Hodge was fluid, he was quick. Instinct kicked in, and he heard the voice of his father screaming in his head.

*Jab to the body!*

Hodge shot a fist down like a knife into Rourke's stomach. The young officer froze, sucked in a great breath, then coughed and gasped as the gum he chewed lodged in his throat. The other two officers stopped and watched. They were close now, but Dodd, with his baton drawn, was closer.

*One! Two!* The voice of his father instructed.

Hodge threw a jab and followed it with a right cross. Dodd stumbled backward but remained on his feet. Now, Hodge turned his attention to O'Malley, who rushed at him.

O'Malley threw a punch. Hodge slipped it.

*One, Two, Duck, Two!* His father called in the recesses of his mind.

Hodge jabbed, threw a cross, ducked as O'Malley threw another punch, and Hodge followed with a second cross. All his punches landed, and Hodge followed with a hook that sent O'Malley down. It had been a long while since Hodge had boxed, but it felt good. It felt natural. His instincts were up. He could take on…

He heard the trunk of wood before the pain spread over his head. The pulsing heat caused his vision to blur, Hodge grabbed the top of his head, and retreated as much as he could. Hodge, feeling dizzy now, turned to see Dodd grinning with his club ready to bat Hodge's head clean off.

Dodd raised the baton in a striking motion.

*Roll!* His father screamed.

Hodge rolled under the baton, crossed to the outside of Dodd's footing, and came up throwing two hard punches to the officer's body.

# 3

Thomas came awake when the fighting began. He hadn't been sleeping, but he knew he wasn't fully conscious either. The drive to the warehouse was a blur. Streetlights, other cars, buildings, and people fogged his mind as they drove in near silence. He remembered the Scrapper asking him questions, giving him instructions, even nudging him for a response, but Thomas couldn't recall a word of them. The car had come to a stop and the Scrapper was gone from his side. Then, a flash of red in the patrol car's headlights, and, just like when he heard him on the radio, the Scarlet Scrapper took over. Thomas sat up, his chin rested on the dashboard, wide eyes took in the punching, the dodging, and the ducking. How did the Scarlet Scrapper move like that? His motions were a blur as he fought off the police. It was just like something out of the adventures he listened to. Only now, Thomas could touch the Scrapper, and it wasn't only confined to his imagination. He didn't even know the Scarlet Scrapper's real name, but the man was everything Thomas had dreamed he would be.

With the dodge of a punch, the Scrapper sprung up and knocked one of the last of the policemen down with a solid uppercut. The only remaining cop was the desk sergeant with the big eyebrows. The Scrapper bent and picked something up from the ground. Sergeant Henry backed up and issued a warning, but the Scarlet Scrapper kept pushing forward.

Thomas got out of the car in time to see the older officer take out his revolver. When the gun hand started to point at the crimson faced hero, the Scrapper closed the distance and beat the gun down with the fallen baton he had picked up from the ground. The gun fell with a metallic clatter and Sergeant Henry gripped his injured hand with his other. The officer continued to back up.

"It's time you gave me some answers." The Scarlet Scrapper grabbed the desk sergeant's tie into his fist and raised the baton, ready to strike. "Now!"

Sergeant Henry did not answer. He looked past the Scrapper at Thomas. He pointed in Thomas's direction with his chin. "It's not about you. It's about the kid."

"I gathered that. Tell me what the hell is going on!"

"The kid's father was a rat. He was going to squeal to some reporter and try to bring down the business of a very dangerous man. Terry and Evie Malloy got it. But their kid didn't." Sergeant Henry looked at Thomas like this was all his fault. He felt his cheeks go flush. Fire lit up in his stomach and the acid there boiled up his throat.

"How did you get involved?" The Scrapper asked.

"Eddie Salazar." Sergeant Henry gave no further explanation.

But the words struck Thomas's heart as he recalled the argument his parents were having right before they were murdered.

*Ter, you can't be going up against Ready Eddie, he's too powerful*, Evie Malloy had said.

*He's strangling us down there. Making it so we can't live, can't survive. I'm going to speak to that reporter. He'll help us*, Terry Malloy had replied.

"Ready Eddie," Thomas said. The Scarlet Scrapper looked down at him.

"You know what he's talking about?"

"My parents were fighting. My dad thought a reporter could help. They hurt my dad, and then they killed him."

There was no helping them now, this Thomas knew, but maybe there would be some justice for them.

"What reporter?" The Scarlet Scrapper was still looking at him. Thomas did not answer. "Come on, kid. What's this reporter's name?"

Thomas shook his head, and the Scrapper turned his attention back to the police officer. Sergeant Henry was still cradling his hand.

"Who's the reporter?"

"I- I don't know. Look, just walk away. Me and the boys will leave you alone. That's all it will take. Just walk away. Take the kid. This isn't worth the money."

"Who pays you? What's his name?" The Scarlet Scrapper raised the baton as if he were going to crash it down on Sergeant Henry's head.

"Edward Salazar. He runs the docks, and he doesn't take kindly to anyone trying to upset that power."

"I'll say." The Scrapper turned to Thomas. "Kid, you know this guy?"

"No, Scrapper. I mean… maybe. I only heard his name. Ready Eddie. But I think I may have played with his son."

"Something sounds familiar there. Henry, where can I find this Salazar?"

"He has an office on the docks. Not far from here."

"Where is it?" The Scarlet Scrapper demanded.

But Thomas already knew the answer. Thomas had been there before. He had visited, even been inside the office.

"Where?" The Scrapper asked again.

Sergeant Henry was not the one to answer though, Thomas was.

"Home," he said.

# 4

Hodge took the keys to the cruiser from Sergeant Henry with the hopes of putting some distance between he and Thomas and the cops. The three fallen officers were beginning to get their bearings when Hodge and Thomas bolted in the cruiser. By the time the tires peeled away, kicking up gravel, two of the officers chased on foot. Hodge heard Henry calling them off, and in the rearview they stopped running. One of the young officers, Dodd, kicked at the gravel and watched the car speed off. In the end he went back to the other cops and Sergeant Henry.

Hodge didn't dare keep the car for any longer than needed, because despite Sergeant Henry's assurance that Hodge could walk away, he doubted the truthfulness of the statement. Especially with Dodd's death stare. He drove as far from the run-down warehouses as he thought safe, to a point where the city felt like a city again. The bustle of cars and people and activity, even so late at night, was everywhere, showing Hodge that he truly lived in the city that never sleeps.

After ditching the car in an out of the way alley, Hodge and Thomas grabbed a cab. Hodge gave the cab driver his address and they sat in silence until they reached his building. He had considered going back to the radio station to ask Jimmy for help. Hodge had no idea what to do with a kid or what to do at all, but he didn't want to get Jimmy caught up in… whatever this was. Hell, Hodge didn't want to be caught up in it, but he was in it now. Deep. Besides, Jimmy was probably home already, and Hodge had no desire to feel Betty's judging stare.

They climbed out of the cab and Hodge walked toward the building, blocking Thomas from viewing the lobby. When he saw the coast was clear, he rushed Thomas to the stairwell and shoved him through the door.

"Move quick, kid," Hodge said.

"What floor are we going to? Why don't we take the elevator, Scrapper?" Thomas looked up at the stairs looming in front of them.

"I don't want any of my neighbors to see you."

"Why not?"

"I'm not really sure what the rules are here, kid. My

neighbors know I don't have children. This could look bad."

"Why could it look bad?" Thomas looked up at Hodge.

"I don't need them to think… just move, it's for your own protection."

*And mine.*

The clomping of their footsteps echoed through the stairwell as they ascended the seventy-two steps to Hodge's floor. Hodge, who kept in shape, never took the stairs to his apartment before, and he hoped to never have to again. Seventy-two stairs, a number he had not known before then, was not much, but when he had been running with no food or drink for so many hours it was a rough climb. Add to that the physical exertion of two separate fights, well he might as well have taken the steps to the top of the Empire State Building. He needed a drink.

They managed to get inside Hodge's door without anyone noticing. Hodge turned the lock and let out the breath he hadn't realized he was holding. Thomas stood near the door. He looked unsure of what to do. Hodge wasn't sure either. *I tried the police, which seemed like the right move, but they were on this Salazar guy's payroll. Who can you trust in authority if the police are out of the equation?* Hodge didn't know, and didn't know what to do next. He looked at Thomas. *What's this kid gotten me into?*

"Scrapper?"

"It's Frank, kid. Call me Frank." Hodge hadn't meant so much venom behind the words, and the kid recoiled like he had been slapped. Hodge closed his eyes and took in a breath trying to calm himself. When he spoke again, his voice had softened. "The Scarlet Scrapper is a character, you understand that, right? I'm a real person. I don't wear a mask or fight crime."

"But you did. You put the mask on tonight, and you whooped them guys." Thomas had hopeful eyes, and Hodge knew the kid had him there.

"Yeah. I did. Even still, call me Frank."

"Frank." Thomas said the name like he was tasting it. "What do we do now?"

"I don't know, but I need a drink before I can come up with anything."

Hodge walked over to a small wooden table in the corner of the living room. He picked up a crystal decanter of whiskey and poured himself the drink he had been craving. He swallowed it down and poured a second one. Hodge sat on the couch. The kid hesitated, but after a moment sat next to Hodge.

Hodge kicked his shoes off and placed them on the coffee table. The kid, in a near perfect imitation of the gesture, did the same. Hodge placed his hands behind his head and leaned it back against the cushion. Again, Thomas imitated him. Hodge smirked. *The kid will be alright.*

"Scrapper… uh, Frank, do you have anything to eat? I'm awful hungry."

"Let's see what we can do for you, kid."

Hodge stood and went into the kitchen. The kid followed.

Hodge opened the refrigerator and called over his shoulder, "You like eggs?"

Thomas nodded.

"Good. That's about all there is."

Hodge took the eggs out, grabbed a bowl and a whisk and got to work. In under ten minutes they were leaning over the counter eating cheese omelets.

Hodge ran through everything that had happened since he met Thomas that night. There were the goons in the alley, the run to the police, the fight with the police, and conversation with Sergeant Henry. Sergeant Henry told him that a man named Salazar was after the kid, and now in turn after Hodge. Thomas had gotten in trouble because of his old man who was going to snitch on this Salazar to a reporter.

"Thomas, are you sure you don't know who your father was going to talk to?"

"I don't know any reporters, Scrapper."

Hodge didn't bother correcting the kid about his name. No, he focused on what Thomas had said. Thomas didn't know any reporters, but "I do."

"What?" Thomas asked through a mouthful of food.

"I know a reporter." Hodge's stomach twisted at the thought of Mary Allen waiting for him outside the Rose Club for a date he had never made it too. "But the question is, will she still want to know me?"

He debated taking Thomas with him to find Mary Allen. If nothing else, the kid would give credence to his story, help his defense, but Hodge decided against it. There were too many unknown factors. One of those unknowns was who was out there searching for them? If it could be the police, then it stood to reason that it could be anyone on the street, and they would be looking for a man and a child. Still, Hodge didn't think he could leave Thomas at his apartment by himself, and he did not want to involve Jimmy. The thought of putting his friend and his family at risk was too much for Hodge to bear. While still a risk, Hodge decided to take the kid to the one place where no one would think to find him.

Their footsteps crunched on the salted entryway. Hodge reached for the door, but it opened from the inside as Cliff hustled out with a smile of greeting. The smile made a quick retreat as it usually did when Cliff realized it was Hodge at the door. A scowl took the place of the smile and Hodge could imagine the scolding that was coming, but then Cliff looked down at the shivering boy next to Hodge, and something softened in his face.

Cliff ushered them inside, but blocked their path forward. He crossed his arms over his chest and looked between Hodge and Thomas.

"What's this? Are you going to tell Ms. Grace that you fathered her child?" He looked down at Thomas. "I don't know how he wrangled you into his affairs, but boy, I would run if I were you."

Thomas didn't say anything, but moved closer to Hodge as if the thought of running from him was the last thing on his mind. And, after all the kid had been through, Hodge guessed it was probably pretty close to it.

"I'm kind of his hero." Hodge tried on a little of his charm. Cliff was still immune to it. "Listen, pally, this isn't about me and Grace, it's about the kid. Thomas here is in a bit of a bind, and I am trying to help him out. But, in order to do so, I need a little favor. I had nowhere else to turn."

Cliff looked down at Thomas again. The boy seemed to have shrunk in on himself while trying to shrink inside of Hodge. Hodge nudged Thomas a little more in view. He wanted Cliff to see how pathetic the kid looked. Really work the pity factor. Hodge watched as Cliff took in the kid's appearance. The stretched shirt, the too large shoes, the scrapes and spatters of mud and blood. The kid cut a pretty sad image.

"I ain't saying yes, but what do you want?"

"The kid needs a place to hide out for a while so I can go figure out how to help him."

Cliff's gaze changed. The pity that had been there was replaced by suspicion. "A bad sort, is he?"

Hodge shook his head. "No. Nothing like that. The kid is in a bit of a bind through no fault of his own." Hodge stepped away from Thomas and told him to stay put. He took Cliff by the shoulder and led him closer to the desk where Cliff could call Grace's apartment. "I need you to call Grace. I need her to look after Thomas."

"What's his story, then?" Cliff locked onto the boy.

"He's all mixed up. He thinks I'm a hero." Hodge said and Cliff scoffed. Hodge decided not to mention it. He scoffed at the notion too. "What I mean is, Thomas thinks I'm really the Scarlet Scrapper. Someone shot his parents in front of him and now they are looking to finish the job."

Hodge looked back at Thomas. The kid was staring blankly at them, but Hodge wasn't sure if he was seeing anything.

"You should be going to the police, not bringing that trouble here," Cliff said.

"We tried that. It didn't work out for any of us." Hodge didn't elaborate, but continued, "Look. It should be just a few hours. I need to go see someone, and I don't think it's safe to take the kid. I just need to stash him for a bit. Cliff, I know we haven't always seen eye to eye, but it's not me you'll be helping, it's Thomas."

The inner turmoil continued to wage a war across Cliff's face, and Hodge knew that the man was fighting between his job and his morals. He imagined the thoughts running through the doorman's head. On the one side, Grace told him that Frank Hodge was not to be admitted, ever. On the other hand, a boy's life was in danger, so it wasn't really about Hodge.

Hodge didn't want to push it, but he felt a gentle nudge was in order. He said, "Cliff, the kid just lost both his parents. I am trying to help him survive. I need your help to do that. *He* needs your help."

"Let me call up."

Without having to be asked, Hodge went back to Thomas. He surprised himself by wrapping his arm around the boy. It wasn't so much the action that surprised him, it was the instinct to do so. He felt that Thomas needed the touch, the comfort and Thomas responded by placing his head on Hodge. Hodge knew at that moment that he would protect the kid no matter what. He was no kind of hero, but the kid had no one else to do it. The feeling was overwhelming.

With the exception of the men he served with, and Jimmy, Hodge had never felt such a keen sense of protection. Regarding those he served with, it was a feeling bred of survival and brotherhood. In regard to Jimmy, he had never shown it, but it was something he felt deep inside. Now Thomas held a spot in his heart that Hodge knew would be there until the day he died.

He barely knew the kid, but that sensation was strong. Hodge felt, for the first time, that he truly had something to live for. Thomas needed someone, and God, or fate, or pure circumstance brought them together.

Cliff came back, and while the battle had subsided, Hodge didn't know which side had won. He stared at Hodge for a moment before opening his mouth to speak.

"I didn't tell her what you wanted, or why. I think that would be best from you. But, I pleaded your case, and she has agreed to hear you out. I'm to escort you up, and not leave your side until Miss Grace makes a decision. If this is some kind of scam, though, you and me are going to have more than words. You understand?"

Hodge bit back a smart remark and nodded his head. "Thank you."

Cliff escorted them to the elevator and all the way to Grace's door.

Even though he had seen her a number of times since the divorce, all those times had been volatile and quick to turn into a screaming match. And Hodge was usually drunk. So, when Cliff knocked on the door, Hodge was rightfully nervous about how the encounter would go.

His nervousness increased when Grace opened the door and the woman behind almost every one of his one-night stands stood in front of him. Grace was as beautiful as ever, and all those placeholders he had woken up to in the morning were poor substitutions for her beauty. But, Hodge also felt something different when he saw her. Or, more accurately, he felt nothing. Grace had lost none of her beauty, but the desire and longing he used to feel was gone.

Hodge had no time to think of this as Grace crossed her arms across her chest. Her red painted lips tightened into a hard line, and her green eyes blazed.

"Hiya Gracie," Hodge said.

"Frank," was all she gave back.

She looked over the assembly at her door. Her gaze stopped on Thomas, and like Cliff, when she saw the boy, something softened in her. She knelt in front of him, and this time Thomas did not shrink away. Grace could be hard and cold, but she had the ability to exude a warmth that a lot of other people didn't have. It was what made her a great teacher. It was one of the things that first attracted Hodge to her. It was one of the things that kept them together long after it should have ended.

"Let me get a look at you."

Thomas stepped forward. Grace looked at him for a moment and then stood again.

No one said a word, but Grace ushered them through the door. Cliff hesitated, but Grace told him to come inside.

"Now, will someone please tell me what's going on?" Grace asked.

"I need to leave the kid, Thomas, here with you for a bit. He's in a world of trouble, and I need to figure out how to get him out of it. I can't do that having him with me."

"What trouble? Did he do something?" Grace looked at Thomas again. She looked deep into his eyes and shook her head. "No, someone hurt him."

"More than you know," Hodge said. "It shouldn't be long. At least, I don't think it should be long."

"Tell me what's going on, Frank."

Hodge told her everything he knew. He didn't bother sending Thomas away this time. He thought it was unfair. Earlier he had done it to spare the boy, but Hodge had the suspicion that the kid knew what was coming and he might as well have been attached to Hodge's leg.

"I need you to watch over him while I figure this out."

"No." Thomas's eyes went wide.

He looked like an animal being forced into a cage.

Hodge knelt in front of him. "I've got to, kid. It will be less suspicious if I go it alone. I can move more freely. If this Salazar guy is out there looking, then they will be looking for a man and a boy."

"No," Thomas said again.

Tears began to well in his eyes, the first two spilling over.

Hodge surprised himself again by pulling the kid into a hug. He said softly in Thomas's ear. "I'm going to help you. I'll come back for you."

He let go of Thomas and looked at Grace. Streaks of mascara ran down her cheeks. She dabbed at her eyes with a tissue. "Frank Hodge caring for a child. Will the wonders never cease?"

Hodge's face flushed. "Will you watch him?"

"Yes. He'll be safe with me," Grace said.

"Please, Scrapper, you can't leave me!" Thomas wrapped his arms around Hodge's legs and squeezed tight.

"Look, I'm not who you think I am. I'm just a guy on the radio. And I know you're scared. Heck, I'm scared, but I need to do this, and I need to go alone. I promise I will do everything in my power to get justice for your parents. For you. I promise that I will be back, kid."

Thomas did not let go, so Hodge pried the kid off and knelt in front of him again. "You found me and thought you found a hero. I'm just a guy, but you gave me some purpose. You trusted me to help you, and I need you to trust me now. This is the best way."

Thomas hugged Hodge. "Come back for me, Scrapper."

"It's Frank, kid."

Hodge pressed a hand to the back of Thomas's head and hugged him back before pulling away. He headed for the door, and called over his shoulder, "Keep him safe, Gracie."

As the door closed behind him, Hodge wiped a tear from his own eye.

# 5

Thomas watched as the Scarlet Scrapper walked out the door leaving him alone with two strangers. He knew now that it was not really the Scrapper; he knew that the Scrapper was just a character on the radio, despite what his schoolmate Johnny said. But Thomas held onto his belief just the same. He had to believe, partly because it was his only hope of justice for his parents, and partly because it was the only thing keeping him going.

The Scarlet Scrapper was his hero, and whether he was just a character or not, Frank Hodge was real. And Frank Hodge was the Scarlet Scrapper.

He caught Grace watching him. While he was anxious about being away from the Scrapper, he also felt at ease with her. There was something maternal about Grace that Thomas liked. Something that reminded him of his own mother. This both warmed him and upset him.

Grace held out a hand to Thomas, and he took it. She led him to a sofa that was much more comfortable than the one at the Scrapper's place. She sat down next to him and continued to hold his hand.

"Do you want anything, Thomas?" Grace asked. He shook his head. "Frank isn't always the best man for the job, but he is a capable man. And, when he sets his mind to something, boy is he stubborn."

"Miss Grace, I left the lobby unmanned." Cliff stepped forward.

The doorman was so quiet that Thomas had forgotten he was there. He stood with his hands folded in front of him, and his head slightly bowed.

"We'll be fine, Cliff. Thank you. If anyone gives you any trouble about being away from your post, just send them to me."

"Thank you, miss. If you need anything, just ring."

Grace stood and walked Cliff to the door. She locked it behind him and went back to Thomas.

"Is there anything I can get you?" she asked again.

Thomas shook his head and Grace sat next to him again. After some silence passed, Thomas looked at her. "How do you know the Scarlet Scrapper?"

Grace laughed at that. "Do you really believe that Frank is a superhero?"

Thomas shook his head. "I guess not. But it makes it easier."

Grace nodded like she understood. "If there is one thing Frank Hodge is not, is easy. He and I were married."

Thomas turned to her. His interest in her story was a welcome distraction to the thoughts swirling around in his head. "What happened?"

Grace laughed again, but it was a sad laugh. Thomas's mother had a similar laugh when things weren't funny. Once he had asked her why she laughed if she didn't think something was funny, or she thought it was sad. She replied that sometimes all you can do is laugh.

"Frank and I had a good time, then we pretended to have a good time, then it wasn't fun to pretend anymore. He has gone through a lot. We all have, but Frank had a rough time of it. Still does, I suppose. Something has changed though. I can feel it."

"What's changed?" Thomas asked.

"You," Grace said. "I think, with the exception of Jimmy, I know Frank better than anyone. In some ways, I think I may know him even better than Jimmy does. I've never seen him the way I just saw him with you."

"Is Jimmy the guy from the radio station?"

"That's right. He's Frank's oldest and dearest friend, even if Frank has a tough time showing it. When Frank cares for someone, there isn't a thing in the world that will stop him from helping them. And I can see that he cares about you."

Thomas could tell that she was holding something back. There was pain in her voice that Grace hid well, but Thomas, going through a pain of his own, recognized the hurt there. After a moment of silence, she cleared her throat and forced a smile.

"Maybe you'd like to lay down for a while?"

She stood up without waiting for an answer. Grace disappeared into another room and came back with a pillow. Placing it on the couch, she fluffed it, patted it, and told Thomas to lay his head down.

Thomas did not feel tired, but he did as he was told. He didn't think he would be able to fall asleep at all, but when he closed his eyes, he was lost in the darkness of the sleep that overtook him.

Behind his eyelids, he saw a brilliant white. The white enveloped him, his surroundings. Thomas stood in that void and looked for a way out. But he was surrounded by nothing.

He spotted something in the distance. Just a dot; he couldn't tell what color it was. He walked forward, but the dot grew no larger. Something shuddered within him. Thomas was trapped in the void. He was scared. His legs worked harder, and Thomas wondered how he could still run after the day he had. How could he still be moving at all. Finally, the dot grew larger, and Thomas pushed, ran faster. The dot grew and he spotted a color. Red.

In that white void, the red dot continued to grow, and a red flower blossomed. The flower began to melt and reshape into the mask of the Scarlet Scrapper. The void began to twist and take shape, and the Scrapper stood before him, a giant now. The crimson mask, like the rose, began to melt. Only this time it did not reshape, it bled down the Scrapper's chest. The Scrapper screamed in pain, in agony. Thomas covered his ears from the scream, but the sound grew louder and louder. Something shook him. Thomas spun around. He was no longer in a white void. He was drowning in a pool of darkness.

"Thomas!" It was his mother's voice. "Thomas, wake up." He felt her embrace take him, felt her warmth.

Thomas's eyes fluttered open while the dream still weighed heavy on his mind. He looked into his mother's face and a smile of relief took hold. But as the dream dissipated, his mother was no longer there. Thomas looked into Grace's eyes and his new reality set in again.

"They killed my mom and dad. They're going to kill the Scrapper." His voice came out rough, his throat was sore.

Grace held him tighter.

# 6

Of course, just because Mary was a reporter did not mean she would know who was working on the Salazar story. Assuming that she would know just because they shared a profession, would be like assuming that Hodge knew Orson Welles personally. He did, but that was beside the point.

Even at that time of night, Hodge could hear the clacking of typewriter keys as he stepped into the offices. Strings of globe lights hung from the ceiling and a plume of cigarette smoke hovered in the air like a gray rain cloud threatening to pour down on the men punching the keys. Hodge roamed the endless rows of tables that led deeper into the office. There were chairs at either end of the tables, and stacked next to most typewriters were books and piles of papers. Ashtrays sat filled with a day's worth of ash and butts and rings of coffee stained the tables.

Hodge, surprised that no one had stopped his roaming, lit his own cigarette as he continued to search for Mary. Most of the heads that looked up from their typing dismissed him as soon as they realized he was not there for them. Others watched him more closely until he walked past, while the rest didn't even bother to look up.

He stepped around a column into the next row of desks and was about to give up when he saw the green felt fedora with a red lace bow tied around it. Her auburn hair was done up in curls and her dress matched the green of her hat. Mary.

She typed furiously at her machine. Hodge took a step closer, but he stopped again when he heard her muttering over the clacking keys.

"Feel sorry for him, and this is what I get. Frank Hodge. Makes me feel cheap. Makes me feel special. Then he makes me feel like I am nothing." A bell in the platen rung and Mary slammed it home again. "Stands me up. Leaves me waiting. I should have given up after fifteen minutes, but no, I waited an hour. One whole hour. So, tell me, Mary, who is the fool here?"

Nervous to begin with, Hodge did not want to interrupt her. He didn't know how long she had been going, but he got the impression that it may have been for some time. He wanted to run away and not look back, but he couldn't do that. He had to help Thomas, and he had to explain himself to Mary. He just needed her to listen long enough for him to do so. Hodge reached out a hand and touched her shoulder.

"Mary," he said.

Mary startled. She spun in her chair, her wide eyes narrowed when she recognized him. Her lips squeezed into a hard line, and she stood up from her chair.

"You've got a lot of nerve coming here, mister."

"I can explain." Hodge held his hands up in surrender.

"I don't know who you think you are, or why you think you can treat people this way, but I waited for you, Frank. I waited for you, and I hoped and hoped you would show up. You just let me down." A look crossed her face that Hodge recognized. Mary wasn't the first woman he let down.

"Please, just listen." Hodge waited to make sure she would let him speak. When she said nothing, he continued. "There was this kid tonight. He needed me."

"I needed you."

Her voice was a whisper, almost lost in the sounds of the office, but Hodge heard her. Hodge felt her words. Hodge knew that she had been burned before.


"This is beginning to sound like an episode of your show, Frank. If you didn't want to see me, why did you put me through that? Why would you keep it up? Just to be cruel?"

"No. I never wanted that. I intended on being with you tonight, Mary. I swear. Thomas needed my help. Still needs it. And now I need yours."

Mary seemed to consider this. She looked Hodge in the eye, and he willed every part of his being to express his feelings. His truth. Something relented in her eyes and Mary shook her head softly. She reached up and took Frank's chin between her thumb and index finger. She turned his face to get a better look at his right cheek.

"Well, you've certainly been fighting someone." With tender care, Mary caressed that cheek. Hodge didn't realize he had a mark; he didn't know when he had been hit. The goons or the cops? Hell, he didn't even realize that he had been hit in the face. "Okay, buster, tell me everything."

Mary sat back down at her desk and took up the same pad she had used during their interview earlier in the evening. Hodge relayed the story as best as he could, telling her again about Thomas and his parents, but adding in more detail now that he had her full attention. Mary finished scribbling some notes and tapped her pencil's eraser against her teeth. Finally, she let out an exasperated breath.

"This is something, Frank."

"I'll say. It's a bit of a train wreck, and I'm stuck in the middle of the carnage."

"Where is Thomas now?"

Hodge had intentionally left that part out. He would like to say that it was for the kid's protection. But, if he were being honest, as he knew he should be, it was because he didn't want to talk about his ex-wife with the woman he intended on dating, if she would still have him.

"He's with Grace." Hodge hoped she wouldn't ask, but knew that she would, so he gave it to her. "She's my ex-wife." Hodge looked down at his feet. He didn't know how Mary would react.

"Smart," she said. "Most people wouldn't think to look there."

She took it well, but Hodge saw that if they were to make a go of it, he would have to open the book about that relationship and let Mary read all the gory details.

"It was my only option."

Hodge's voice held a note of defense that made him wince as soon as the words left his mouth. Mary didn't seem to notice, or ignored the tone.

"What do you need from me?"

"One of the cops said that the kid's father was approached by a reporter, or maybe he approached a reporter, I'm not sure which. This reporter might have the goods on Edward Salazar, and maybe with that, I can get the kid in the clear."

"You want to confront this guy? This Salazar?" Mary asked.

Hodge hadn't really thought of it, but now that the words were out there, he guessed, yeah, that was how he felt. He didn't like a bully, and this guy had put Thomas in danger, and that put Hodge in danger. Also, something about the kid had grown on him. He didn't know when it happened, but he found himself caring for Thomas. It might have been the shared experience of being in a life-threatening situation with the kid, but it felt even stronger than that. Hodge liked the kid.

Thomas was smart, tough, and needed someone on his side. Fate must have played a joke on the kid, because it gave him Hodge, the so-called Scarlet Scrapper, but damn it, Hodge would give the kid his all.

"I don't know, Mary. I just know that I need to keep Thomas safe."

"If what you've said is true." Hodge opened his mouth to protest, but Mary held up a hand silencing him before he could start. "And I do not doubt that it is. Then, this Edward Salazar is a powerful man. If he has the police on his payroll, I'm not sure even the Scarlet Scrapper could save the day this time."

"I just want to talk to this reporter. See what he has on Salazar, see if he is working with anyone else in authority. Then I take it from there. I know I'm no hero, but Thomas needs justice. He has had enough taken from him already, I don't think he should have to live scared for the rest of his life. Do you?"

Mary appeared to think about it for a minute and the decision was written all over her face. With a nod, she said, "Let me see what I can find out."

# 7

Thomas could not sit still, so he made circuits around the perimeter of Grace's living room. She watched him in silence, but when he glimpsed her face, he could tell that his pacing was making her uncomfortable. Thomas couldn't help it. He had a knot of nervous anxiousness that started in the pit of his stomach and spread like wildfire through the rest of his torso and into his limbs. His mother would say that he had 'ants in his pants.' Every time Thomas passed the window in the living room, he would look out and down at the street as if he would see the crimson mask of the Scarlet Scrapper heading through the entrance below.

He knew that was why he was nervous. The Scrapper wasn't there with him. Thomas had no idea how long the Scrapper had been gone, but days passed in every minute. Worse, he didn't know where the Scrapper was. What if someone had followed them? What if they snatched the Scrapper and were torturing him even then? It would be all Thomas's fault.

It had always been a dream to fight alongside his hero, and when that time had come, all Thomas could do was cower.

Grace was a nice lady and all. She did a good job making him feel safe, at least for a short time. But Thomas didn't want to be safe. He wanted justice. He wanted to be with the Scarlet Scrapper, helping to bring down the men that had taken his parents, his innocence, his world.

Two things stood in the way of his leaving to find the Scrapper. One, Grace would not willingly let him leave. Thomas figured he could get out of there without an issue, though. He had even thought of some ways to distract the Scrapper's ex-wife. Thomas's second hurdle was that he did not know where the Scarlet Scrapper would be. His only thought on that matter was to find the guy from the radio station. But the only place he knew of to find him was at the station itself. Would he still be there after so many hours? Thomas didn't think so, but thought it was as good a place to start as any. If he couldn't find this Jimmy guy there, he would try to figure out where he lived.

Grace still wore that uncomfortable facial expression. She wanted to help him, but Thomas could tell she did not know how. He wasn't sure anyone could help him but the Scarlet Scrapper. And now, he knew he had to help the Scrapper too.

Thomas, for the first time since his parents were murdered, felt a sense of purpose, of hope. He should have insisted on going with his hero to begin with. But, like adults always do, the Scrapper assumed he knew what was best for a child. In some regards, Thomas was sure that was true, but deep in his bones, he knew that this was his only path. Being with Frank Hodge, the Scarlet Scrapper, when he brought his parents' killers to justice was what Thomas needed. It was the only way he would feel whole again.

First, he had to get out of there.

Thomas stopped in front of Grace. "Thank you for helping me."

Grace's smile was sad and warm. "Thomas, no one should have to go through what you are going through. I just wish I could do more."

"Can I have a glass of water?" Thomas asked.

Grace nodded and looked glad to have something to do. She stood up, squeezed his shoulder, and went into the kitchen.

As soon as she was out of sight, Thomas started for the door. When he heard the water start to run, he turned the lock and twisted the doorknob. He glanced over his shoulder just in time to see Grace looking around the living room for him.

"I'm sorry," Thomas said and took off at a run.

She called after him, but he couldn't stop. He wouldn't. He would make it up to her somehow later. Right now, Thomas just needed to find the Scarlet Scrapper.

When he hit the lobby, the doorman from earlier was sitting

at the desk, a phone pressed to his ear. Cliff locked eyes with Thomas as soon as he left the elevator. Thomas started walking toward the door as if he had every right to. He guessed he did, but another thing adults liked to do was to take away even the basic rights of kids. He was not a captive, he was not a prisoner, he was not being held for ransom. Thomas had done nothing wrong, so he should be able to come and go as he pleased. None of these people were his parents.

Cliff hung the phone up and stood from his chair. Thomas was just passing his desk.

"Thomas, you need to go back up to Miss Grace, now." Cliff started to step around the desk. "Come on, I'll walk you back up."

Thomas took off at a run. He felt freezing air coming through the glass of the door. He pushed through the door and went right out the lobby onto the sidewalk. The blast of cold was overwhelming.

Though he had been inside for hours, the chill from the cold never seemed to have left his bones. Now that he was back outside in the cold, his body began to shiver with renewed purpose. The cold weather set off a burning itch in his fingertips, and pierced the cheap shoes given to him by the police sergeant. Thomas was unsure where exactly the radio station was, but he took off at a run when he sensed movement coming from the glass lobby door.

Cliff called after him, but when Thomas looked over his shoulder, he saw that the doorman was not following him. That was good. He slowed his run and tried to figure out what to do next.

# 8

Hodge waited at Mary's desk while she went to try to get information. He was leaning back in her chair with a cigarette hanging from the corner of his mouth. His neck and shoulders were so tight, he felt if he moved the wrong way something would snap like a rubber band. The more he tried to relax them, the less he felt relaxed. What he needed was a long, hot soak and an even longer night's sleep. Maybe a drink or two to ease him. Hodge thought that he would feel a sense of relief when Mary came back. A sense that he was making some progress toward whatever goal he was working toward. But when she approached the desk, Hodge only felt his muscles tighten further. Part of the problem was that he had no idea what result he looked to achieve. He knew he wanted to help Thomas, in any way he could, but he really had no idea what that entailed.

Hodge stood from the chair and waited for Mary to say something. She wore a look of concern that Hodge didn't like one bit. An eternity seemed to pass in those few seconds.

"Mary what is it? What did you find out?"

"Not much," Mary said. She looked at her hands, indecision written on her face.

"Tell me," Hodge urged.

"I didn't find out much. Nothing really, but I am still not sure if I should share what I do know."

Hodge told her that she should.

"Albert Graves is the reporter who is trying to bring down Edward Salazar. He is as dour as his name implies. Albert has gone home for the evening where I imagine he is spending a humorless night with his wife listening to the radio."

"Mary, please stop stalling," Hodge said.

Mary Allen let out a sigh. "As I said, there is not much I can tell you without talking to Albert, but some of the boys gave me an address and rumors about Edward Salazar. He is also known as Ready Eddie, though that is a nickname stemming from the days before he was a *legitimate* businessman. Apparently, he does not take kindly to being called that anymore. His right-hand man, since they were kids in a gang called the Docktown Dukes, is named Gus Gusterson. He is also known as Gus Gus."

She looked at her ever present notebook and then back at Hodge. He motioned for her to continue.

With another sigh, Mary went on. "Salazar runs the local longshoremen's union, and Thomas's family is not the first to suffer such a fate. It seems that anytime someone comes close to bringing Edward Salazar down, they suffer an unfortunate accident. Never anything as blatant as straight murder, not until now."

"But what is Salazar really doing on the docks?" Hodge asked.

"That, I don't know. There are rumors, of course, but nothing confirmed. From what the guys have gathered, he controls the docks. Makes it so you don't work, and then you're forced to take a loan out from him. Then you need to work. He is squeezing them, Frank. There is probably more, but that was all I could get without talking to Albert. The last thing I have is the address for his office."

"What's the address?"

"Frank, we haven't known each other long. If we are being honest, we don't know each other at all, but I can see it in your eyes. I've seen that look before. You are desperate. You want to make something happen and… and I'm scared that if you do, it will not end well for you."

"Please. What is the address?"

Mary hesitated again, but she relented. Hodge jotted the address down using a pencil and scrap of paper he found on Mary's desk. He folded the paper and tucked it inside his suit jacket.

Hodge gripped Mary lightly by the shoulders, leaned in and kissed her on the cheek.

"Thank you."

Their eyes locked for a moment, and he flashed his charming smile, let go of her arms and walked away. He was only a few paces away when she called after him.

"Frank, wait!" Mary rushed over. She hesitated again, but pulled Hodge into an embrace and a deep kiss. "Just be careful. Don't do anything stupid."

The kiss did wonders to reinvigorate Hodge's spirits. His smile amped up to its full power. "I'm just going to check his place out. No big deal. Scout's honor."

Hodge gripped Mary's hand and began to walk away. She held onto him until their arms were fully extended and their grips slipped. He did not look back toward her until he reached the elevator. While he could not see her, he knew she was still watching in his direction.

The warmth he took from the kiss of Miss Mary Allen had long worn off as Hodge walked from the chain link fence of the docks and passed the first warehouse on the right. He blew into his hands, but it did nothing to abate the stiff coldness that had overtaken his joints and burned his skin.

The wind cut through the cheap material of the suit he had worn at the appearance earlier in the evening. If he didn't wrap this up soon, whatever this was, he would be dead from the cold. And speaking of dead, no one was out on the pier under Salazar's control. Hodge guessed they'd have to be fools to be out there on such a cold night, and so late, or early depending on how you looked at it.

Waves crashed against the dock pilings, as the wind howled below and beneath them like the cry of a banshee. The pier was mostly dark with the exception of the evenly spaced lights high up on poles and the dimmer lights centered above each warehouse door. Hodge scanned his surroundings. He really could not understand why he thought he needed to go there. Not in the dark. Not in the cold. It all seemed so foolish now. He was sure it was foolish earlier, when Mary had told him it was.

But he needed movement. He needed motion. Hodge needed to feel like something was being done. This was not just for Thomas's sake, but for his own. He hated feeling stagnant. That was why he couldn't stand to wait until Albert Graves came in the next morning. He wasn't sure what that would accomplish anyway. At least now, this way, he felt like he was getting somewhere. Even if that was just his imagination.

Hodge hated feeling like he was powerless to do something. Anything. That was why he was there. He walked into the lion's den when he knew the lion would not be home.

Or was it?

At the end of the dock stood a small wooden shack set apart from the warehouses. A light burned behind the square, frosted windows of the shack. From a chimney pipe through the roof, black smoke rose. It was barely visible in the inky black sky, but the smoke was just a little darker. *Is Salazar here after all?*

This complicated things for Hodge. He was prepared to check out the territory and then figure the rest out in the morning. He had hopes that this Graves fellow would have contacts within the police department; men they could trust to help. He knew that the smart move would be to leave now. Come back during the day when other people were around as witnesses. Maybe, if Albert Graves had the resources, he would come back with people in authority.

Of course, Frank Hodge was never known for making the smart move.

Even as Hodge continued toward the shack, he told himself it was just for a peek inside. He wanted to do the smart thing for a change. Or the semi-smart thing, as he knew that looking would be a risk in itself. He wanted to get a look but did not want to be seen by whomever was inside the shack. He could still just turn around, find someplace warm and grab a drink. Mary would probably still be at the paper just waiting for news from him, hoping that he would not do something stupid.

Hodge approached the small shack. He carefully followed a small walkway that led around the building. More than once, he nearly slipped on ice that had formed from the splashing waves, but managed to right himself before plunging into the water.

At the back of the building, on what Hodge assumed was the opposite wall from where the furnace would be, there was another window. This one looked like the porthole of a ship. He pressed closer to the building and stayed put for a few moments. The warmth seeping through the walls was welcome and inviting. He managed to pull himself away from the comfort and stuck his head in front of the circular window.

The furnace turned out to be a wood burning stove and was located where Hodge guessed it would be. Opposite that stood an unoccupied desk decorated with piles of paper. The chair was facing to the side as if whoever had occupied it had just stood up. Leaning back against a wall near the stove was a heavy-set man in a newsboy hat. In the corner of his mouth was an unlit cigar. The heavy-set man folded a newspaper and smacked it as if in disgust. He looked up, his gaze sweeping the window as his attention was drawn to the side of the room. His gaze quickly darted back in the direction of the porthole and locked there.

Hodge moved quickly and nearly slipped on the ice again. From the front of the shack, he heard a door bang open and voices.

"I'm tellin' ya, I saw something."

"Probably a bird. I'm not too fond of freezing my keister off out here, Gus."

"There was someone in the window."

Hodge waited until he heard their footsteps on the wooden planks before setting off. He hoped that the steps would tell him which way to go, but sound was weird on the docks, and the clunking of wood sounded like it came from all directions.

Without thinking, Hodge reached into his jacket pocket and pulled out the contents. His face grew warmer, and he picked a direction. Unfortunately for Hodge, he chose poorly as he came face to face with Gus, Hodge assumed. Another assumption was that Gus would be taller, but the man was not only egg shaped, but short.

The second man, the one who didn't want to freeze his keister off, was nowhere to be seen. Gus held a .38 revolver pointed in Hodge's direction. Hodge recognized it from the props on the show. He had even handled one on a few occasions. Hodge was not a fan of guns.

A second set of footsteps came from the other direction. Hodge turned and saw a slim man that exuded power. He wore his hair slicked back and in the dim light Hodge was having trouble picking out many features of the man's face. But, though there was no smile in place, there was a sort of humor etched in the man's facial features, as if he were forced to wear a pleasant-faced mask all the time, or the world just amused him.

"What the hell is this?" The tall man said.

"That ain't a bird, Ready," Gus said.

"I know. Sorry Ed. Force of habit."

"Let's bring him into the light. I want to… see him better." Edward Salazar said in a confused tone. He shoved Hodge toward Gus. For the third time, Hodge nearly slipped on the ice that coated the dock.

Back on sure footing, Hodge held his hands up near his face. He did this to emulate surrender, but also because it got his hands in the right direction of his fighter's stance. If they were going to get into it, he wanted to be ready.

Salazar began to circle him, and Hodge's face grew hotter and hotter. He realized that he was having trouble breathing. Hodge's mind, already running a marathon, could not grasp why his breath felt hot and short.

Salazar stopped in front of him, a look of confusion on his face that matched the tone from earlier. Gus stood solid, like a statue, revolver pointed at Hodge's chest.

"What's with the mask?" Salazar asked.

Hodge touched his already raised hand to his cheek. He didn't recall pulling the mask over his face. He didn't even remember taking it out of his...

His pocket. He had reached into his pocket when the two men were getting out of the office. Hodge didn't like that he had put the mask on, but he had no time to think of the implications. He thought of them anyway. *Have I gone nuts? Going down to the docks alone; pulling on the mask of a radio show's silly character. Truth, justice, and all that is good. What a joke.*

"You there? You some kind of nut? What's with the mask? You trying to rob us? No one robs Edward Salazar."

"Eddie, this is the guy from the radio," Gus said. When Salazar did not respond, Gus continued, "You know, the one with the kid."

Recognition dawned on Salazar's face. "The Scarlet Scraper!"

"It's the Scarlet Scrapper," Hodge corrected.

"I don't care what you call yourself. I want the kid. Unless I get him, you can call yourself dead."

"As you can see," Hodge began, his voice full of a false bravado, "I don't have him. Why is he so important anyway?"

"Frank Hodge. Sergeant Henry told me about you. That you came in with the boy in tow. Said that you and a group of your friends fought off three armed men despite him telling you that you could leave. So, why is the boy so important to you?"

Hodge didn't call out the lie, and he had no answer for the question. He knew that taking care of Thomas had awoken something in him that he had not felt in a long time. Something that he wasn't sure he ever truly felt. The need to protect. When he was overseas, he felt it for his brothers in arms. They had to protect one another in order for them to live another day. Of course, that did not go as planned as Hodge was the only one to walk away, and that just barely. When he was with Grace he felt a sort of protectiveness, but if he was honest, that was more about ego. He didn't want anyone else to come between them, and it was mostly about jealousy. But with Thomas it was different. He felt the need to protect, but also to nurture.

Hodge didn't think that this Edward Salazar would understand, so he remained quiet.

"You care for Thomas Malloy, don't you?" It was more statement than question. "I always liked him too. He and my boy used to pal around in the summers. Thomas would come to work with his old man, and my little Ollie would be here waiting with a ball and a stick. He's a good kid. Both boys are."

"Then why?"

"It wasn't supposed to go this far. The two idiots I sent were just supposed to send a message. You know, throw a scare at Terry Malloy. Things got out of hand, and now the kid is a liability. I don't like it. I don't like to hurt kids."

"You almost sound sincere," Hodge said. "Thomas had nothing to do with any of this. His old man may have been talking, but Thomas, he's innocent. Let him walk away. No one will bother you."

"Now," Salazar shivered as if suddenly chilled, "I guess you're right. He is just a kid. I mean, what could he do to me, right?"

"That's right," Hodge said.

"Come on, we'll walk you back to the gate." Salazar began to turn. For just a moment, Hodge allowed himself to believe it. For just a moment, he thought things would turn out okay. He had gone there to help Thomas, and maybe he had done it. Maybe, now, Thomas would be safe.

But Salazar stopped midturn. He held up a finger as if a thought suddenly had come to him. He pointed that finger at Hodge. "The only problem is, and I want to believe you, but, one day he won't be a kid no more. One day he'll be a grown man."

"So, you'll kill him because of something that might happen in the future? Be reasonable man."

Salazar jabbed his finger in the air. "You're right. You're right. But, if Thomas isn't going to be a problem, then why are you here on my docks?"

Salazar lifted his thumb and dropped it like the hammer of a gun. He made a gunshot noise.

Hodge heard the actual gunshot right after he felt the impact of it. An invisible hand lifted him and tugged him back. His body felt like it hovered in the air, then gravity took hold again. Before the fall, he had a moment to think about the giant canes that would pull a lousy act from a vaudeville stage. Then, he was engulfed in fiery, ice water and everything went black.

# 9

Thomas tried the front door without much hope that it was unlocked, but the knob turned, and he stuck his head inside. The long hallway was empty, and he could hear no sounds coming from the building. He stepped in, glad to be out of the cold. He headed toward the door at the far end of the hallway and hoped that his luck would hold out and he'd find Jimmy. While Thomas wasn't sure if Jimmy could help him, he had a gut feeling that the Scarlet Scrapper would eventually go to his friend.

Thomas twisted the handle and pressed his ear against the door, and it opened.

The room was dark. The only light, a crack from a door

slightly askew. He thought he heard some noise, but it was too faint to make out. The noise was repeated, and then repeated a third time. A fourth. He did not recognize it. He opened the door a crack and peeked in. There was no one there, but the noise was louder. It sounded like when one of the kids in the neighborhood would try to imitate a professional ball player by slapping a catcher's mitt against their leg.

"Hello?"

Thomas regretted calling out as soon as the word had left his lips. But there was no response. He pushed ahead and heard the slapping sound again. This time he heard something along with it. A whimper. Thomas made his way toward the light and the slapping sound was more prominent. So was the whimpering.

Then he heard muffled conversation. The words became clearer as he got closer. Two men were arguing.

"If you hadn't shot the guy, we wouldn't be in this situation, Nicky."

"What part of message don't you understand, *Tony*?" Nicky said in a mocking whine.

"I could ask you the same thing. How do you deliver a message when the guy getting it can't understand anything no more? Because you killed him."

Silence was the only response.

"What, nothing to say to that?" Tony asked.

"It sends a message to anyone else trying to go up against Ready Eddie Salazar."

"The boss would kill you if he heard you call him that. We're in enough trouble as it is because of you."

Throughout the whole argument, the whimpering continued. Then a weak, crying voice said, "Please, just leave me alone."

"First you got to tell us where he is," Nicky said, and

another slap followed.

With every word, the voices became more distinct, and Thomas recognized them. The men who killed his parents. And Thomas knew who was begging too. It was the Scrapper's friend, Jimmy. Thomas wanted to rush in there and hurt those men, but he knew he couldn't stand up to them. He fought the impulse and hung back. If he revealed himself, he wouldn't be able to help the Scrapper, or Jimmy.

"I... I don't know where he is. I haven't seen him for hours. Since you were all in the alley!" Jimmy's voice was weak, but he still managed some force in his statement.

Another slap, this one louder, harder. And again, Jimmy whimpered. He begged. Pleaded.

Thomas wanted to go in there but knew in this instance to be strong was to stay put. He hated it, but Thomas would only get himself killed and probably Jimmy too. Then he would never see justice for his parents.

"You don't know where he is," Tony said. "Fine, tell us where he lives."

"N-No. I can't do that," Jimmy's voice took on an edge of panic.

"James Stephen Childers." Nicky read the date of birth and the address.

"No." Jimmy's voice sounded pathetic.

"Look, there's a picture in here too. That is a beautiful wife, you got there. Two beautiful kids. Take a look, Tony," Nicky said.

From Tony came an appreciative grunt.

"No." Jimmy repeated.

"We might have to head over to the Bronx," Nicky said.

"No. Please."

"Then maybe you want to give us a different address." Tony said.

Jimmy let out a defeated whimper. This one held more pain than the ones before. He gave them an address. Thomas didn't know if it was the Scrapper's, but he thought it was. He couldn't blame Jimmy. These guys were not playing fair.

"I'm going to hold onto this, James. If it turns out you're lying, we will pay your family a visit. You understand?"

"Yes." Jimmy's voice was desperate, hurt, small like a child.

Without another word Nicky and Tony's footsteps headed back toward the door. Thomas tucked himself in the corner. When the door swung open, he was hidden behind it. He slipped in as the door swung back closed.

Jimmy was already standing, and openly crying. He had not seen Thomas, and Thomas thought that for the better. He wanted those guys out of there before either of them started talking.

Thomas kept his eyes on the door, half expecting them to come back at any moment. He only relaxed when he heard the outside door click shut.

When he turned to look at Jimmy Childers, Jimmy still hadn't noticed him. His eyes had a glazed over look, and Thomas wasn't sure that Jimmy was seeing much of anything at the moment. He wanted to make his presence known, but he worried that he would startle the already frightened man.

Jimmy started walking toward a door on the other side of the room. His legs appeared wobbly, and he started to teeter to one side. Thomas rushed over to help steady him, and Jimmy jumped with a cry. He ended up falling over anyway, and Thomas was nearly crushed under the weight of the small man.

"It's okay," Thomas said. "I'm here to help."

"Who are you?"

"I'm a friend of the Scarlet Scrapper." Thomas tried to puff his chest out in a heroic fashion.

"Frank? Oh God, is he okay?"

"I'm more worried about you. I think we need to get you to a hospital."

"No! Those animals know where I live. I need to get home to Betty."

Jimmy started to rise, but he fell off balance again. He squeezed his eyes shut and sat still. When he opened them again his gaze appeared clearer.

Thomas stood up first and held out his hands. Jimmy gripped them in his own and after two false starts, he managed to get onto his feet.

"What are you doing here? You said you were friends with Frank?"

"The Scrapper saved my life. I came here looking for him. I thought if anyone knew where he was, you would, being that you're his best pal," Thomas said.

Jimmy started toward the door again, and Thomas walked next to him, his hand on the small of the man's back, like he had done before when his father came home with a mean drunk on.

Opening the door, Jimmy smiled down at him and nodded. Thomas could see that it hurt to do so, but the message was clear. Jimmy had it from there. Through the door, Thomas could see a toilet stall and a urinal. He stepped back and the door closed behind Jimmy.

Behind the door water ran. A few moments later Jimmy came out again. He dabbed at his eyebrow with a wet paper towel. He rushed to a coat rack and pulled on a long tan coat.

"I have to get home," Jimmy looked at Thomas, "I think you're coming with me."

Thomas followed without argument.

Under other circumstances the car ride may have been fun, like a ride at the fair. Jimmy sped around and through the light city traffic, and on more than one occasion, the wheels slid this way and that, causing the car to fishtail down the icy roads. But, at the moment, Thomas's stomach twisted and turned as much as the car. Every bump and bounce was like driving over mountain ranges and Thomas thought he would be sick on more than a few occasions.

Jimmy finally slowed the car down when they headed over the Henry Hudson Bridge. Thomas figured the thought of taking a dive into the river was not an appealing one; especially since the goal was to make it back to his home to protect his family. Dying on the way there would not help achieve that goal.

He lost count of the turns and streets they had taken as his eyelids grew heavy. Thomas didn't remember the last time he slept, or the last time he ate. He knew the Scarlet Scrapper had made him an omelet, but he had no idea what time that was. He had no idea what time it was now.

What Thomas did know was that he was hungry and tired, and more scared than any other time in his life. His parents' death felt more real with each passing minute. Whenever his mind had a chance to slow down he saw them, and the image wasn't one that he wanted to see.

Thomas preferred to pull from his memory a happy moment. Mom and dad sitting on either side of him on the Wonder Wheel. Dad teaching him to throw a ball. Mom letting him lick cake batter from her mixing spoon. But each of those images was replaced by red flowers blossoming in a field of white; by a head snapping backward and falling forward with a demonic Cheshire cat's grin, a dribbling of blood down between the eyes.

Thomas fought the images, but the harder he fought, the harder the images came. The more he tried to focus on the good memories, the more they were replaced by his most recent memories of his parents. His father being shot down before he knew what was happening, and his mother yelling for him to run. And Thomas was just as powerless to stop these images as he was to stop his parents from being murdered.

He didn't know if bringing the men who hurt him to justice would bring him peace, but Thomas felt that it would be a start.

In the books, and movies, and on his shows, that was where the healing began. Now, Thomas needed that healing for himself. He would never forget his parents. They weren't perfect, but they were his. They did their best, and Thomas knew he had been loved.

He noticed the difference in the car's driving. Things were moving smoother now. Less bumpy, less erratic. Thomas looked out the window and saw that they were in a neighborhood of brownstone row houses. Jimmy slowed the car to a stop and with a last skid and sputter of the engine, he shut the lights and car off. He placed his head back on the seat and didn't move. For a moment, Thomas thought that he had fallen asleep, but he shook his head.

"I'm not sure how I am going to explain this to Betty," Jimmy said. "She'll want me to go to the police, but I don't know if that is dangerous or not. These men know who I am. Know where I live. Know I have a family."

"The police are with them," Thomas said.

Jimmy lifted his head from the seat and looked at Thomas.

He let out a snort. "Well, this should make a good script for Frank. Maybe he won't complain for once. Well, what do you say, kid, you want to meet my family?"

"Not sure I have a choice, sir," Thomas said.

"There's always a choice. But, I think you should come inside. In fact, I think I need your help to get me inside." Jimmy laughed, but the laugh had no humor in it.

Thomas climbed out and went around the car. He opened the driver's side door and Jimmy used him as a crutch. They started to walk across the street. After a few steps, Jimmy let go of Thomas.

"I think I'm okay on my own." He took another step.

Thomas did not.

"What are you doing, Thomas? It's freezing out here."

"There's someone hiding in the corner of the porch."

Thomas could not take his eyes from the black shape crouched in the corner of the front stoop. It wasn't moving, and he couldn't tell if it was a man or a woman.

Jimmy stopped walking and leaned forward as if that would give him a better view.

Without a word, he turned back toward the car.

"What are you doing?"

But Jimmy did not answer. He went straight to the car's trunk, stuck his key in and opened it. He took out a baseball bat and limped back toward his front door.

"They will not hurt me again. They will not harm my family. Stay here, Thomas."

The injuries that Jimmy had sustained were forgotten as he held the baseball bat on his shoulder, ready to swing. Thomas, though told to stay put, followed behind him. He didn't want to get in the way, but he wanted to be ready to help if he could. He wouldn't cower behind anymore. He wouldn't be a victim to anyone else again, not even himself, or his fear.

"What are you doing here?" Jimmy asked.

His voice was strong but faltered in the middle. There was no answer from the shape on the stoop. There was no movement.

"I asked you a question. What are you doing? This is my home, and you are not welcome here." Jimmy continued forward.

"Say, pally, you invited me over for dinner." The voice was slow, and shaky. "How about a night cap?"

"Frank?"

Jimmy ran to the Scarlet Scrapper and Thomas followed right behind.

"Jesus, Frank, are you okay?" Jimmy started pounding on the door. "Betty! Betty get out here!" He continued slamming his fist.

"Scrapper, what happened?"

"I'm fine kid. Just a scratch." The Scarlet Scrapper reached a hand up and patted Thomas's cheek. The fingers were stiff and cold, like rubbing against a block of ice. "Just a scratch."

The Scrapper's hand fell away, and his eyes fluttered before closing.

# EPISODE 3

# FALL OF THE
# SCARLET SCRAPPER

# EPISODE THREE
## The Fall of the Scarlet Scrapper

From the episode "And the Kid Makes Two" in
*The Adventures of the Scarlet Scrapper*
— November 4, 1942

**TANAKA:** Ah, the great General Beahr (pronounced bear). What brings you to my secret lair?

**GENERAL BEAHR:** This secret is too easily found.

**TANAKA:** What is to say I do not wish to be found?

**GENERAL BEAHR:** You've escaped the Scarlet Scrapper already, and you wish to be caught again?

**TANAKA:** (laughs) That is where you are mistaken, my dear general. I will not be caught, but I will catch our Scarlet clad friend.

**GENERAL BEAHR:** What will be different this time, Tanaka? How do you expect to succeed where we have all failed before?

**TANAKA:** Come look at my newest invention.

**F/X:** CHAIR SCRAPES AGAINST THE FLOOR

**GENERAL BEAHR:** It looks like a box. What are these dials on the side and what is this red button?

**TANAKA:** No, no general. You mustn't push that button. Watch, I will push this button here.

**F/X:** A LOUD CRACKLE FOLLOWED BY ELECTRICITY RUNNING

**TANAKA:** And then we just adjust the dials like so.

**F/X:** A LOW WHINE EMITS

**GENERAL BEAHR:** But what does it do doctor? What is that purple light?

**TANAKA:** Please, General Beahr, step over there. Yes, step into the purple light.

**GENERAL BEAHR:** Well, alright, but I don't see… Now, just a minute. I can't move. It's like the light is making me freeze. It-it's an effort just to talk.

**TANAKA:** You see now? When the Scarlet Scrapper shows up in my secret base here, a secret base of which the location has been spread to those with loose lips. Then we will place him in the light field, and he will be powerless.

**GENERAL BEAHR:** Okay, okay, now let me out of this, Tanaka.

**TANAKA:** Not so fast, general. Watch what happens when I twist the dials.

**F/X:** WHINING IN DIFFERENT TONES

**GENERAL BEAHR:** I can move now, but it's like walking through a pool of molasses. My arms and legs feel so heavy.

**TANAKA:** That is correct. By turning these dials, I can increase or decrease the ability to move muscles. With this dial on top of the machine, here, I can increase the field of light to a greater volume.

**GENERAL BEAHR:** Doctor Tanaka, that is genius! How many men can it hold?

**TANAKA:** With the light field at its maximum power, it can hold four grown men. And, it can crush them to death if I will it.

**GENERAL BEAHR:** Then it's true. The Scarlet Scrapper will finally meet his doom.

**GENERAL BEAHR and TANAKA:** (laughs)

**F/X:** A WHOOSH OF AIR FOLLOWED BY A CRASH AND SMALL EXPLOSION

**TANAKA:** My machine!

**SCRAPPER:** Thanks for explaining how that contraption works, Tanaka. It's a shame you'll never put it to use again!

**TANAKA:** No! How did you find me so soon?

**GENERAL BEAHR:** Let's get him together, Dr. Tanaka. We'll show this do-gooder what happens when he crosses us.

**SCRAPPER:** I've taken you both on before, and I can do it again!

**GENERAL BEAHR:** You've never fought against us together, Scrapper. This time you will not win.

**SCRAPPER:** We'll see about that.

**F/X:** PUNCHES AND A SCUFFLE

**GENERAL BEAHR:** I've got him, Tanaka. Quick knock the Scrapper out.

**F/X:** THUD

**SCRAPPER:** (groans)

**TANAKA:** We've done it! We have defeated the Scarlet Scrapper, and this time, he will not escape our clutches.

MUSIC UP and FADE

*End of Excerpt*

# 1

Edward Salazar took his time undoing the cuff link of his right sleeve. He then rolled the sleeve up to his elbow. He repeated the same process with his left sleeve, all while looking the man tied to a chair in the eyes. The man, for his part, looked back with defiance and anger in his eyes. That was just a mask though, because Salazar saw something else there. He saw the man's fear. Salazar felt fear of his own. Not of the man, but of the situation. *I've been at this game a long time, and never has anyone come so close to tearing down my operation as now. And all because of a child and an actor; the timing could not be worse, either.* Salazar shook his head. He had to understand, and that brought him to the man tied to the chair.

"How did this happen, Nicky?" Salazar took Gus's chair from the wall by the door. He turned it so when he sat, he sat backwards on the chair. Despite the cold outside, he felt a fire burning hotter inside of him than the one in the wood stove in the corner.

Nicky did not answer. He looked at Gus standing like a silent specter in the corner. Gus was a squat figure with a face like a bulldog. His bark was just as fierce. Gus, who normally would handle this sort of thing, was sidelined though. Salazar wanted this. He could have sat back and let Gus do the work, but what kind of message would that send? He was never one to shirk responsibility, to shy away from getting his hands dirty. Edward Salazar was never afraid to show his strength.

"Don't look at him. You look at me. You should be happy he's not the one standing in front of you. I've grown soft in my old age. Gus, he is just as ruthless as he ever was. So, look at me, and tell me what happened."

Nicky pulled his gaze away from Gus but did not make eye contact with Salazar. Salazar lifted the tied man's chin, so they were looking eye to eye.

"Talk."

"We… we were just doing like you said."

Salazar's hand slashed out and slapped Nicky across the face. It wasn't a particularly hard hit, but it was humiliating enough to throw a shock into the captive. A moment passed where nothing happened. When Nicky opened his mouth to speak again, Salazar slapped the other way. The last shred of defiance washed away from Nicky's face.

"Think before you speak, my friend. You were doing as I said?" He looked over his shoulder. "Gus, did I tell these two idiots to go shoot anyone? To do it so obviously that even the stupidest detective in the world could figure out who was responsible?"

"Not that I'm aware, Ready." Gus chewed a fat cigar.

Salazar shot a look at Gus. It wasn't the time, but he guessed he'd have to have a talk with his old friend about using that nickname. Edward Salazar was no longer the kid that went by 'Ready' Eddie. The Docktown Dukes were a thing of the past. While Salazar didn't fool himself into thinking he was a respectable man, he wasn't a kid no more, either.

"Where's Tony?" Nicky's split lip dribbled blood and spit. Tears filled his eyes.

"Don't worry about Tony." Salazar turned his attention back to Nicky. "Now, tell me what happened."

Nicky looked down into his lap. "We went there to deliver the message, like you said. Things j-just sort of got out of hand."

"Let's see. Two people are dead. We still don't have the kid to wrap this mess up once and for all. And, apparently, this kid found help. The cops could be here any minute to arrest us. Yes, I'd say things got out of hand."

Salazar didn't add in the unrelated deal he had going with the Germans. Recently, some Krauts had approached him with a deal. They were 'renting' out a back storage unit of one of his warehouses. This didn't sit too well with Salazar, but if he was being honest, he didn't feel he had much of a choice. Sure, he was being paid for the space, and paid well, but he knew these Germans were up to no good and it could only be for one thing, sabotage. Salazar was not a good man, but he was not a traitor either.

While he couldn't figure out what the plan was, it was obvious that the first men who came to him were handlers, but whoever showed up next would be the ones to really watch out for. Salazar kept his men on a rotation to watch the warehouse. He wanted to know about any activity. He didn't know what he would do about it, but he felt he needed to know.

If harboring spies wasn't bad enough, now he had this Malloy situation on his hands, and it was all thanks to this idiot in the chair, and his partner.

"Why'd you shoot them, Nicky?" Salazar placed a hand on the back of the chair where Nicky could see it; where it would be a reminder that he could get hit again. Nicky locked onto the hand.

"It wasn't supposed to go that way," Nicky said.

Salazar didn't say anything. He let the silence build. Nicky wanted to say more, and Salazar thought he knew what his *soldier* would say. Tony was the one that pulled the trigger. Salazar still said nothing. In his experience, silence led to blabbing. Nicky did not disappoint.

"Me and Tony we was supposed to just scare Malloy. Make a threat. Rough him up a little. Have him back off."

"And why would that be the message?" Salazar asked.

"Because you already knew that Malloy was a snitch. He was seen with that reporter, but, like you said to us, Malloy didn't do nothing yet, so you just wanted to scare him off."

"That's right. Unnecessary heat is never a good thing. If Terry wasn't going to say anything, then he didn't have to get hit. If he wasn't hit, then no one would know better. Now people will know. Now people do know. You left the kid alive."

His words were cut off with another slap from Salazar. Salazar stood up from the chair and thought again about the Germans. *Are they watching? Will they care about this business? They chose his territory to hide and made veiled threats. Will this make them come through on those threats?*

"You stupid, son of a bitch." Salazar's teeth clenched and he began to savagely punch Nicky until he had no more breath to swing a fist.

Nicky groaned in his chair, and Salazar stood over him panting. He could have started punching again, but the moment felt over. He looked over at Gus.

"What time is it?" Salazar asked. Gus told him. Salazar shot a look at Nicky. "Keep me updated. I'm going to be late."

He unrolled his sleeves and threw his jacket on before leaving the small office.

# 2

Mary Allen paced the area where the elevators let out. She could have just waited at her desk, but when she got in that morning, she dropped her belongings and decided she couldn't bear to sit there yet; it felt like she had never left from the night before. After Frank had left the office, Mary stared at the words she had written for her story. She stared at all that blank space where more words needed to be written, but nothing came to her. Her mind was so focused on Frank Hodge that everything else seemed to play second fiddle, even her job. Mary thought about that, and knew it was unhealthy territory. *How could I have fallen so hard and so fast for a man that I loathed on first impression? It's his eyes. There was just something damaged there, something lost, but there was the sparkle that wanted to come through. Frank fought hard to be aloof, to not care about the people and things around him. He wanted to be hard, so as not to be hurt, like a stray dog, he would hide when he felt threatened. In Frank's case, it's the emotion that was the threat. And damn it, that sparkle is just so attractive.*

Mary had always had a thing for strays. Her hands were grasped in front of her. When she noticed that, she took a deep breath, and smoothed her dress. She wished her stray were standing in front of her now.

The ding of the elevator pulled her from her thoughts about Frank Hodge. While her reasoning for waiting dealt with Frank, she had to put on her reporter's hat now and interview Mr. Albert Graves.

A crowd of men stepped off the elevator, and trailing behind them, looking down at a folded-up newspaper, his dour expression in place like a stone mask, stepped Albert Graves. He wore a drab gray suit and the light from above shone off his bald scalp. Albert's eyes lingered on Mary's legs for far too long, and then the rest of her figure. When their eyes finally met, Mary had to fight to suppress a shudder. She knew it was time to play nice.

"Miss Allen, what a pleasant surprise. How are we this morning?"

"Good morning, Albert," Mary said, knowing how Graves would react from the lack of formality.

A look of distaste crossed Albert's face, as Mary knew it would. She would play nice, but that didn't mean that she couldn't have a little fun with the grave man.

"Yes. Well, I do have work to do." He started to walk by.

*too*

"Albert, I need your help."

"Hmm. Yes, well, why don't we step over to my desk and we'll see what this is about."

Mary began to let go of his arm, but he clasped a hand over it as if he were escorting her on a date. Albert led her the long way

137

around the office to his desk. Mary was not blind to the eyes that watched them, she wished she were.

At his desk, Albert placed his briefcase down and plopped onto his chair. The chair protested his presence as much as she did as it groaned from the weight.

Albert Graves took the moment to look Mary over again before asking, "What can I help you with, Ms. Allen?"

"Edward Salazar," Mary said. "I need some information."

His face grew defensive, territorial. Albert adjusted his glasses, and his eyes took on a hard squint. "That's my story."

"Yes. I know. I also know that you were talking to a Terry Malloy before he and his wife were murdered. I also know that you are looking for their son, Thomas. And I know where he is." The last part was true. Frank had told her where Thomas was. She'd be lying if she didn't admit that she felt a pang of jealousy when Frank told her that he went to his ex-wife for help. But she also understood. What was a guess in her statement was that Albert Graves was the reporter talking to Terry Malloy in the hopes of bringing Edward Salazar down. He was working on a story about Salazar, but that didn't mean he had spoken to Terry. It could have been any number of reporters in the city.

That guess paid off though. Mary could see that Albert wanted to know how she knew. He wanted to know where Thomas was. She had hooked him.

"I do not share bylines, Ms. Allen."

*So, he wants to play hard ball*, Mary thought, *I can accommodate that.*

"I have no interest in sharing the byline, Mr. Graves. I was simply asking as a professional courtesy because a new angle in the story has crossed my desk. An exclusive, but if you have no interest… very well."

Mary turned to walk away.

"Miss Allen," his chair groaned again as he shifted, this

time even louder, "these are not men to be trifled with."

"Thank you for your concern." She kept walking and in a few short steps, he caught up and stopped her.

"Maybe you should come sit down." He looked down, this time at his own shoes and not her legs.

"Very well." She smiled.

They walked back to his desk. Once seated, she took out her notebook and flipped to the notes she had taken when Frank had laid the story out for her.

"As I said, I am not looking to share a byline, or to write the story. What I am looking for is information."

Albert Graves's face relaxed just a little, but there was still suspicion hiding in the lines around his eyes.

"What exactly are you looking for, Miss Allen?"

"As I said, information." When Albert made no reply, Mary continued, "I know that this is a dangerous man, and I know he has influence with the police department. My source said that he was nearly killed when he went to the police for help."

"And who, might I ask, is your source?" Graves removed his own little notebook and a pencil from the inside pocket of his suit jacket.

"No, you may not ask. Let's just call him an interested party, who happened to be in the wrong place at the wrong time. Now, if Edward Salazar has the police in his pocket, my question to you, Mr. Graves, is who can help bring him down?"

Albert Graves placed his notebook and pencil down. He meticulously straightened them on his desk before looking at her. He didn't say anything until Mary's discomfort had her opening her own mouth to speak.

Graves got there first, "I will help you, but you must give me something in return."

There was a gleam in his eye that Mary didn't like. Not

one bit. She already knew what he would ask, and while she was reluctant to agree, she knew it was the only way. She said nothing as she waited for his fat, greedy lips to open and utter the words she knew were coming.

"I want the exclusive story. I want interviews with all interested parties: your source, the Malloy boy, everyone involved. And I get the full story."

It was the type of story she desperately needed if she ever wanted to get away from being assigned puff pieces about fashion, or novelty pieces about how little Scotty organized a victory garden for his neighborhood. It was the type of story one doesn't come across too often. It was the type of story that would see her taken seriously around the newsroom. The type of story that could make a career. Her career. She even had a title all worked out: Reluctant Radio Hero Saves the Day.

"It's yours."

*Damn you, Frank*, she thought as she looked into the nicotine-stained smile of Albert Graves.


# 3


When his son was born, Edward Salazar thought he could never be happier, but watching Oliver grow and mature, Salazar knew he had been mistaken. As long as his boy was there, as long as he continued to teach him and watch him grow, he knew the happiness he felt would continue to grow. Everything he did, he did for his son. That wasn't always true, of course, it used to be for selfish reasons, money, and power, or just for the thrill of it. But being a parent changed things. Being a parent made him mature in a way he never even considered when he started the Docktown Dukes.

Salazar wanted his son to grow up strong and self-sufficient, but he wanted his boy to also be a good man. Oliver was not disappointing in that regard. Oliver read books, asked questions that no eight-year-old should. The kid was smart. He was sensitive, but strong. He cared for other people in ways that Salazar never had. And he was, overall, a good kid. Salazar wanted to keep him that way.

So, he had made it a point early on in Oliver's life to always be home for dinner; to always be around for his son. This was something that Salazar's own old man never did. His old man had been a louse. He never cared about anything but work and his drink. His old man worked late and came home even later smelling of piss and booze. His own father abused him. Beat him. Until Salazar was old enough and strong enough to fight back.

On that day, his father came in drunk and mean because he lost a ton of money playing cards. Salazar took the first punch in the jaw, but he quickly fought his father down. Standing over his father, Salazar trembled, teeth clamped shut.

"You can't touch me. You've done your worst, and I'm still standing. You ever try to touch me or mom again, and I'll kill you."

His father began to sob, and Salazar never found out if it was because his father felt proud or beaten.

Edward Salazar never wanted Oliver to feel the pain and fear he had felt as a kid. He wanted to always be there for his boy. That was why he protected his operation so fiercely. That was why he had zero tolerance for rats and snitches. For his son's sake, he could not be caught.

"What'd you do in school today?" This was Salazar's favorite question to ask his son at dinner. The way the boy's eyes lit up with excitement recalling the little details that made up his day. Things that were trivial to an adult meant the world to a child.

The phone rang before Oliver could answer, and Salazar gave it a look like he could silence it with his glare. The phone continued to ring, and Alice stood to get it. She listened and nodded. Alice looked over her shoulder at him, and Salazar knew his night at home was over. Too much was happening out there, and until things settled down it would not be the same.

He stood from his chair and took the phone from Alice. Neither said a word.

With his back to his family, Salazar said, "Yeah."

"Our guy is here. Says he has some information for you. There's another... interested party."

"This thing is getting too big, Gus. If the Germans find out about all the heat, what's going to happen?"

"I don't know. They want to keep a low profile too."

"Exactly. And the way things are going, it doesn't feel that low to me anymore. We need to end this quickly. We need to find the kid before this goes any further, before the krauts find out."

"Our guy doesn't know where he is, but he says he can find out. Some reporter was asking questions about you. Talked about the Malloy kid and some actor."

"I don't like it. It's getting too big." Salazar repeated. "Meet me at the office."

Things were moving, and they were moving fast. He dropped the phone back in the cradle and went to his son.

"Sorry, kiddo, I've got some problems at work."

"Will you be back to read to me tonight?" Oliver asked.

"I'll try, but I'm not sure." Salazar bent and kissed the top of his son's head, then ruffled his hair. "I love you, Ollie."

"I love you too, pop."

Alice walked with Salazar to the front door. The look on her face told Salazar that she was worried. He was too. While Ollie was sheltered from what his father did for a living, Alice was not. She knew about the Malloy situation and the Germans. Their relationship went as far back as the Dukes, so Alice knew everything. In all that time together, her fears never went away.

Salazar saw them come to the surface every time he headed out the door.

"Be careful," Alice said. "I love you."

Salazar hugged her tightly and kissed her hard. He stepped outside as the first flakes of snow lazily fell from the sky. It was a cold night.

# 4

Albert insisted on going with her to visit his contact with the police, a detective named Harry Cooper. He assured her that his man wanted to bring down Salazar more than anyone.

"Detective Cooper grew up with Edward Salazar, even ran with him in the Docktown Dukes for a while. But when Salazar had made a bad call and gotten Cooper's brother killed, Harry broke away from the gang and joined the cops. Both Salazar and Cooper grew in their respective ranks. Salazar in the underworld of the city, and Cooper with the police." Mary frowned at the bravado in Albert's tone, but her interest in his story held her tongue. "Harry Cooper still holds a grudge, and now a badge. Harry Cooper still wants justice for his brother." As they approached the car, Albert added, "So, he and I teamed up with the Herculean task of bringing Edward Salazar down once and for all."

On the ride to meet with Detective Cooper, Albert informed Mary that he and Cooper had worked on finding a source inside of Salazar's organization. They were ready to give up hope, to find a new angle of attack, but then Terry Malloy had presented himself. Graves never found out how Malloy knew about him, or that he was trying to bring down Salazar, but he held onto the suspicion that one of the dockworkers under Salazar's thumb, who had met with an 'unfortunate' accident, had given Malloy the reporter's name.

The taxi pulled to the curb and Mary climbed out, followed by Albert a moment later. A tall man stood with his back to the wall, looking up and down the street, his eyes were restless. The man wore a long tan raincoat and a black fedora. When Albert led the way over to him, he took the hat off revealing sandy blonde hair buzzed around the sides with a side part on top. He looked young, but Mary assumed the man had to be in his mid to late thirties, the same as Salazar. He had the look of a man in uniform, with the rigid straight back and intense, serious eyes.

Albert held a hand out and the man shook it. "Detective Cooper."

The detective looked at Mary with some suspicion, and she had to fight not to look away from his gaze. After he sized her up, he said, "And this is the young lady you called me about? The one working for you?"

Mary, feeling like she was not passing whatever test this Cooper fellow had silently placed over her, stepped around Albert and held a hand out taking charge of her own introduction.

"Mary Allen. I am a *colleague* of Albert's."

Something shifted in Cooper's eyes, but Mary couldn't tell if it was a shift in her favor or not. She hoped that a little control would help Cooper's estimation of her, but she also knew how some men were with a strong woman. They could not accept it.

Cooper nodded. "It's good to see you ladies stepping up while our boys are overseas."

While she'd give just about anything for the war to end, and American soldiers brought home to reunite families and loved ones, she knew that the soldiers fighting overseas was what gave her the chance at her job to begin with. She didn't say any of this though. She just smiled and gave a slight nod.

"Let's take a little walk," Cooper said.

He started off before Mary or Albert could respond. They fell in line on either side of him.

"Where are we headed?" Mary shivered in the cold.

"This is my old neighborhood," Cooper said. "Over there, that row of houses, that's where I grew up. No one I know still lives around here. At least, no one I care to know. See that one on the end? That was Eddie's house. The one right around the corner was Gus. They were like brothers. Hell, their relationship was closer than I was to my actual brother."

Cooper stopped at the corner and turned to Mary. She had the impression that Albert had heard this already. "Alex, he was my brother. He didn't want to join up with Ready Eddie. I did. It started out with the four of us fighting each other almost every day. Me and Alex against Eddie and Gus. I don't know if we were trying to establish the block as our turf, or if we were bored, or just wild boys looking to prove something. From that fighting grew a grudging respect, a veneer of friendship, then finally the four of us were thick as thieves. Especially when we were stealing." A grin crossed his face.

"What happened?" Mary asked.

"Alex had never been comfortable with the path we were taking. It was like something out of a Cagney movie. I was all for the criminal life, but Alex wanted to be a priest. He wanted to help people, not hurt them. Even the ones that deserved it, my kid brother wanted to save. So, every job we pulled, the more he pulled away. Eddie started getting tired of the little smash and grab jobs we were doing. He wanted a big score. He wanted us to get into the big leagues, you know? I was for it. So was Gus, of course. But, Alex, he wanted to sit it out. He wanted the two of us to sit it out. The score seemed perfect. Eddie had me convinced, but not Alex. I was the one that convinced Alex." He stopped and his eyes took on a pained look. A haunted one.

"What was the job?" Mary asked.

He did not answer at first. He stared at the row of houses. A sad smile whispered across his lips.

"Eddie wanted to rob the *actual* big leagues. It was a poker game with some extremely dangerous people and very high stakes. He and Gus had the whole thing planned out. It sounded good to me, but Alex wanted out. Know how I convinced him?"

"No." Mary, feeling Cooper's anguish, felt tears well up in her own eyes.

"It didn't take much, really. I told him that I needed him with me. Or maybe that was everything. I needed him with me, and now I will never have him again."

"What happened?"

"Things were moving fast. We took care of security outside. No one was hurt, not really. Sure, they'd have a headache and bump, but nothing serious. Then we went inside expecting just the card players. We had this image of stacks of bills and poker chips. We had a plan. We get in there, each of us covering a player at the table. Only one is missing. Alex turned to me. He looked me in the eye and shook his head. He knew. Somehow, he knew it was about to go south. I trusted in my brother as much as he trusted in me.

"So, I turn to Eddie and tell him we should split. He doesn't want to hear it. Gus neither. We keep going. We disarm the men at the table, and Alex starts taking the cash and shoving it in the bag we brought. Thousands and thousands of dollars. More money than we had ever seen. There was something else that we didn't see. The missing player came out, and like he had some vengeance against Alex, he pointed his gun and just shot Alex. Then he shot again and again.

"I can still see Alex standing there with the half full bag of cash just hanging in his hand. He looked at me, and I will never forget the look in his eyes. He blamed me, but I read something else in those eyes too. He wanted me to be better; to do better. I stayed with Alex, even as Eddie and Gus took off. I expected that I wouldn't walk out of there alive, but these men didn't lay a finger on me. I wasn't sure why, and when I asked, they didn't respond. One of them, the one who shot Alex, helped me take him out of there. When we were out in the street carrying my brother, he looks me in the eyes and says, with all sincerity, 'no hard feelings, kid'.

"As much as I hurt, as much as I wanted to kill this man who had shot my brother, the only good person in my life, I nodded. I thought of Alex and what Alex would have wanted. He would not have wanted revenge; we were the ones in the wrong. He would want me to forgive, to pay my penance. So, I did what I thought my brother would have wanted. I did better. I became a better man. I knew I couldn't walk the line of a priest like he would have, but I dedicated my life to cleaning up the streets."

Cooper said no more, and Mary knew he didn't have to. She could fill in the blanks on her own. She guessed Cooper was a soldier and saw some action. When he came home, he joined the cops and worked to honor is brother by cleaning up the streets, being a better man. And he wanted Salazar brought down. For Cooper, Salazar was his penance. Mary got the feeling that Cooper blamed and punished himself, even today, for the death of Alex. But she knew that Salazar had become 'the great white whale' for his part in Alex's death.

Cooper who had been staring into the past, came back to the present. "Now that you know my story, why don't you tell me how we can help each other?"

# 5

By the time he pulled onto the pier, the snow was falling hard. The flakes were so thick, it looked like something fake, out of a movie. Each flake was so big you could see their individual shapes. Salazar knew that Ollie would love it. He also knew he had to keep his head in the game. This could be the break he had been waiting for, hoping for. This could be the end of his troubles.

Tires skidded on the ice as Salazar pressed on the breaks, and for a moment, he thought he would end up driving through his small office and into the icy river beyond. That would be a shitty, pathetic way to go. He wondered if it would be a fitting end to all the lousy things he had done throughout his life. Would it be a just ending to all the pain he had caused? Salazar did not think so. He always saw himself going down in a hail of bullets. Fighting until his last breath. He didn't want to go down at all, and he knew that the visions of glory were romanticizing the issue. Dead was dead, and there was nothing glorious about it.

It didn't matter none, because the car did stop and Salazar closed his eyes to compose himself after he put it into park.

He climbed out of the car and into the cold, taking care as he walked to the office as to not slip on the ice. Inside, Gus had the fire in the wood burning furnace blazing. Nicky was no longer there, but the chair and the ropes that had bound him were. The ropes lay where they must have fallen when Nicky was untied, and the chair was now occupied by a face that felt vaguely familiar. It took Salazar a moment to recognize the man.

One of the Germans who had come in after the initial man. One of those packs with the identity and money belonged to him. Salazar had never seen the man in person, but he had seen photos.

"Ready, we have a guest."

"Enough with that name already. And I'm not blind. Who is this?" Salazar decided to play dumb about their *guest*.


But the German stood from the chair and cut Gus off. He extended a hand and said in a near perfect New York accent, "I am Joseph Smith."

The name was laughably generic, but Salazar guessed it was as good as any, especially if these men were trying to keep a low profile. Salazar shook the man's hand. He would be lying if he said he wasn't scared of the men who he knew could not be on American soil for any good reason. If they were, then they would not have slipped into the country under the radar. And they would not have had bags of money and identification papers hidden in one of his warehouses. So, why was this man here now?

"But," Smith continued, "You already knew that. As, I am sure you recognize my face, yes?"

"I don't have a clue who you are." Salazar lied.

"Your men took my picture. I'm sure they showed you."

Salazar opened his mouth to say something, but nothing came to mind. He had no explanation. He was caught, what more could be said? He closed his mouth again.

"I understand." The German held his hands up and issued a reassuring smile. "My people would have done the same. In fact, we have." Smith reached into his pocket and took out an envelope of pictures. He dropped them on the desk and photos of Salazar, Gus, the dockworkers, and Salazar's *other* men slid out.

Smith reached out to the photos and selected one. He held it up for Salazar to see. The photo showed a man that looked much like the other longshoremen, but Salazar did not recognize the face of the man.

He shook his head. "I don't follow."

"You do not recognize this man?" Smith held the photo up a little higher. The glossy image caught the dim glare of the bare bulb hanging from the ceiling. "That's because he is mine. He keeps tabs on things around here." He finished his sentence with a shrug.

"Why are you here?"

"We are here to sow the seeds of chaos," Smith said.

Salazar almost wanted to laugh. It was like something out of a propaganda film. "Why are you here tonight?"

"My superiors want me to help you with your troubles."

Salazar shook his head. "I don't have any troubles, friend."

"What about the child and the actor? They are not troubling you?" Smith smiled; this one was less than reassuring.

"Everything is under control. It's not trouble, and it is certainly not your trouble."

"It is too late for my people to find another safe house, so anything that might bring 'the heat' as Americans say, is my trouble."

"I handle my business." Salazar's tone was insistent, strong.

Smith looked at him and nodded. "I will give you time, but when I feel that you can't handle your business, I will be back."

It didn't sound like a threat, but it sure felt like one. Smith turned toward the door where Gus had taken up position. Smith said nothing, but Gus looked over the German's shoulder to see what Salazar wanted to do. Between the heat from the stove, and the conversation, Salazar just needed air. He needed Smith to be gone. He needed to go back on their deal and end the tenancy of the Germans on his docks. Salazar, too hot for the cold, felt suffocated. He nodded his head and Gus stepped away from the door.

Smith looked back wearing a polite smile and then disappeared out the door.

Salazar gripped the chair at his desk. He squeezed. He wanted, no needed, to hit something. He needed to scream. This would not be his ruin. This would not be how he went down.

"Where are Tony and Nicky now?"

"They're cooling off in one of the warehouses. Mazzo's on them."

Salazar knew cooling off meant that they were being guarded. No harm, or additional harm rather, was being done to the two men who put him in this position.

"Good," Salazar said. "It's time for them to redeem themselves. Get them in here."

Gus left without a word.

# 6

Mary laid it out for Harry Cooper, much the same she did with Albert Graves. She held onto the same information she had about where Thomas was now. Even in the short time she had known Cooper, she felt he was trustworthy, but she didn't want to put the innocent boy at risk. And she had no idea where Frank had gone off to… or if he was even alive. She knew at this point; she should not worry. Frank was supposed to meet up with her in the morning, or at least call the paper if he couldn't go there, and she had not heard from him either way. But it was still morning, so, with much difficulty, Mary tried not to focus on Frank's whereabouts. Instead, she tried to focus on the situation at hand.

Could they really bring down Edward Salazar? Before Frank had come to her with the story, Mary had heard whispers around the newsroom about the man; mainly when one of the dockworkers had an accident. The crime reporters liked to boast about the dangerous men and sometimes women they were investigating. For them, it was like a badge of honor. Mary didn't understand it, she guessed it was some kind of male ego thing. A way of measuring one's self against others, if you will. While Albert Graves didn't often join the boasting, he did not shy away from the talk when the other men asked about what he was working on. When Albert dropped the name of Salazar, the other men of the newsroom offered appreciative whistles and claps on the back.

But, to Mary's knowledge, Albert had been working on the story for some time now, and still Edward Salazar was a free man, a free and dangerous man. This led her to wonder how much progress he and Cooper could really be making. Which then led her to wonder if there wasn't something else going on. Mary didn't see it though. She didn't believe that Albert was a bad man, despite her own feelings and distaste for him. Still, if the police and a good reporter were on the job why wasn't Salazar already behind bars?

Cooper called her name, dragging her from her thoughts.

"I'm sorry, what?" Mary looked back and forth between Cooper and Albert.

"I asked if you cared to grab some breakfast with Albert and me to talk about this some more?"

She shook her head. "Thank you. I should go see if my source has made contact." She didn't know why she had called Frank her source, maybe to distance herself from worry, but both Albert and Cooper looked at her strangely.

"Are you okay?" Cooper placed a hand on Mary's upper arm. He gave her bicep a light squeeze.

Mary nodded.

"Yes. Tired is all. I didn't have a decent night's sleep."

Cooper still looked concerned but nodded his head. He removed his hand from her arm and the three said their goodbyes and parted ways. Mary headed in the opposite direction of the two men, and the feeling that something was off came rushing back. There was something about the way they were acting that she didn't like, but she just couldn't put her finger on it. Was it both of them? Or just Cooper? She did not know, but she pushed the thought down, hoping her subconscious would play with it and come to a conclusion. She hoped that conclusion was just her tired imagination playing tricks on her.

Mary hailed a cab as she turned the corner. She took another look back the way she had come, but Albert and Cooper were no longer in sight.

# 7

He watched as Nicky and Tony left the office. They each had a look in their eyes, aside from the fresh bruises and lacerations, a determination set on their faces. They wanted to please him. They wanted to make up for their mistakes and the problems they caused. Salazar didn't know if he should trust them again, but he explicitly told them no killing this time. If they did, then they would be dead by the end of the night. This thing was too hot already. Besides, from how they described this guy, he was a fat little pissant who shouldn't be much trouble. If they applied a quarter of the pressure he laid down on them to this guy, he should roll over no problem. They just had to find out where this actor was or might be. Shouldn't be much trouble at all. Still, Salazar had his doubts. Nicky and Tony have proven that they probably shouldn't be relied upon. The thing with the Malloys was not their first mistake, it just happened to be their worst mistake. Possibly one of their last mistakes.

"What do you think the likelihood of them screwing this up is?" Salazar asked Gus. Gus sat in his chair to the side of the doorway. He, as usual, was reading the newspaper.

Gus dropped the paper from his face and looked at the door as if he were peering into the future. "They've done work like this before. They should be fine."

"Putting the scare into Terry Malloy was supposed to be like this and look how that turned out. Not fine."

"Eddie, they got this. If they don't, we'll figure it out, or that German offered to help."

"Absolutely not. That comes at a price I am not prepared to pay. He stays out of it. It's bad enough that he is on my docks. We take care of our own problems."

"It's not like this Scrapper guy is just going to waltz up to the office here and offer himself up. If you're worried about it, we've got to do something," Gus said. "While we don't know this Joseph Smith's mission, he obviously doesn't want any heat either. From what we pieced together; this guy is the real deal."

Salazar fought back his impatience. He knew they had to do something, and the more time that passed with Nicky and Tony being the ones he sent out to do something about it made him nervous. They hadn't been gone long, probably weren't more than a mile or two away, but Salazar already felt it was a mistake to send them. He figured they wouldn't want to screw up again. They knew what would happen if they did, but what if they were so eager to do it right that they screwed up worse than the last time? Could he really rely on Joseph Smith? Should he? The spy's handlers couldn't even come up with a better name.

No. He would not ask Smith for help. Not yet anyway. He didn't want to think about that just now. He and Gus had to make it work without the German. It was his business, and he could not show a sign of weakness.

"We leave the German out of it. If things get… desperate, then we consider it. You hear me? No outside help." Salazar looked at Gus until the heavyset man nodded. "Good. Now let's think about this. What are our concerns?"

"So, we got the kid. He saw everything. Then we got this actor, Hedges, or something."

"Hodge."

"Sure, Hodge. We don't know who else they may have told. It's possible that the guy from the radio station knows something. Nicky and Tony are handling that. At the least he'll know where to find the actor."

"In other words, we don't have shit."

"What about the cops, boss?"

Salazar shook his head in confusion. Go to the cops? He never really considered himself a criminal, at least not anymore. He always thought of his organization as a business, and himself a businessman. Big business did questionable things all the time, so why couldn't he? They broke the law and made more money. He lived under that same principle. Sometimes things went south, sure, but he took care of his community. He cleaned it up. Kept the drugs out. Kept the… undesirables out. But, when he did think about the cops, it scared him. All the little lies he told himself rushed to the surface. He had people hurt. He had people killed. He ran a racket. What he did was frowned upon in the eyes of Johnny Law, so how could he really consider himself legit?

And why would Gus suggest going to the police? The police brought questions. The police brought suspicions. He couldn't buy off everyone.

"Sergeant Henry and his guys. We ain't heard back from them." Gus said.

Salazar wasn't sure if more had been said before that, but Gus's intentions clicked home. Gus hadn't meant to go to the police to report, he had meant to go to the police to get a report. Without a word, Salazar picked up the phone and within moments was being connected to his man on the cops.

"Yeah, Henry, it's me." That was all that needed to be said, and Salazar wouldn't have wanted to say more.

"He had help." Sergeant Henry's voice was hesitant.

Salazar stayed silent, but he wanted to scream at the man on the other end. This was not a report. This was no information at all. Henry did not continue, forcing Salazar to ask. "What do you mean, Sergeant?"

"We had him. We had them both. I offered to take the kid off his hands, and then Hodge would never have to see us again. He didn't go for it."

"And?"

"And then we were on him. We got a couple good hits in… but… but he had help. Four, five guys came out of nowhere, must of followed my patrol car. They grab my guys, and a fight happens. We were lucky they didn't kill any of us. This Hodge fella stole my car and drove off with the kid. His men disappeared as easily as they had come in. Lucky, we found my car not too far away."

"Lucky? I fail to see any luck in this situation. Are your boys out there looking for him?"

"About that. We're done. I'm on my way out of all this anyway, but the boys got a long way to go. This is too hot, and too risky. You keep our last bit of pay as a gesture of good will and peace," Sergeant Henry said.

"You're not going to do anything, Eddie. You are powerful, but you are a crook. We've got insurance. We've got badges if you know what I mean. We're out."

The line went dead. The muscles of Salazar's hand cramped from squeezing so hard. He replaced the phone in the cradle and looked at Gus.

"Apparently this guy has friends. It's a no go with Henry and the boys. They're out."

"Do we hit them?" Gus asked.

"Nah, too risky. Things are bad enough as it is. Besides, we may be able to save the relationship. With some of them, at least."

"What now, Ready?"

"Damn it! Ready Eddie is dead. We ain't kids no more. Gus, for the first time in a long time, I'm feeling a little lost here. I don't know what to do. I feel…" His words trailed off. He looked at his old friend. Salazar was not the type of man who wore his heart on his sleeve. He was not the type to share. He always wanted the image of strength. But this was Gus.

"I feel like we're trapped in a burning building with no way out. You know what I mean?" Salazar made sure to keep eye contact.

Gus broke his gaze away. A look crossed his face that Salazar did not like. He showed his weakness, and Gus was eating it up. Gus was disgusted. Now, on top of everything else, Salazar had to worry about his old friend making a move.

He opened his mouth, but Gus held up a hand before Salazar could utter a word. Salazar closed his mouth. Gus held a finger to his lips in a shushing motion and then tapped his ear. He had Salazar's attention. Gus pointed to the door and drew a square in the air with his finger. Salazar thought he understood, and then he heard the noise from outside. Just as the sound registered in his ears, Gus pointed his index and middle finger down and made like they were walking.

Footsteps.

"Someone at the window." Gus said in a whisper.

"Probably a bird or something."

Salazar stood up from his chair the same time as Gus stood from his own. Like it was rehearsed, they both reached into their jackets and came out with a gun. For Gus, a Colt .38 revolver, for Salazar a Smith & Wesson. He motioned with his head and Gus went to the door. Salazar took aim at the door, and Gus pushed it open. They were met only by the gust of cold air that broke up the heat of the fire as if it were never there.

Salazar stepped slowly through the door, the S&W at the ready. No one was in sight. He looked at Gus and shook his head.

"I'm tellin ya, I saw something."

"Probably a bird." Salazar repeated, but with the way things were going, he had a bad feeling that it was someone peeking in. "I'm not too fond of freezing my keister off out here, Gus."

He wanted to dismiss the whole thing.

But the sound came again. Outside, even with the wind blowing, the sound of footsteps was unmistakable.

"There was someone in the window." Gus's eyes widened and his expression said *now do you believe me*. Salazar did. He motioned for Gus to go one way and he would go the other. Gus nodded and the two men separated.

With his S&W held at the ready, Salazar began his trek around the small office. He made sure to be careful on the slick, wet boards. He turned the corner so that he was on the backside of the little shack he called an office, but there was no one there. Salazar pushed on.

Turning the final corner, he watched as a tall man in a black suit reached into his pocket. Salazar was about to pull the trigger of his gun, expecting the tall man to be reaching for his own, but when the man's hand came out it held a red handkerchief.

The tall man lifted his hand as if he were going to blow his nose, but he pulled the fabric tight and down over his head. It was not a handkerchief, but a mask.

Salazar took another step, and the man froze. He turned and looked back at Salazar. Salazar, for his part, put on a smile. The menacing one that he used when he came across someone who didn't want to fall in line. Inside, Salazar was confused. *Who is this guy? How could he be so brazen and foolish? What's with the mask?*

"What the hell is this?" Salazar asked.

"That ain't no bird, Ready," Gus said.

"I know. Sorry Ed. Force of habit." Gus shrugged.

"Let's bring him into the light. I want to… see him better." Salazar was confused. He had feared that the German was spying on him. That Smith was trying to muscle in on the operation, or just kill him outright. He had not expected a man in a mask.

Salazar shoved the man forward. The man walked, and when he was back on level ground, he held his hands up near his face as if surrendering. Salazar's mind was all over the place. He began to circle the masked man, until he stood in front of him. Gus stood to the side; his own gun pointed at the masked stranger.

"What's with the mask?" Salazar asked.

The masked man touched his cheek as if he just realized he were wearing a mask at all.

"You there?" Salazar prodded when the masked man didn't answer.

This was getting weirder by the minute. "You some kind of nut? What's with the mask? You trying to rob us? No one robs Edward Salazar."

He thought again of the German. How many of them were there? Would his business be of interest to them? Would they make a move against him?

"Eddie, this is the guy from the radio," Gus said. "You know, the one with the kid."

"The Scarlet Scraper!" The red mask suddenly made sense... sort of.

"It's the Scarlet Scrapper," the guy said.

*What is his name? Hedge... no, Hodge. Frank Hodge.*

"I don't care what you call yourself. I want the kid. Unless I get him, you can call yourself dead."

"As you can see," Hodge made a show of looking around. "I don't have him. Why is he so important anyway?"

"Frank Hodge. Sergeant Henry told me about you. That you came in with the boy in tow. Said that you and a group of your friends fought off three armed men despite him telling you that you could leave. So, *why* is the boy so important to you?"

Hodge did not answer, but Salazar took something from his silence. The boy meant something to this man. Salazar recognized the love of a father for a son. He almost felt bad. But he was doing it for Ollie. Even though when Ollie found out the Malloy kid was dead, it would hurt him.

"You care for Thomas Malloy, don't you? I always liked him too. He and my boy used to pal around in the summers. Thomas would come to work with his old man, and my little Ollie would be here waiting with a ball and a stick. He's a good kid. Both boys are."

"Then why?"

Salazar's mind was still on the two boys. "It wasn't

159

supposed to go this far…" He kept talking, but he thought of all the mistakes that led him here. He *did* like the Malloy kid. Liked his old man too. If he had just gotten to talk to him first. If those idiots hadn't done what they done.

Hodge continued to talk, and Salazar continued to respond, but he was only half there. Words struck his ears and mind. Innocent. Just a kid. Let him walk. Salazar had to bring himself back. He needed to decide about what to do with this man. He was just as much a threat now as the boy was.

"So, you'll kill him because of something that might happen in the future? Be reasonable, man."

Maybe the Malloy kid wouldn't be an issue. Maybe this would just all go away. Salazar said, "You're right. You're right." Thomas Malloy might not be a problem down the line. He knew it was true. The kid would never forget, but that didn't mean anything. On the other hand, if he looked at the trouble that this whole situation brought upon him, how could he take the chance? "But, if Thomas isn't going to be a problem, then why are you here on my docks?"

Salazar, who's gun hand was now at his side, lifted his empty hand and pointed it like a gun at Frank Hodge. He dropped his thumb like the hammer of a gun and made a gunshot noise. Gus fired a second later and the actual gunshot left a ringing in his ears.

He watched as Frank Hodge's body lifted from the docks, seemed to hover before gravity took hold and the radio star disappeared into the icy, black water.

When Salazar looked over the edge, the body was nowhere to be seen.

# 8

Frank was not at her desk when she entered the newsroom, and there was no message on her desk blotter. Mary went to the office secretary to check if she was holding any messages, but the young woman said it had been a slow day and popped her gum. Mary didn't say goodbye as she walked away. As two professional women, there should be a sort of kinship navigating this man's world, but Mary never did get that from the young woman at the desk. She only got a sort of dismissive attitude like Mary was somehow just a burden in the secretary's day. When one of the men went up there, it was all smiles and fluttering eyelashes. Mary shook her head and went back to her desk.

Sitting down, she stared at her empty typewriter. Then she looked around the office. She felt at a loss for something to do. She had to wait for Frank, or for Albert to get back. Either way she had to wait, and she was never very good at being idle. Mary switched her roving gaze from the bustle of the newsroom to the clutter of her desk. How could she be expected to just sit in the closed in world of the office when she had no idea what was going on outside?

"Oh," she muttered under her breath, "Where are you, Frank?"

Through the clutter of papers, notes, and scribbles on her desk, Mary spotted something that could be some forward momentum. She grabbed a scrap of paper with a phone number scrawled on it, then snatched the phone from the corner of the desk.

She got an outside line and dialed. The other end rang, and rang, and finally a woman answered.

"Yes?" The woman asked.

"Hello. I am looking for the Childers residence. I need to speak with Jimmy Childers," Mary noted the desperation in her own voice, and did not like it one bit.

"Mr. Childers," the woman's voice turned defensive, "is currently indisposed. May I take a message?"

"Um. No. That won't be… Yes. Please. This is important. My name is Mary Allen. I am a reporter with the New York Daily. It is important that I speak with Jim… With Mr. Childers."

Mary listened. Her heart thumping into her ears as her temples throbbed with her rising blood pressure. *Will nothing go right today?*

"Hello." She said, again the desperation in her voice noticeable. "Hello."

"Ms. Allen?"

Mary recognized his voice right away. The excitement she noted when they had met was replaced by a wariness and pain, but Mary knew who had come on the line.

"Jimmy," she said. The pressure that had been building released as if someone had slowly turned a valve. "Jimmy, I can't find Frank. He was supposed to contact me this morning. It is vitally important."

"Ms. Allen, Mary, calm down. Frank is here. He's… he's okay."

The valve was fully released, and Mary sagged in her chair. She could hear that there was more to the story than Jimmy was saying, but Frank was okay.

"Has he filled you in?" Mary asked. Jimmy told her that Frank had. "Can we meet? The three of us?"

"I'm not sure that is possible," Jimmy said.

Mary didn't respond. She knew something was wrong but had no idea what. The silence on the line grew. Mary could tell that someone had covered the phone's mouthpiece. The silence was broken by more muffled conversation with the same impatient, angry woman who answered the phone. Then, as if the hand had been ripped from the phone, Jimmy's voice came through the receiver loud and clear. One snapping word, or more precisely a name. "Betty!"

"Jimmy?" Mary asked.

"We think you should come here. I think we all have a lot to discuss and catch up on. As I said, Frank is here. He is hurt Mary, but he'll be fine. Thomas is here as well. I think we'd all like to know how to make this all end."

"Well, Jimmy, I may be able to give you that much, or at least a start."

Mary wrote down the address as Jimmy dictated it. She then jotted down a note to Albert Graves that told him where she was going, without giving him the address. Mary still could not shake the feeling that something was amiss with Albert or Cooper, so she wanted to play it close to the vest. Besides, while the Salazar story may be Albert Graves's, The Scarlet Scrapper was Mary's.

She dropped the note onto the desk of Albert Graves and rushed to the elevator, through the lobby and out into the street. Mary hailed a cab. In such a rush to get going, she didn't even notice Albert step up to her until his large, round belly bumped her elbow.

"Why the hurry, Ms. Allen?"

"Albert, I have to go," Mary started to turn toward the cab, but Albert placed a hand on the door.

"Is this related to *my* story?"

Mary thought about lying, but as soon as Albert Graves went to his desk, he would know the truth anyway. Mary had no time to get into it with him right there on the street. She had no schedule to keep but getting to the Childers residence felt crucial.

"Yes," Mary relented. "I'll fill you in on the way."

If Mary had not been so distracted by the sudden appearance of Albert Graves, she may have noticed Larry Cooper running in their direction.

# EPISODE

# TRIUMPH OF THE
# SCARLET SCRAPPER

# EPISODE FOUR

## The Triumph of the Scarlet Scrapper

From the episode "The Counterfeit Caper" in
*The Adventures of the Scarlet Scrapper*
– April 24, 1943

**F/X:** MECHANICAL PAPER PRESS AND SHEETS OF PAPER RUFFLING

**ADAM:** Say, would you look at this. They look perfect.

**PAULIE:** Aces! They sure do. These counterfeit war bonds are going to make us rich. That General Beahr (pronounced Bear) only wants a small percentage back for the equipment.

**ADAM:** Why's he doing it, though, Paulie? He gives us the equipment, he gives us this old, abandoned sheet metal factory as a base of operations. He sets us up completely. So, I mean, he could be making a fortune on this himself.

**PAULIE:** I don't know. I don't care. Let's collect these samples and start printing the next batch.

**F/X:** METALIC SCREECH OF A DOOR OPENING

**PAULIE:** Someone's here. Take out your gat and face the door. Be ready now.

**ADAM:** There's nobody there!

**PAULIE:** Just keep ready.

**F/X:** PIPE ROLLING ON HARD SURFACE

**PAULIE:** Over there!

**ADAM:** There ain't nobody there, either!

**F/X:** A DISTANT CLANG

**PAULIE:** We're surrounded.

**ADAM:** Is it the coppers?

**PAULIE:** How should I know? (shouts) Where are you?

**SCRAPPER:** (from behind) Say fellas, what do you hear, what do you say?

**ADAM and PAULIE:** Huh?

**F/X:** PUNCH; PUNCH

**SCRAPPER:** So, you want to know why the kraut General Bahr gave you the equipment and asked for almost nothing in return, do you?

**F/X:** SCRAPE OF METAL

**ADAM:** He's got our guns, Paulie.

**PAULIE:** I can see that, ya nincompoop.

**SCRAPPER:** Your friend General Bahr is nothing but a kraut spy set on the destruction of the United States. His only goal is to see America and the Allies fail to stop the Germans and Japanese. Can't you see what you're doing? By selling these counterfeit war bonds you are not only hurting ordinary citizens, but you are hurting your country.

**PAULIE:** Can it, Scrapper, we don't need none of your patriotic babble. Do we, Adam?

**ADAM:** I don't know. What the Scarlet Scrapper says kind of makes sense. We can make money some other way. We don't need to hurt our country.

**PAULIE:** Traitor!

**F/X:** RUNNING FOOTSTEPS FOLLOWED BY A WHOOSH OF AIR AND A PUNCH

**SCRAPPER:** No, Paulie, you're the traitor! You're a traitor to your friend and more importantly, you're a traitor to your country.

**PAULIE:** (moaning)

**SCRAPPER:** Adam, is it?

**ADAM:** Yeah, Scrapper.

**SCRAPPER:** Let's shut this down. I'll put in a good word to the cops for you.

**ADAM:** Say Scrapper, that would be swell!

**SCRAPPER:** I can see you learned your lesson. Nothing in life is worth betraying your ideals and values. It's worth something to work hard for what you earn. If it comes easy, it isn't worth it.

**ADAM:** Thank you, Scrapper. From this day forth, I will follow your example and fight for what is right.

**SCRAPPER:** If we all do our part, we can win this war.

### MUSIC UP and FADE under Announcer

**ANNOUNCER:** And so ends the Case of the Counterfeiters on the adventures of the Scarlet Scrapper. The Scarlet Scrapper is a copyrighted feature that brings you radios most thrilling character in suspense, mystery, and adventure. Oh, be sure to listen when you hear the cry to ride with the Scarlet Scrapper!

### MUSIC UP and FADE under Announcer

**ANNOUNCER:** The role of the Scarlet Scrapper is played by…

*End of Excerpt*

# 1

Frank Hodge awoke to darkness. He could not feel any part of his body, aside from the fierce burning on his side. For a moment, just a moment, but it was enough, Hodge thought he was back in the war. And, for that moment all the fear, anxiety, and pain flooded through him. The lost friends. The explosions. The fire. The blood. But the war for him was over; at least that war was. He was suffocating as he lay there; slowly drowning as if someone held a wet towel tight over his mouth. Hodge swiped at his mouth, but the towel held on. He tried again and his finger snagged on something obstructing his mouth. The mask. He managed to pull the sopping fabric over his mouth and nose, and the clear air that hit his lungs was invigorating.

When his vision finally came back to him, he did not recognize where he lay, but he remembered how he got there. Salazar had shot him with his finger. That couldn't be right, but that was how Hodge remembered it. Hodge lay still for a moment. He wiggled his toes, moved his feet, his legs, fingers, and arms. He couldn't feel much aside from the burning in his side, but everything seemed to be working.

Even with the numbness coursing through him, Hodge managed to pull his soaking corpse out of the ice water and onto a rocky shore. He crawled over the rocks barely feeling as the jagged stone cut into his hands.

Clear of the water, Hodge's strength gave out and so did his arms. With his face planted to the sand gritted ground, Hodge was tempted to just lie still, but he knew that if he did, it would be a death sentence. He rolled to his right, because the pain was on his left, and got his knees under him. He pushed out with his hands, feeling the sharp rocks bite his palms and fingers. He would not die there. He got one foot planted and started to rise. Slowly, he got to his feet. Weak and dizzy, Hodge stood there. When he took a step, the rocks made for bad footing, and he almost fell again. Hodge managed to keep himself upright. He found his way to the street where he leaned against the side of a building.

Even with his unclear mind, Hodge knew he had to get warm. His shivering was uncontrollable and the chattering in his teeth caused his jaw to ache. He needed to get somewhere warm, and fast.

Headlights turned a corner at the end of the block. The car moved in Hodge's direction. Hodge could not make out the details of the car, but he felt sure it had to be Salazar looking to finish the job he had started. He knew he couldn't run; he wouldn't make it far. He let his body sag against the wall of the building and slide down to the ground. Hodge closed his eyes.

The car pulled to a stop. A door opened and heavy footsteps came his way. Still, Hodge kept his eyes closed. The cold air mixed with the fire burning on his side was enough to just want it to end. So, he decided he would not fight it.

The footsteps stopped and there was silence.

"You alive?"

Hodge didn't recognize the voice, and he didn't answer.

"Hey? You alive, buddy?" The voice asked.

His foot was nudged, and Hodge finally opened his eyes. A tall, skinny man wearing a hunting cap with the ear flaps down was standing with his hands on his hips looking down at him. Hodge looked beyond the man to the car at the curb. It was yellow. A taxi.

"I'm not sure. Check back with me in a few," Hodge said.

"You're fine. A little drunk, and soaking wet, but you'll live."

"Okay," Hodge said.

"You got money?" The cabdriver asked. Hodge nodded. "Then where am I taking you, buddy?"

Hodge hadn't even felt the cab driver get him to his feet, but they were already halfway across the sidewalk. Hodge muttered an address, and the cab driver closed the door to the cab. The sensation of movement overtook his body. The jerk of the cab in motion sent fresh, intense pain coursing through his entire being. Hodge closed his eyes again and felt nothing anymore.

"Hey Mac, we're here. You'll have to sleep it off inside."

Hodge awoke with a start. His eyes fluttered open, but he could not focus. His mind was still muddy, and his speech wasn't much better.

"Much owe you."

The cab driver looked over the seat at him. He eyed Hodge up and down, taking in his appearance. The bemused driver held up some sopping wet bills. "You already paid, pal. We're square. You need help getting in?"

Hodge looked down at the wallet he held in his hand. He didn't remember taking it from the inside pocket of his jacket and did not remember handing the cabbie any money. The driver looked over the seat at him, the hand resting on the back of the seat still holding the wet money.

"I'm good." Hodge threw open the cab door. He grabbed the frame and pulled himself out. Unsteady, but standing, he walked across the street and up the steps. The cab sat for a moment but took off leaving Hodge alone.

He faced the door and raised a hand to knock, but his wobbly legs gave out and Hodge fell hard to the concrete steps below him. His head rolled on his neck, and everything went black.

In his dream, footsteps approached. There was the murmur of two voices, one young and one older. There was a threat issued. And still, the footsteps got closer. Even in the dream, all he could see was darkness. Someone called his name. Then there was a pounding, like a fist on something wooden. Another name was called, Hodge thought it sounded like Eddie, but not quite.

His eyes began to open as the dream began to recede, but Hodge realized that he was not dreaming at all. Two dark figures stood over him. It took a few moments for his muddy mind to catch up, but when it did, Hodge smiled.

Jimmy and Thomas were there. Jimmy was close, lightly slapping his face. He called toward the door again, "Betty!"

So, it was Betty, not Eddie. Hodge looked at his old friend and smiled. "Say, pally, you invited me over for dinner. How about a night cap?"

There was a little more conversation, but none of it registered for Hodge as his mind drifted off and someone shut out the lights.

He heard movement and opened his eyes. The ceiling light burned them. Hodge squeezed his eyes shut again. He lay there fighting his muscles into a standstill, as every movement sent flares of pain up and down his side. It was a feeling he remembered too well, and one he still dreamt about too often. Despite a rising desire to go back to sleep because the movement stoked the burning in his side, the light now cut through his eyelids when he closed them. He heard the movement again and tried to ask whoever was there to turn off the light, but all that came out was a dry croak. Hodge shifted his weight and the fire burned more intensely.

"Water," he managed to whisper.

Tiny footsteps replied. A moment later, his eyes still closed, Hodge felt a cool glass against his lips. He took a little sip at first, and then a second. He would have started to gulp it down, but the glass was pulled away. Hodge rested his head back down.

"Please, turn off the light."

Again, tiny footsteps replied and a moment later the harsh light no longer cut through his eyelids. There was still light in the room, but it was dim now; daytime with the curtains drawn. He still refused to open his eyes. Off to his right, the crackle of a burning fire gave off a different sort of heat than the burn he felt on his left side.

With sleep not in sight, Hodge opened his eyes slowly. He was scared even the dim light would burn them, but they were okay if a little out of focus. When his vision cleared, he spotted a tiny face looking shyly over the armrest of the sofa he found himself laying on. The little imp looked familiar, but Hodge could not place her. As his focus returned, he realized the entire room looked familiar. Even the loose-fitting bed shirt that lay unbuttoned on his chest, he recognized. The arms were too short, and the stomach would be too big on him, but not on Jimmy. Hodge knew where he was and knew who had given him the water.

"Aggie?"

The imp poked her head up higher and giggled. The imp, as it turned out, was Jimmy's youngest child Agnes Ruth Childers. Hodge was the only one that called her Aggie. She came over to him and placed her tiny fingers on his arm. He wrapped his hand in hers and marveled, as always, at how tiny she was. Hodge normally did not like children much. It was one of the reasons his relationship fell apart with Grace. Granted, it was a minor part, as his disconnection and alcoholism were the driving forces. But Aggie was different. Hodge took an immediate liking to her as soon as Jimmy placed her featherweight body in his arms on that first day baby Aggie came home. Hodge was hesitant at first, but she reached her little fingers up and tickled his mustache and then she smiled. It was love at first sight.

"Fra," the girl said, and Hodge laughed and winced at the pain that shot through him. Like he was the only one to call her Aggie, she had called him Fra since she started talking.

"Aggie, go get your daddy. Can you do that?"

Aggie nodded, tickled his mustache just like that first time, and ran off pleased with herself. Frank took a moment before he reached down to his injured side. He felt the bandage there. When he looked, he saw the blotch of blood staining the white. He lifted the bandage and barely felt the sting from the tape pulling at his skin.

The bullet had carved a deep trench in his side just above where his belt would have been. His entire side was discolored a purplish yellow that sat on top of the pink scar tissue, this mixed with the dried blood created a gruesome canvas to that which already painted his torso. The skin was sensitive to the touch, and Hodge didn't think exploring it too deeply would be a wise idea. Even the lightest of prodding caused his eyes to lose focus.

"Frank?" Jimmy asked from somewhere behind him, and in a louder voice, "He's awake!"

"How long have I been out? What time is it?"

Jimmy took out his pocket watch. "It was late last night. It's afternoon now. Betty!"

Jimmy's wife Betty came into view next. She was a plump, pleasant looking woman, except when it came to Hodge. Whenever he was around Betty had a hard time hiding the distaste she felt for him. Betty had never approved of Hodge's drinking, womanizing, how he spoke, how he talked to Jimmy, how he dressed, his smoking… well, she didn't approve of Hodge on any level. But, when Hodge looked at her now, he saw something different on Betty's face. Betty was concerned.

"How ya doing, Betty?" Hodge asked.

"Jimmy, please take the kids out of here. Make sure they know that I am helping him," Betty said. She turned to Hodge. She looked him in the eyes, the look of concern turned to worry and sadness. "Frank, I am going to hurt you." The words were slow, enunciating each sound so she was clear.

Hodge wasn't sure he heard her. He opened his mouth, but his words were replaced.

Hodge screamed as Betty did something painful to his left side. His numb side flared into full awareness. It subsided and throbbed a moment later. But Betty was at him again, and the pain flared red and subsided. Red and subsided. Hodge no longer screamed, but whimpered like a hurt, hungry puppy. Days passed with each red-hot pain, and seconds passed when the pain subsided. Betty moved him this way and that and stripped him of the bed shirt. On the coffee table next to him, was a mounting pile of bloodied rags and his old bandages.

It went on and on. At times, Hodge was out completely. Then, from some distance, he heard Betty say, "You'll be okay, Frank. You'll hurt, but you'll be okay."

Hodge tried to answer, but he was falling again. Everything faded until it was all black.

# 2

Thomas could not manage to put it all away. After what he saw happen to his parents, and now seeing the Scrapper with a bullet hole in him too, he wasn't sure how he hadn't crawled up into a ball to disappear from the world. Mr. and Mrs. Childers told him the Scrapper would be fine. That the wound was not as bad as it looked, but Thomas didn't fully believe it. Adults always said stuff like that. Still, at the urging of James, Jimmy's oldest son, Thomas found himself outside in borrowed clothes watching a snowball fight unfold between the Childers children. Thomas watched but did not participate. The feel of the Scarlet

Scrapper's icy skin, images of his pale face were too similar to that of Thomas's own murdered parents. *How could the Scrapper pull out of this? How could skin so cold, skin so pale be that of a living person?*

"Frank will be okay," Mr. Childers had said. "Betty is a nurse. She knows how to take care of him."

Something about him calling the Scrapper by that other name made Thomas fear the wound even more. It made the Scrapper, Mr. Hodge, more real; more human. It made the trench dug into his side with a bullet more painful to look at. *How could anyone survive that?*

But Frank Hodge was the Scarlet Scrapper. Frank Hodge had done so much to help Thomas, even though they were complete strangers. He put his life at risk again and again to fight for justice. Frank Hodge was the Scarlet Scrapper, and the Scarlet Scrapper would not be taken down so easily.

Something inside of him shifted again. The core of his being felt like it was in a malleable state; constantly moving, reforming, trying to find a permanent form to take hold. Thomas lifted his head. *The Scarlet Scrapper would not go down so easily.* Whether he was Frank Hodge or the Scrapper, he was a hero, and he would get up again, because that is what heroes do. Thomas's chest puffed out a little. His shoulders squared. Everything would be alright with the Scrapper on his side. His lip began to pull back into a smile.

An avalanche of snow rushed over his head, the debris fell into the neck of his borrowed jacket and melted slowly down his back. Thomas froze, his muscles tensed from the shock of the cold. He looked up, but there was no indication that the snow fell from above. He looked around, aside from himself and Jimmy's kids, the street was empty. It was like the world no longer existed outside of the bubble of people Thomas had found himself with. Then, he heard the laughter. James pointed a finger at him, a large grin spread across his lips.

"Gotcha!" James was already bending to gather more snow.

There was that shift inside Thomas again. The shock of the snowball wore away, replaced by a sort of childish glee. Thomas ducked down and pushed his own snow into a ball. He formed a second one and rushed James, his snow ammo in hand. James picked up his younger sister, Agnes as a shield. She laughed in delight as he whirled her through the air. Thomas took a shot and then another. The first snowball clipped Agnes on the shoulder. The explosion of snow caused her to laugh harder. The second snowball knocked James's hat clean off his head. Snow shrapnel ran down his face.

"Get him, Agnes!"

James put his sister down and Agnes squished snow in her hand in an attempt to make a snowball, before clumsily running toward Thomas. Thomas ran away in mock fright as Agnes caught up and pressed the sopping snow in her hand onto Thomas's back. He fell to the snow and laughed as she leapt on him.

Thomas had no siblings, and the closest he had to a brother had moved away in a rush, but this, he thought, was what it must feel like. He had just met the Childers's children the night before, but they instantly accepted him. He didn't know if they saw the pain, saw that he needed the connection on some level, and if he was being honest, he didn't care because he appreciated it. Thomas knew that he would be forever grateful to them for allowing him to forget about his real life even if it was short lived.

He rolled with Agnes in the snow. The two of them laughing even as cold, wet snow made its way through the layers of their clothes and down their collars and open sleeves. James rushed over and the snow flinging began again.

# 3

Hodge's knees shook when he saw the kid. He gripped the heavy fabric curtains that hung from the windows and squeezed tightly until he felt some strength return. He told himself that the weakness he was feeling was due to the gunshot wound he had in his side, Hodge understood it was really the shock of seeing Thomas. The fact that the kid managed to find Jimmy felt like a dream. Hodge had thought it *was* a dream when Jimmy had found him on the front stoop more than half frozen and slipping in and out of consciousness. First, he had seen Jimmy looking ridiculous carrying the baseball bat, looking like he had just received a beating from it. Then, he had seen Thomas just before everything had gone black.

Now, he saw Thomas again. He was real, and while a weight of sadness still held the boy down, the smile he wore as he and Jimmy's kids exchanged a barrage of snowballs looked genuine.

It was in that moment that Hodge realized he not only cared for the kid and his well-being, but he loved the kid. They had a bond now. Hodge knew nothing of being a father, and his own father was no example to go by, but he had seen the unconditional love that Jimmy held for his kids. He understood that he was not at the unconditional yet, but he knew that if he were given time and a chance he could easily get to that point.

Thomas smiled and laughed along with Jimmy's children, and, though he could not hear the laughter, Hodge felt it. The pain throbbing in his side seemed to ease and a different warmth flushed through him.

"Frank?" Betty's voice held the usual tone she reserved for Hodge, a little scolding, a lot of bitterness and distaste. But her face held a note that Hodge had never seen when it had come to him: concern. "I told you not to move around. Your wound might not be as bad as we first thought, but you still suffered a great ordeal."

Hodge looked back outside, and Betty was at his side. She started to pull him away but noticed his gaze out the window. Her face softened as she walked him back to the couch. Hodge sat down with a grimace. Betty kept looking at him. The coldness in her eyes melted more.

"He'll be okay," she said. "He suffered, but children are resilient, and they can come back from almost anything. All he needs is someone to care for him. I think the same could be said for you." She looked at Hodge earnestly. Her eyes conveying the message that had hit Hodge as he watched Thomas outside. Somehow, when all this was over, he would have to take Thomas in. If they managed to survive, that is.

"Careful Betty, I might start thinking that *you* care for me," Hodge said.

"Don't count on that," she said, but she was smiling. The first real smile that Hodge could remember directed his way in a long time. Maybe ever. "But he cares for you. God knows why."

The sound of the phone ringing broke the moment. Betty stepped around Hodge and grabbed the phone from the cradle.

"Yes?" Betty remained silent, but her face took on a look of suspicion. Jimmy stepped into the room. "Mr. Childers is currently indisposed. May I take a message?"

Hodge and Jimmy exchanged glances. While Hodge could not hear the other end of the conversation, it looked like Jimmy was in trouble. Hodge himself had been in trouble with Betty for most of the time they've known each other, he pitied his friend.

Hodge and Jimmy looked at each other and said in unison, "Mary."

Jimmy was by her in a flash. He grabbed the phone from Betty's hand.

"That's Mary Allen," Jimmy said as if that explained everything. It didn't. Hodge eyed the phone. He was tempted to snatch it from Betty's hand himself, but by the time he was going to make a move, Betty and Jimmy had settled the argument and the phone was in Jimmy's hand. He shot his wife the sternest look that Jimmy could muster up and held the phone to his ear.

"Ms. Allen," Jimmy said it in an overtly formal tone. Hodge guessed this was for Betty's benefit more than anything. He opened his mouth to talk further but closed it as Mary spoke. Jimmy looked at Hodge and was finally able to speak again. "Ms. Allen, Mary, calm down. Frank is here… He's okay."

"I'm not sure that's possible." He removed the phone from his ear and covered the mouthpiece. He looked from Hodge to Betty but could not meet her eyes for long. "She wants to meet."

"Absolutely not. This whole thing endangers our family, Jimmy. We took Frank in because he was injured, and we took Thomas because he is just a boy. But I don't want you out there. What if these people spot you? Look what they did to you already. What if she's one of them?"

"She's not. We need this to end, so we can all be safe. They know where we live, Betty. That brute made it a point. We will only be safe when this is over, and Mary can help us. Mary has been helping."

"Betty!" Jimmy looked as shocked as Hodge and Betty at his outburst. Hodge felt a certain amount of pride in seeing Jimmy stand up for him and stand up for himself. While Hodge understood Betty's concerns, her worries, Jimmy was right. They were all in danger until it ended; until Salazar was put away. "Sorry, but this is how it has to happen."

Jimmy took a second to compose himself and held the phone back to his ear. "We think you should come here." He looked Betty square in the eye, as if daring her to argue again. Hodge decided he was more than *just* proud of his friend, though he couldn't think of a word to convey such a feeling. "I think we all have a lot to discuss and catch up on. As I said, Frank is here. He is hurt Mary, but he'll be fine. Thomas is here as well. I think we'd all like to know how to make this all end."

*My sentiments exactly*, Hodge thought.

Jimmy gave Mary the address. Betty glared at him but did not say another word.

# 4

He dressed in the black suit he had been wearing since the appearance. His bloody shirt had been discarded, and in its place was a white button down that Hodge kept at Jimmy's if a bender ever happened to bring him there. Hodge just tucked the shirt into his pants when his legs could not hold his weight any longer. Hodge knew this was as much from the thought of Mary seeing him in that state as the weakness from the injury and swim through the frigid, icy waters. He didn't know where the two of them stood at this point in the game, and Hodge knew that should be the least of his worries, but he could not help but think about what could have been; what might still be between himself and Mary. Something had awakened in Hodge since meeting her. Something that he knew was missing but did not know to what extent it had been. Then the kid came onto the scene and that missing something deepened. But, like cement poured for the foundation of a home, the hole was being filled and hardening into a new resolve to do better and be better; to accept other people into his life.

Hodge realized that he had not done that, not with Grace, not with Jimmy, certainly not with the parade of women that followed him to bed like he was the Pied Piper. He had constructed a wall long ago, and while no one had broken through, some peered over the top or around the sides. With Mary Allen, with Thomas, he could see the wall coming down. He wanted it to. He wanted to be better for them, and better for Jimmy.

"Frank, you okay?" Jimmy placed a hand on his shoulder and looked at Hodge in a way that made him think his mind was being read.

"Yeah, pally." Hodge looked down in his lap and said words that had never come easy to him. "I'm sorry, Jimmy." He was afraid to look his friend in the eye but forced himself to do so.

"Sorry?" Jimmy asked, and sat on the couch next to Hodge. "What for?"

Hodge laughed. With a more cynical person, Hodge would think that they were delighting in his apology. That down the line they would hold it over him and never let him forget. But not Jimmy. Jimmy always saw the best in people, even when they were at their worst. Jimmy would fight for his friends and the things he cared about until his dying breath. If he loved someone or something, that person would always get the benefit. This was Jimmy's greatest quality and greatest flaw.

"For everything, pally. I have not been a good friend to you, and you've been a brother to me. You've held me up, sometimes literally, you've kept me going. I have never repaid you for it. And now I got you involved in this mess."

"Frank Hodge, there is nothing else I would rather do."

"So, you've enjoyed all the drunken verbal lashings over the years? Or having your face rearranged by a couple of toughs? Oh, and that you and your family are in danger?"

"I'd do it all again."

"Liar."

"Yes. Yes, I am."

"I love you, Jimmy."

"I know, *pally*." Jimmy patted Hodge on the back.

A throat cleared at the living room's entrance. Both Hodge and Jimmy looked toward the sound. Standing in the doorway was Ms. Mary Allen. She looked stunning in a navy-blue blazer with gold buttons down the front, and a matching skirt.

"I hate to break up the moment, boys, but I think we have some things to discuss," Mary stepped into the room. She looked directly at Hodge. "And I have a date to reschedule."

Mary was followed by a round, egg shaped man that Hodge immediately recognized as Albert Graves, despite never meeting the man. Mary confirmed this with an introduction and a scowl on her face. Hodge got the impression that Albert Graves was not an invited guest.

"How do you do?" Albert Graves asked.

"I think we've been better," Hodge replied.

Graves looked over both Hodge and Jimmy. He nodded his head.

"I see your point," he said inclining his head.

Jimmy stood up and shook Mary's and Graves's hand. Hodge started to stand, but tentacles of pain grabbed at every part of his body. The pain was intense, but it wasn't as bad as it had been earlier.

"Sit down."

Mary shot Hodge with a stern look that allowed no room for argument. Hodge saluted her and sank back into the sofa. When he settled, he let out the breath he had been holding. The pain eased.

"Why don't we all sit down?" Jimmy gestured to the armchairs on each side of the sofa. Mary took the one closer to Hodge and stole a glance before seating herself. Albert Graves lingered for a moment. He looked around, Hodge could not understand what he was looking for, but finally the large man settled into the other chair.

"Now," Hodge said. "Let's all get caught up."

# 5

"And Thomas is here? Now?" The look of amazement on Mary's face caused Hodge to grin. He knew the feeling, having felt the same sort of relief when he saw Thomas playing with James and Aggie outside. He nodded. "That's… incredible. I can't believe after all that he managed to find you. It's almost like…" Her words trailed off.

Hodge didn't know what Mary had been about to say, but he had a guess. Throughout this whole ordeal, Hodge had felt like he had somehow been transported into an episode of his own radio show. He had survived on minor amounts of skill and a lot of dumb luck. But the fact that Thomas had managed to find Jimmy, and then find Hodge himself was damn near a miracle. Which was Hodge's guess as to where Mary's words might have led. It was a miracle that Hodge was alive. That Thomas had not been caught and managed to find his way back to him. Maybe there was something to this Scrapper business after all.

"The boy is here? Can we talk to him?" Albert Graves had listened to the story with intense interest. He scribbled notes throughout Hodge's telling. Hodge thought nothing of it, the man was a reporter, and Mary had done the same. But there was an eagerness in the egg man's tone that Hodge was not fond of.

"I'm sure you'll get the chance." Hodge hoped he disguised the wariness in his voice.

While he knew he may be overcautious, he thought at this point he had every right to be. This whole ordeal had taught him something about blind trust. Never would he have thought that the police would be on the payroll of a man like Salazar. Hodge wasn't naïve though, he knew that there were cops on the take, but the first police officer he had gone to? That seemed like too much. He would not trust so easily again.

Mary was another story. Mary had come around before Hodge even knew that Thomas Malloy existed. She was there before he had ever heard of Edward Salazar and the trouble that name would bring. Plus, she was helping. Whereas Albert Graves, even if he was not in the pocket of Salazar, was out for himself, out for the story. He didn't really care about Thomas, Hodge or Jimmy and his family. He cared about getting himself ahead, and if Hodge was correct in reading Mary's face when the two entered the room, Graves invited himself along for the ride. Hodge made a mental note to ask about that if he was able to get Mary alone.

As if she knew he was thinking about her, Hodge felt Mary's eyes on him.

"Frank, you okay?" Mary asked.

"Yes, I'm fine."

"You seemed to disappear for a moment there." She leaned forward and placed a hand on his knee. A new warmth spread through him. Hodge was sure he was blushing.

"Just tired."

"Do you want us to let you rest?" Graves stood up from his chair, the look of eagerness still etched on his face.

"No. It's okay," Hodge said.

"Then, would it be okay if I took a break. I could use the... um... facilities."

Jimmy, who had been silent for most of the interaction, stood up with a smile. "I'll show you where it is."

He looked between Hodge and Mary as if he expected a thank you. Hodge replied with a simple nod. Jimmy shot him a wink and led Albert Graves out of the room.

After a moment alone, Mary stood from the chair she was in and moved to the couch next to Hodge. She looked him over. She looked worried.

"Oh Frank, what did you get yourself into? I thought you were just going to *case* the joint. Not going to get into any trouble." She raised an eyebrow like a teacher scolding a student.

185

"It's not like I intended to go out there and get shot," Hodge said. "It was late at night, I figured gangsters and crooks kept banker's hours." He tried on a smile.

Mary's face remained stern, but soon melted like ice. "I'm just glad you're okay."

"We're not out of this yet. What's with your friend?"

"He just sort of invited himself. I met the detective. There was something strange there. I couldn't quite put my finger on it, but something felt off. He had this sort of righteousness that felt... put on. I want to do some more digging into him."

"I'm not sure that's a good idea. If he is in with Salazar, you could be the next one to get shot, and you may not be as lucky as I was."

"Then I guess it's a good thing I have my very own superhero to save me."

"Mary," Hodge held her gaze. "I am not kidding here. This man is dangerous. We don't know enough about him, and I won't have you risking your life for me."

"You don't get to do that. If I decide to look into it, then *I* decide. And it's not all about you, Frank. I'd be doing it for Thomas. That boy needs some sort of closure, or he will spend his life with a chip on his shoulder so big that he will just topple over. I don't want to see that for him. Do you?"

"Of course not. I want Thomas to be safe. I want to help him. To protect him." Hodge stopped talking and looked down to the floor, as a thought that had been bothering him came back to haunt his mind. "What will happen to him when this is over?"

"Most likely he will end up in an orphanage and from there, who knows," Mary said.

While Hodge suspected the answer, he didn't like it; not one bit. Mary must have noticed the look on his face. Her hand squeezed over top of his. "Unless someone decides to adopt him."

Hodge looked up. He had never considered children. He

always figured that he would not be a good father because of his own upbringing, but in the brief time they had known each other, Thomas had changed him. Hodge wanted to keep Thomas safe, not just now against odds that were too big for the both of them, but until the kid could take care of himself. He thought that Thomas might like that too. But Thomas thought that he was a hero; that Frank Hodge was the Scarlet Scrapper in real life. Was that some sort of defense mechanism for the kid? Did he need that fantasy to help cope with the murder of his parents? Or did the kid really believe that Hodge ran around the streets at night donning a red mask? The most important question for Hodge, though, was, did it matter either way?

He didn't think it did and the words stumbled out of his mouth. "Doesn't matter." He said.

"What?" Mary was looking at him closely. "You drifted again. What did you say?"

"What if I want to take him in?" Hodge stood up. He felt he could no longer remain seated. His side felt like it was ripping open, but he had to move as his mind raced. He could be better than his own father. What he felt was love building for the boy. Like a flower budding in the Spring, Hodge's love would continue to grow, especially if he nurtured it. He would not be his father. He would be Thomas's. "Is that possible?"

"It might be. I know someone who may be able to help with that."

"Let's get through this first, and then we'll see what Thomas wants."

Mary nodded as Jimmy stepped back into the room.

"Where's Albert?" Mary stood from the couch.

Hodge, exhausted from the movement, plopped back down.

"He had to use the phone. Had to call his wife." Jimmy locked onto Hodge, and for the first time Hodge noticed the tears running down his cheeks. He quickly dabbed them away.

A moment later the egg-shaped man filled the entryway into the living room. Graves looked like he was ready to go, as if he had gotten all he needed. He looked over the three in the room. He stepped to the chair and lifted his coat and briefcase.

"Now, if we can talk to the boy, Thomas, then I think we'll have everything. Yes?"

Jimmy looked at Hodge and Hodge got the impression he was asking permission, or for direction. Hodge didn't want Graves to talk to Thomas, but he also did not know why he felt that way. Hodge could think of no reason to stop Albert Graves from speaking with Thomas. This was the entire point of reaching out to Mary and in turn the other reporter. They needed someone to trust, and Hodge did trust Mary. He looked at Jimmy and, with a nod, gave Jimmy permission to get Thomas.

When Jimmy left the room, Albert Graves took his seat from earlier and wore a satisfied smile that redoubled Hodge's doubts.

# 6

Thomas watched from the upstairs window of James's bedroom. He still shivered from the cold outside, but his body was thawing. He hadn't liked the look of the fat man who stepped out of the cab after the woman. Where she was pretty with a kind face, if not a little worried, the fat man's eyes had a greedy look to them. Thomas had seen similar looks in the faces of his classmates when they were trying to please the teacher. Who was the fat man trying to please?

He crept to the door. James, who was lying on his bed with a Hardy Boys book, *The Flickering Torch Mystery*, to his nose, looked at him.

"Where you going?"

"I just want to check something out."

No further explanation needed; James disappeared behind the book again. Thomas made his way down the hall to the stairs. He listened but heard nothing. He peaked into the room at the end of the hall. There Mrs. Childers, and Agnes lay napping on the bed. Thomas knew that Mrs. Childers was up most of the night taking care of the Scrapper. She had done what she could when they pulled him into the house, James had been woken to help, and she did the rest when the Scrapper woke himself. Thomas thought it was a well-deserved rest.

He took his first step down onto the stairs and made sure to hug the side closest to the wall. He had learned in his short time there that some of the steps had a creak to them. James told him the trick. James used it to sneak into the kitchen at night for cookies, or sweets, or, on occasion, to sneak out of the house to meet up with his friends. James told Thomas this was to solve mysteries like the Hardy Boys. Thomas had used this trick once already to sit next to the Scarlet Scrapper as he slept fitfully on the sofa, murmuring and grunting and crying in his sleep. Thomas had cried too. The Scrapper was hurt, and he had gotten hurt helping him.

At the bottom of the stairs Thomas made his way toward the voices. The hushed tones became clearer as he got closer to the living room where the Scrapper had lain injured. From the direction of the kitchen, Thomas could hear men talking. He went that way and looked through the doorway. The fat man was headed into the bathroom, and Jimmy stood looking in the icebox. Thomas went back to the living room in time to hear the Scrapper talking.

"What if I want to take him?" This was followed by a grunt and a pause. "Is that possible?"

What did that mean? Who did the Scrapper want? Thomas knew on some level that he was the subject of the conversation, but he did not want to believe it. On one hand, how could Thomas accept another man as his father? On the other hand, Thomas had been concerned about what would happen to him now. And the Scrapper, Mr. Hodge, was the only man he trusted completely. He knew he would willingly accept him if Mr. Hodge really wanted him.

Sounds from the kitchen drew his attention away from the conversation in the living room. Thomas ran to the stairs and went up far enough so that he wouldn't be easily seen. He waited until he heard the conversation start again before making his way back to the living room to listen.

"Now, if we can talk to the boy, Thomas, then I think we'll have everything. Yes?"

Thomas didn't recognize the nasal toned voice, so he assumed it was the fat man. A moment later Mr. Childers appeared around the corner.

"Thomas, what are you doing down here? I was just coming to get you."

Mr. Childers placed an arm around Thomas's shoulder and began to walk him into the living room. "Well, there is someone in here who we think might be able to help. A friend of ours, Ms. Allen, she brought him. They are reporters."

Thomas said nothing but allowed himself to be led into the living room.

"Hiya, kid," The Scrapper said as Thomas entered the room. Seeing the Scrapper up and, while he still looked pale, looked stronger than he had. Thomas ran to him and threw his arms around Mr. Hodge. He felt his hero's body tense, but it soon relaxed, and the Scrapper's arms were wrapped around him as well. "Alright kid, I still need to be careful here."

Thomas let go and sat only after the Scrapper did. The pretty woman from the taxi sat on the opposite end of the couch.

"Hi Thomas, my name is Mary." She held a handout. Thomas shook it. "This is my associate, Albert. He is going to ask you some questions about the things that have happened to you. He is going to ask you about your parents. Is that okay?"

Thomas nodded. He didn't want to talk about his parents, but he knew that it was necessary, especially if these people could help him and the Scarlet Scrapper get justice for his folks.

# 7

The questioning covered a lot of the ground that Hodge had already gone over with Albert Graves, but he guessed it was a way to corroborate the story. Police use a similar tactic for criminals in interrogation rooms. Thomas, for his part, held up well under the questioning. There were moments where his voice took on a monotone lilt, and other times where tears welled up in the kid's eyes, but Hodge was impressed by Thomas's resolve.

There were parts of the story that Hodge had heard, but they were told with some distance now, as if the kid was closing himself off, blocking out some of the memories. Hodge didn't know if this was a good thing or a bad thing. He blocked off hard memories from the war and look what had happened to him. He was a mean drunk who slept with women who reminded him of his ex-wife. Not really a healthy situation.

Albert Graves cleared his throat. "Well, I think that is all I have for you. Thank you, Thomas." Albert inclined his head.

He took his time putting his notebook and pen back into the briefcase. He shuffled paper around before closing the case and looked at them. He made no move to stand up. No move to leave. Albert took a handkerchief out of his pocket and dabbed at his forehead.

"Albert, should I call you a taxi?" Mary stood up.

"Oh no. Thank you Ms. Allen." He offered no further explanation.

Mary stood for another few moments and finally sat down.

An awkward silence, louder than the conversation recently held, filled the room.

"Don't you want to call Detective Cooper? Get the story written up?" Mary tried again.

Hodge looked between Albert Graves, Mary and Jimmy.

Apart from Graves, the other two wore the same expression that Hodge imagined he wore.

Hodge stood up. He started toward the window, but Jimmy beat him to it, so he turned back to Graves. "Who should be here any minute?"

The egg man didn't answer. He looked into Hodge's eyes with a satisfied smirk curling his lips. The situation felt so odd that Hodge could think of nothing to say, and the deafening silence of the room was back. He didn't have to wait long because Jimmy spun away from the window.

Hodge hurried to the window. Pain ripped his side. He recognized all four of the men. It was Salazar and his cronies. The two who had hurt Jimmy were the same two from the alley. Hodge turned back to Graves.

"What have you done?"

Hodge threw a quick jab into the egg man's nose. There was a satisfying cracking sound, as if he had broken the shell of an egg. Blood poured from the nose and Graves took his handkerchief out again pressing it to his nose.

"Albert, how could you?" Mary asked. "You know what that man has done. You know the people he has hurt!"

"I am truly sorry, Miss Allen."

Hodge had to admit, he did sound sorry, but that wasn't enough to quell his rage. He was on Graves again, the egg man's collar wrapped tightly in his hand. Hodge pulled back his fist and was ready to let fly, but Jimmy stopped him.

"They're coming up the steps!"

Jimmy reached into his house sweater and took out a small pistol, a .22. Jimmy fumbled with the small gun, and looked a little sheepish when he caught Hodge watching him.

"You know how to use that?" Hodge's voice was harsher than he intended it to be, but he didn't have time to worry about that.   Jimmy just nodded. "Good, grab Betty and the kids and go out the back." He looked at Mary and Thomas. "I want you two to go with them."

"Frank, you're coming too," Mary said.

There was no invitation for debate in her voice.

Hodge debated anyway. "I need to try to hold them off. Give you all a chance to escape."

"It's no use Mr. Hodge." Graves stepped forward. His handkerchief, now more red than white, was still pressed to his nose. "These men will kill you and then take care of the rest of them."

"Albert, why are you doing this?" Mary asked.

Hodge didn't wait for a reply. He drove his fist into the egg man's thick stomach and felt the satisfying whoosh of wind out of his mouth. Graves bent in half and coughed.

"Mary, I need you to go." Hodge turned and pointed toward the back door.

A pounding came from the front door. Hodge looked into the hallway. The door was vibrating in its frame. He didn't know how long the door would last. From behind he heard Mary gasp. Before he could turn back, something solid came crashing down onto his head. Hodge's legs disappeared from underneath him. The impact to the floor hurt more than the blow, and Hodge grabbed at his side. He felt a wet warmth spreading there.

"Albert!"

Mary went to shove the egg man away, but he caught her arms, and in a swift motion, spun her into a choke hold and pressed the barrel of a pistol against her temple. It was no .22.

"I am going to open that door and let them in. The faster we do, the faster this business will be over." Graves, with Mary in tow, headed to the front door.

The floor beneath Hodge vibrated as a parade came running down the stairs. James was the first one down, followed by Betty carrying Aggie and Jimmy trailing behind.

"Go out the back door." The .22 was still in Jimmy's hand. He held it with a little more confidence but made sure it was pointed at the floor. Everyone froze. Jimmy surveyed the scene. Hodge on the floor. The pounding at the front door. Albert Graves with a gun to Mary's head. He jumped into action. "Betty get the kids out the back."

Jimmy raised his own gun and pointed it toward Graves and Mary. Hodge sure hoped his friend knew how to shoot, or didn't have a twitchy trigger finger.

No one said a word until Betty and the kids were out of there.

"Mr. Graves, I'm going to need you to drop the gun now and let Ms. Allen go," Jimmy took a step closer and the gun in his hand steadied.

"Not now, Frank." It was a tone that Hodge had never heard his old friend use. It was sure, steady, and strong. Words that Hodge would never use to describe Jimmy a day ago. "I'll ask again. Please drop the gun."

The egg man didn't comply.

A crack of wood sounded. With the intensity of the situation, Hodge hadn't realized there was still pounding at the front door. The door crashed in, and Jimmy whirled in that direction. Salazar stood there with his cigar chomping guard dog standing right behind him.

"Looks like we're just in time for the party, Gus." Salazar said as he crossed the threshold into the house.

A silence took hold, but it was short lived.

As if in answer, Betty's scream broke through.

Jimmy looked at Hodge, and Hodge stared straight into his friend's eyes and shouted one word, "Go!"

Jimmy took off toward the kitchen.

# 8

Thomas heard Mrs. Childers scream from the backyard. If he had thought about it, he probably would not have run in the direction of the scream. He would have probably frozen, like he had done before. But he didn't think about it. Someone was in trouble, and Thomas had decided that he would not sit idly anymore. He had done that already and his parents were murdered. The Scrapper had to fight his battle, and then the Scrapper got shot. Jimmy was hurt, and Thomas had done nothing. He would not be responsible for anyone getting harmed again.

Mr. Childers rushed past without a look in Thomas's direction. He ran out the back kitchen door leaving it wide open behind him.

With the kitchen light on, there was an open mouth of blackness where the back door had once stood closed. Thomas ran to the open doorway and saw Jimmy and his family being backed against the house. Mr. Childers had the small gun raised, but he did not fire at the two men who approached him and his family. They were the same two men who had killed Thomas's parents.

Thomas looked around the kitchen for a weapon of any sort. He almost gave up his search but spotted a broom behind the open door. He said he would clean up the mess he had caused.

Creeping through the door, Thomas held the broom like he was ready to play stick ball again with Pat Kenzie. When he stepped behind the one who pulled the trigger on his parents, Thomas swung the broom in the same manner as when he played stick ball with his friend, wild and with everything he had.

The broom stick landed with a crack of splintering wood. Half of the stick flew off into the darkness. The tall man turned, shock in his eyes, but he made no move beyond that. Thomas wasn't done though. With all his might, he launched a foot into the groin of the tall man. The shock turned into a glazed sort of look.

An odd squeal sounded from deep in the tall man's throat. He fell to his knees and Mr. Childers brought the pistol he was holding down hard on the man's head. The tall man fell the rest of the way to the ground.

His partner reached into his jacket, but Jimmy aimed the gun at him, and another crack broke the silence of the night. The second man gripped the shoulder of the arm that had been reaching for the gun. Mr. Childers fired again, this time into the man's foot and he joined his friend on the ground.

Seeing them there, blood staining their clothes, caused a blind red rage to fill Thomas. Still grasping the broken broomstick in his hand, Thomas began smashing from one man to the next. Each swing caused a whoosh, and each strike made a noise like a *thump* as it hit the men.

Thomas was about to bring the broomstick down again, but arms wrapped around him and lifted him lightly from the ground. Thomas fought the grip. He wanted to hurt these men. Hurt them so bad that they would feel how hc felt. The grip tightened, and Thomas fought harder. He kicked and elbowed and thrashed.

A grunt and exhale sounded in his ear. Then a breathless voice caused him to calm, but just a little.

"Dad, I can't hold him," James said.

"Thomas, we got them." Mr. Childers's voice was warm. He made no move to stop Thomas. Thomas's eyes began to register details again. "We got them," Mr. Childers repeated.

Breathless, Thomas dropped the broomstick to the snow. He blinked once. Twice. And then the blinking became uncontrollable. The tears fell warm down the cold skin of his face. The arms that tried to restrain him before embraced him now. Thomas let the tears flow freely as he placed his head on James's chest.

Mr. Childers placed a hand on each of the boys' shoulders. Thomas felt himself relax more. But with that relaxation came the realization that they had left Mr. Hodge alone with those men inside.

# 9

Hodge was powerless to stop Albert Graves from dragging Mary through the front door. The burning and throbbing in his side was debilitating, and Salazar stood with a gun pointed at him. He knew he needed to act, but there was not much to be done while staring down the barrel of a gun. Hodge was not bullet proof, and he'd have the scar to prove it.

"Mr. Scarlet Scrapper," there was mockery in Salazar's voice, "I see Gus should have aimed a couple inches higher and a little to the right. If you take another step, I won't make that same mistake."

Hodge stopped. He couldn't help Mary, or Thomas, or anyone if he was dead. He needed a way out of this. Hodge needed a distraction.

As if on cue, shots were fired outside. The moment caught the three men off guard, but the moment was fleeting as Hodge let his mind worry if Jimmy, Betty, or any of the kids were hurt. That worry gave Salazar enough time to bring his attention back to Hodge.

"No mask tonight?" Still with that mocking tone.

Hodge's hand moved of its own accord, feeling the pocket that held the mask. It was there, but he fought the impulse to pull it out. Salazar smirked with a knowing smile. Somehow this show of weakness on Hodge's part, and recognition on Salazar's, made Hodge even more angry, frustrated and scared. It was like a perfect storm brewing inside of him; a feeling close to what he felt in the war.

"Just leave these people out of it. It's me and the boy you want. The family that lives here is not involved."

"Judging from the shots back there, they are very much involved. And now so is the pretty reporter. Albert told us all about how he used her to see what you knew. Not much. This almost seems like a waste of energy."

"Where did he take Mary?" Hodge demanded.

"Knowing Albert, he took her to the docks to await further instructions. He is a good little soldier. Now, let's get this over with. If we work fast Gus and I can have this all wrapped up with a neat little bow tonight."

A clap of thunder from the front door knocked Gus off balance. His hand shot up to his shoulder and he fell to the floor groaning.

"Eddie, I'm going to need you to drop the gun!" A tall man with a sandy blonde side part stood there. His gun aimed between Hodge and Salazar. Hodge didn't know how he might appear threatening, but he guessed he could understand the man being cautious. Hodge could even respect it, but still, he needed to get out of there to find Mary.

"Hi Coop. I see you're still holding that old grudge."

"You killed my brother. Now, drop the gun."

"That's not how I remember it," Salazar said.

He bent and placed the gun on the floor, but Hodge saw his other hand reaching toward a blocky shape at the small of his back. He couldn't know for sure if it was another gun. He couldn't be sure that this Coop wouldn't fire on him. What Hodge was sure about was that he needed to act now, or this guy would be dead.

Fighting through the pain, Hodge leapt forward with a left-handed straight that caught Salazar in the chin as he pulled a small pistol from the holster on his back. The gun went skittering across the floor. Everyone locked onto the pistol and froze.

Edward Salazar was the first to make a move for the gun, but the man with the sandy blonde hair shot it. Salazar stood up straight again and raised his hands in defeat.

Hodge stood up straight himself and a new wave of pain caused the room to spin, and his stomach wanted to force up the slices of toast and coffee that was the diet set out for him by Betty. When the waves that had overcome him dimmed to a minor annoyance, Hodge started for the door.

"Have you got these two?"

The man named Coop moved the barrel of his gun in Hodge's direction, but Hodge could tell by the look in the man's eyes that he would not fire. At least he hoped not.

"Where do you think you're going?" The gun wavered as he asked.

"The fat man has Mary."

"Ms. Allen?"

It was clear from the look that crossed his eyes that this man had become smitten with Mary Allen too. Hodge felt a new wave rush over him. This one a hot wave of jealousy. He knew he didn't have time for it. He had to go after them.

"Yes. I need to stop him before it's too late."

Hodge took another step toward the door when his name was called from behind. He turned to Jimmy's voice, though he desperately wanted to run out the door.

"Jimmy, is everyone okay? Is Thomas—"

"Everyone is fine. Except for the goons who came with these two. They'll both need some time in the medical ward of Sing Sing." Jimmy looked toward the man with the gun. "Who's this?"

With his gun still levelled, Coop reached into his jacket and pulled out a badge. "Larry Cooper. I'm with the police."

Hodge was growing more impatient. Every moment wasted meant more time that Mary would be in danger. He was about to express this concern, again, when Gus made a move.

The heavyset man, mostly forgotten since he was shot in the arm had grabbed his gun and started firing. His aim wavered and no shots struck home, but it gave Edward Salazar enough time to shove past them and make a run for it out the front door.

Hodge took up the chase. "He's getting away!"

He was out the door and into the cold. His left side was on fire and a painful pulse tore through him whenever he put his weight on that foot.

When Hodge made it to the street, Salazar was already climbing behind the wheel of a big mint green Cadillac. Hodge, with no car of his own, had to rush back in and get the keys from Jimmy. The scene he walked in on was a satisfying one as in the brief time Hodge had been out of their presence all of Salazar's henchmen were lined up against the hallway wall. They all looked worse for wear.

"Jimmy, keys!" Hodge held a hand out.

There was a slight hesitation from Jimmy, but he reached into his pocket and handed Hodge the keys. Hodge headed back outside.

"Wait," Larry Cooper called. Hodge didn't want to waste any more time, but the man had saved his life. "I'll come with you."

"You need to stay here with them."

"I have men on the way." To Hodge, Cooper's voice came out like a whiney child. Hodge shook his head.

"Then come after they get here. Salazar said they would be heading back to the docks." Without another word Hodge rushed from the front door. When he hit the street again, he touched the bulky pocket of his suit jacket. The pocket that held the mask. He left it where it was. For now.

Hodge didn't bother checking both ways when crossing the street. It was icy and cold, and the neighborhood might as well have been deserted. That is aside from the red taillights at the end of the block. Hodge jumped into Jimmy's car and slammed the door shut. So focused on catching Salazar, he didn't notice Thomas scurrying into the back seat. When he rammed the key into the ignition and turned it, the car sputtered, but kicked into life. He threw it in reverse and made a three-point turn. Hodge floored the petal, the tires taking a moment to catch any traction, and then, the car rocketed off. As he rounded the corner, the flash of red and blue reflected into his mirrors.

Salazar's car swerved on the ice, and it wasn't long before Hodge almost lost control of his own vehicle. He followed Salazar onto Atlantic Avenue and knew they were headed toward either the Manhattan or Brooklyn Bridge. They would have to drive through Lower Manhattan, Soho, and Hell's Kitchen before making it to Salazar's dockside office. The drive would normally take about an hour. It should be longer due to the icy conditions, but Hodge figured they would make it there in record time.

He sped up the car to help prove his own point.

Salazar must have noticed his tail because his car sped up and gained more distance. Hodge could hear the roar of his enemy's engine even from so far back. Hodge wanted to stop Salazar before he made it back to the pier. A monster was strongest in its lair, and that was exactly where this monster was headed. And Mary was there too.

With no thought of going over the side himself, Hodge pushed harder on the pedal. It was touching down now, and the car rocketed forward. It managed to keep its grip on the pavement, but the rear did fishtail.

He was gaining.

It was too dark to see into Salazar's car, but Hodge pictured him stealing glances into the mirrors. Every now and then Salazar swerved just a little, as if he were not paying attention to the road. Hodge continued to gain on him.

When he finally caught up, the bumper of Hodge's car tapped the bumper of Salazar's. It wasn't much, but just enough for the car to shimmy before righting itself again. Hodge didn't know how far he should push it but decided to push it a little more. He pushed the bumpers together again. This time both cars shook with the collision.

At full speed, Hodge pulled to the side of Salazar's car and swiped it. Salazar looked over at Hodge as if he were crazy, and Hodge *did* feel a certain amount of crazy at the moment. He also felt desperate. He knew that if he got to the docks, he could probably handle Albert Graves, but with the action he had already seen that night, he didn't know if he could take down both Salazar and Graves.

He rammed into Salazar again. Both cars shook and swerved. Hodge hit the brakes and his own car swerved more violently. He held the wheel tight, but the car was headed toward the side of the bridge. Hodge twisted the wheel sending his car into a spin. Both his feet slammed onto the brakes, but the car kept spinning. After two rotations the car came to a stop. It was skewed, but facing in the right direction. Salazar hadn't gotten much of a lead.

They were nearing the end of the bridge now, and Salazar sped forward. Hodge let him get ahead. His loss of control scared him. He knew where Salazar was going, and if he had to fight the man, he would. He would be no good to Mary dead.

Salazar was in his sights the whole time. Not once had the brake lights flashed on, and Salazar had gained some great distance, so Hodge knew the man was still speeding along the icy city streets. Hodge had no idea how big Salazar's operation was; how many men he had involved, and he hoped he wasn't about to find out. He kept on after Salazar regardless. It would end that night, no matter what the outcome was. Hodge just hoped that the cop from Jimmy's place would send some of those patrol units this way.

From up ahead there was a screech of tires and roar of engine, all followed by a loud crash of crumpling metal. Salazar had crashed into a light pole. The wood cracked and the top half of the pole fell to the roof of the car, caving it in. He hoped the man had been crushed in the impact. Hodge pulled in behind Salazar's crashed car. The tires skidded and his car didn't stop until it bumped into Salazar.

Shrieking metal screamed through the empty night when the driver's side door was forced open. Edward Salazar placed a foot outside of the car. He gripped the roof and pulled himself out. He looked back at Hodge and his eyes went wide before he shielded them against Hodge's headlights.

"Son of a bitch," Hodge muttered.

Fighting through the pain that every step brought, Hodge ran past warehouse after warehouse on the pier as Salazar made no attempt to thwart his chase. Hodge felt a moment of panic. *Is Salazar scared about the unravelling of his operation? Is that why he isn't stopping to fight? Or is it something else? Could there be a trap ahead?*

But Hodge didn't think so. There had been no way for Salazar to call ahead and let his people know that there was trouble. From what Hodge knew of Salazar, his confidence and ego wouldn't allow him to even consider the possibility of failure at Jimmy's house. Hodge had seen the shock and disbelief on the man's face. He had not expected a fight at the house, and certainly had not anticipated a chase.

Still, Hodge had to be careful, he was on his enemy's turf now. They were both injured, but Salazar still held the advantage.

Salazar disappeared behind a warehouse. Hodge knew from his last visit, which he did not want to think about too hard, that the office lay back there. He had to hurry. Who knew what Salazar might have hidden in that office? He sped up enough where the pain in his side did not increase too much. When he turned the corner of the warehouse, he saw a swaying light through one of the front windows. As he got closer, Hodge heard raised voices. Two men, and Mary.

With the assumption that the men were Salazar and Albert Graves, Hodge's confidence rose a little. Graves was not much of a threat, and Salazar was injured, so the playing grounds might be more even than he had initially thought. None of that mattered though. All that mattered was getting Mary out of there and safe. Whatever came after would come whether in Hodge's favor or not. He did know one thing though; Salazar's goose was well and cooked.

Hodge took the red mask from his pocket. He ran his fingers over the material, almost lovingly. He knew it was ridiculous, but he felt a sort of comfort now in wearing the mask of the Scarlet Scrapper. It worked on different levels. It was a shock to the men he went up against. They looked at him as if he were a lunatic, and maybe to some extent he was, but it kept them off balance. But it also would help to hide the pain he felt with every movement. Something his father once said came back to him: *When you're in the ring, hide the hurt. Shove it down. Don't allow your body to feel it until you're done with the fight. Make them think you are a machine. A fight is more mental than technique. We know you have the technique, now show them how strong you are up there.*

He took a deep breath and pushed the pain away. He would feel it later. Hell, he probably would be in bed for days. Even now, it was still there, but it felt duller now. More of an inconvenience than anything. He caressed the fabric of the mask one more time before pulling it over his face.

Hodge threw the door to the little shack office open. Salazar stood behind his desk frantically rummaging through one of the drawers. Albert Graves stood, his mouth wide open as if he were singing opera, and Mary sat in the chair that had been occupied by Gus on his first visit.

Hodge rushed into the tiny room and threw a cross into the weak chin of Albert Graves. The egg man's head snapped to the side and rolled back to face Hodge. Graves dropped like someone had removed his legs. His face planted onto the top of the desk a small pool of blood forming on the white blotter, before the large man's body rolled to the floor. The motion of the punch tore at Hodge's side, but he swallowed it down.

"Frank?" There was surprise in Mary's voice. "Is everyone okay?"

Hodge didn't turn away from Salazar. "Everyone is fine. Everyone besides the men he brought to Jimmy's." Now speaking to Salazar, "Get away from there."

Without argument, Salazar did as he was told and took a step back from the desk. His back was against the wall now. Salazar's hair, perfect the two times Hodge had seen him before, was disheveled and Edward Salazar had a wild desperation in his gaze. His eyes darted here and there, but what he was looking for could not be found.

"This ends tonight. You should have left well enough alone, Salazar." Hodge felt a rage boiling in him. "You could have let us walk. You could have let Thomas lead a normal life, but instead he'll have more trauma than just the death of his parents to deal with."

Salazar held his hands up in surrender. He took slow steps from behind the desk until he stood at its side. He looked down at the limp body of Albert Graves on the opposite side of the desk.

"You must pack quite a punch there." Salazar took a small step forward.

From outside, bright lights lit up the small interior of the office. It also managed to light up the intent on Salazar's face. Hodge knew that Salazar was going to make a run for it a split second before the man did so.

He barreled into Hodge, shoving him out of the way as he ran into the cold night outside. Without thinking Hodge followed. As he ran through the office door, Mary yelled his name. This gave Hodge pause.

"You can't just go out there," Mary said. "You have no idea who else is here. That looks like an awful number of cars, Frank."

For the first time since he had entered the office, Hodge got a good look at Mary. She did not seem hurt, but her hands and feet were tied to the chair.

"I'm not sure it matters anymore. This is going to end tonight, one way or another. If Salazar has his men here, then I am a dead man. But you don't have to be."

Hodge looked around the office. When he didn't find anything to cut Mary's bindings with, he got to work on the knots.

"What are you saying?"

From the look on her face, Hodge could tell that Mary knew exactly what he was saying.

"If I fall, you have to promise me one thing." Mary opened her mouth to respond, but Hodge shook his head. "Make sure Thomas is taken care of."

He got the ropes from her feet free and then her hands. Hodge stood up. Mary stood with him. He turned to the door, but her hand on his arm caused him to pause. She looked up into his eyes behind the mask. She lifted it from his mouth. They kissed hard. Mary pulled the mask back down and with a sad smile that spoke volumes, she said, "Go get him, Scrapper."

Hodge went through the door and out into the light.

# 10

Thomas hid in the shadows between warehouses as a parade of cars entered the pier. Peering through the darkness it looked like the cars were all filled with men. Thomas worried that the Scrapper would be sore with him for hiding in the car but he had to be there when Ready Eddie went down.

Now his concern was not how the Scrapper would react to his hitching a ride, but how to warn the Scrapper that he had company.

The cars began to park in a semicircle around the office of Edward "Ready Eddie" Salazar. Thomas remembered playing in that office. He remembered how nice Oliver's dad had treated him. Thomas was even told to call him Eddie. *None of this Mr. Salazar garbage*, the man who murdered his parents had said. Now, like most of his childhood, it felt like a lifetime ago.

The men began to climb out of the cars. Though it was dark and hard to differentiate them, Thomas began to count the men. He counted twenty-two before their shadowy forms began to blend and merge into one as they walked like the mob in *Frankenstein*. All they were missing were the torches and pitchforks.

In a crouch, Thomas pushed forward. He ducked behind any cover he could find, but pushed on without hesitation. He didn't know how much time he had before those men would go in and hurt the Scrapper. He drew closer and closer to the last car in the half circle that surrounded the office. The headlights flooded the little office and the large area outside of it. Thomas ducked behind the rear bumper of a car and peered around the side.

A man burst out of the door of the office. Ready Eddie's face was whitewashed with the blaring lights washing over him. The lights so bright that Thomas could see almost every detail of the man's face.

Eddie Salazar ran into the middle of the open area and stopped. A hand raised to shield his eyes. A big grin spread across his lips, and something that wasn't there when Eddie had left the office, slowly took hold of him. He dropped the hand shielding his eyes. His chest puffed out, and his chin went high.

"Good," he called out. "Now that you're all here, you can help me with a little problem I'm having."

Salazar turned to face the office. The other men tightened their circle. Salazar placed his hands on his hips and waited.

The Scarlet Scrapper came out of the building, and speaking over his shoulder Salazar shouted, "Get him!"

# 11

Even as he did it, Hodge knew running out of that office might be the dumbest thing he had ever done in his life. And he had done some dumb things in the past. He took an odd comfort in the knowledge that he might not live long enough to regret it.

Hodge had no intention of dying, but if the cars outside were what he thought they were, he probably wasn't going to make it. He just hoped that Mary would find a way to get off the pier unscathed. *Where the hell is Larry Cooper?*

The lights outside were blinding. Silhouetted against that light stood a figure that Hodge instantly recognized as Edward Salazar. With the light at his back, Salazar's features were cast in grim shadow making his face look like the face of a skull. A skull wearing a big grin. He stood with his hands on his hips, like he hadn't a care in the world, like he was in charge of the world.

"Welcome to the party, my friend." Salazar's voice was as confident as the smug smile he wore. Hodge wanted desperately to punch that smile from his face. "Let me introduce you to the boys. Boys, this is the Scarlet Scraper! Scarlet Scraper, the boys."

"It's Scrapper, you buffoon." Hodge's breath warmed the inside of his mask. The skin of his lips beginning to chafe from rubbing against the tight material.

"It doesn't matter. You are about to be dead." Salazar turned toward the crowd behind him. "One hundred dollars to the man who brings me that mask." He turned back to face Hodge.

Nobody else moved. Through the dim wash of light, Hodge recognized the men not as Salazar's goons, but as men of the working class. These men were on Salazar's payroll, but they were paid for a legitimate job. They were the longshoremen who called the pier their home.

Something crossed Salazar's face, but, like a slate, he wiped it clean, and that big grin returned. Still facing Hodge, he said, "You boys strike a hard bargain. Two hundred dollars to bring me his mask."

A man looked down at his feet, and then around the crowd of other men. He took a step forward, but another man held out an arm blocking his path and shook his head. The man who had taken a step looked down at his feet again. Hodge could feel his hesitation even from that distance. The man stepped back.

Salazar turned to face the crowd of men once more. "Two fifty."

The crowd of men moved in closer as if of a hive mind. They closed the space between themselves and Edward Salazar.

"Now we're talking. Who's it going to be?" Salazar reached into his pocket and took out a wad of cash. He counted out the money. The men closed the gap even more.

As the circle of men drew closer, Hodge felt a pit of doom as heavy as a building drop through his stomach. He was done for, that was certain. Yet not one man took the money Salazar had offered. In fact, they stopped a man who was going to try. The pit in his stomach dissolved as Hodge started to put together what was happening.

*The longshoremen have been in a sort of stranglehold with Salazar in charge. Their ranks were being picked off one by one, whether through extortion, murder, or whatever other nefarious deeds Salazar and his goons ran on the pier. No one has taken Salazar's offer of money and lord knows they need it. These aren't gangsters, just hard-working men.* This meant he and Salazar were on an even playing field. These men were just as curious of the outcome as Hodge was.

"What's with you guys? I offered some serious cash for this masked moron. Now someone do it!"

Still, no one moved.

"It looks like it's just you and me, Salazar!"

Hodge felt his blood pumping, roaring through his veins.

He rolled his head, stretching out his neck. Without thinking, he was on the balls of his feet, his knees slightly bent, his weight shifting back and forth.

Salazar began to undo the cuffs of his shirt. He slowly and deliberately rolled his sleeves up to his elbows. "You think any of this is going to matter? You think you can bring me down? You're in my world now, Scarlet Scrapper. No matter how you shuffle the deck, down here, on the docks, I am always king!"

"Yeah, well, it looks like we'll be playing with a new deck." Hodge got into his boxer's stance and stepped forward.

Both men closed the space between them. The crowd of longshoremen closed the circle tighter. It all felt familiar to Hodge, like being back in the ring again. The crowd of men, no longer silent, but grunting and cheering, like they were at a prizefight.

Hodge and Salazar began to circle, like animals in the wild. Hodge sized Salazar up, and was sure the other man was doing the same. They were both injured, Hodge from his gunshot wound, and Salazar from the collision with the light pole. Without any knowledge of Salazar's prowess in a fight, Hodge guessed they were pretty evenly matched.

But Salazar was a showman. While Hodge circled in his boxer's stance, the stance his father had drilled into him since he was a child, Salazar had his chest puffed out, his shoulders back and his chin held high. He walked like he hadn't a care in the world, like this was just a small obstacle in an otherwise obstacle free day.

The crowd around him disappeared. Hodge could still hear them, but everything in the world blacked out except for Ready Eddie Salazar. It was always like this for him, whether he was in the ring, or at the mic in the studio, the world vanished as if it were never there, and it was just him and his goal. In this case, the goal being to knock Salazar senseless.

Hodge, chin pointed down, kept his eye on Salazar as they circled. He stepped in with a jab that briefly knocked the grin from

Salazar's face. The grin came right back, as if it had never left. But the jab must have rocked Salazar more than he let on, because his arms were now loosely raised to block any other incoming punches.

"You really think you can win this? You're an actor, for Christ sakes!" Salazar rushed in. His movement was that of an untrained fighter. Sloppy, but there was power behind it. Hodge blocked the blow easily and countered with another jab. This time Salazar caught it on his forearm.

"And you're just a rabid dog that needs to be put down." Hodge jabbed again and followed it with a cross to the body.

Salazar's breath burst out in a whoosh. The noise from the crowd, smelling blood, amped up. Salazar staggered back in an attempt to get his air back. It looked like he was going to throw up. Hodge closed the distance and pulled back for another punch. But Salazar recovered fast. He grabbed Hodge's collar and threw a punch of his own.

The punch, though wild, connected with Hodge's eye. Golden dots floated in front of his vision, but at the same time something inside of him clicked. Like a machine, Hodge was in and out again. He landed a left to Salazar's nose, and a right to his stomach. Hodge rolled under a counterpunch and landed one of his own.

The crowd around them, still blacked out in Hodge's vision, roared in approval. Hodge was out for blood, but they were out to see the public execution.

Hodge was in and out. He moved here and there. The pain in his side disappeared like the men who were crowding the fight had. The only things that existed in his tunnel vision were himself and Salazar. Hodge moved from action to action. Enacting the devastating combos his father had drilled into him. Every punch, pivot and duck was for one singular purpose: to bring down Salazar. Reading the movements, the intentions of his opponent, Hodge felt unstoppable.

But Salazar endured the jabs, the crosses, the hooks. He threw and landed punches of his own, but if this were a real match, in a ring, the round would have gone to Hodge. As if it were a real match, and the round bell had rung, both men backed off and began to circle each other again.

Hodge was breathless. His body lathered in sweat. He kept his eyes on Salazar as they walked around each other. Salazar wore that self-assured grin, but Hodge could see a sort of panic in his eyes too. This was not how he expected his night to go.

Salazar was the first to break the walk. Punch after punch came at Hodge, and Hodge never struck once. He covered up, blocked, ducked, and clinched the other man in order to take a breath and protect himself. While every movement Hodge had made had a method, Salazar's attacks were wild, but they sure did bite when they landed.

They broke apart again. Both men breathless. Blood flowed down open cuts on Salazar's temple and nose. There was a slit just under his eye. Hodge had no way of knowing if the hot sticky wetness under his mask was blood or sweat, but he tasted blood in his mouth.

Salazar pushed the attack and kept pushing. His breaths were growing short as he threw heavy punches with little finesse and no particular aim. It seemed as long as the punch was in Hodge's general direction and landed anywhere on his body, it was good enough for Salazar. For Salazar's part, he did not leave much for Hodge to strike back with.

But one punch missed the mark, leaving Hodge an opening.

Hodge threw a hook, his arm arcing horizontally, all his weight thrown into the half-pivot of his body. Salazar went down hard to the snowy ground. He rolled onto his back and crawled away backward. Hodge advanced on him, stood over him, and grabbed the fallen man's collar.

"You're through, Salazar. I hope you're *ready*

A searing, twisting pain rushed through Hodge's right side.

It spread up and down his body. Then another twist. Hodge looked down at his side. Salazar's hand pulled away covered in blood. It took a moment for Hodge to realize that the knife was still in him. He stood up straight, but the pain made him want to lay down and never stand again.

He looked at the handle protruding from his side. An odd sensation ran through him as his mind focused on the thought that there was a piece of sharpened metal in his body at that moment. He knew he should be focusing on backing up, getting away, but his mind just kept repeating it over and over. *I've been stabbed.*

Salazar stood up as Hodge wrapped his hand around the hilt of the knife. Salazar's hand enclosed Hodge's.

"Let's leave that in there. Just a little longer." Salazar pressed the blade harder.

The pain, unbearable a moment ago, faded into a numbing pulse, but still Hodge felt paralyzed by his thoughts. And the new one to enter his mind. *I'm really going to die tonight.*

As if his body was just waiting for his mind to catch up, Hodge collapsed. His vision blurred. A blackness at the edge of his vision started to pulse with the pain and throbbing of both his injured sides. He felt overheated and freezing at once, and a soreness took hold.

*I've been stabbed. I'm really going to die tonight.*

Salazar threw a punch into Hodge's side. He put Hodge down with another punch, this one to the face. "You are going to die tonight."

As his vision continued to darken, Hodge believed him.

# 12

Thomas watched as the Scarlet Scrapper went down. He had shouted a warning when he saw Eddie Salazar reaching into his pocket, but the crowd of men were too loud. Thomas shoved through the crowd as best as he could. He went between, pushed around, and even went under the legs of the dock workers, but he still could not make it in time. Now, the Scrapper was down holding his side and Salazar was on him, punching him in the face. The grin Salazar usually wore had turned vicious, and blood painted his face.

The Scrapper fought to block as many of the punches as possible, but Thomas could see that he grew weaker and weaker. His arms moved sluggishly as he tried to block the incoming blows.

Thomas made it to the front of the crowd, and watched as the Scarlet Scrapper was being murdered in front of his eyes. He knew that he was about to witness another death, but Thomas could not tear his eyes away. The Scrapper was all he had left in the world.

He wouldn't let him die.

Thomas ran forward with the intention of knocking Salazar off the Scrapper, but he only made it a few steps before a strong hand stopped him.

"Hey, hey, hey," a familiar gruff voice said. A second hand clamped onto him. Thomas was lifted and spun in the opposite direction of the fight. He thrashed wildly in the grip. "Thomas!"

At the sound of his name, Thomas settled down. He looked over his shoulder, the Scarlet Scrapper was still fighting back, but his situation had not improved. The gruff voice said his name again and Thomas looked into a familiar face to match the familiar voice.

"Mr. Kenzie?" Thomas looked around as if his old friend Pat would be standing by.

"What are you doing here, boy?" Mr. Kenzie asked.

"M-my parents…" Thomas could get no other words out. Seeing Mr. Kenzie after all this time; another reminder of the past. Seeing the Scrapper in a losing fight, it all became too much.

"I heard. But what are you doing here?"

"It was him!" Thomas struggled to get away from his grip again. He almost succeeded, and Mr. Kenzie put him back on his feet, but did not let go. "I have to help the Scarlet Scrapper."

"There's nothing you can do, boy."

Thomas fought again, and again, the grip tightened on him. Feeling helpless, and vulnerable, Thomas watched as Salazar pressed his attack.

"NO!" Tears fell in a steady stream down his face. "Get up, Scrapper!"

But the crowd was too loud.

# 13

The world around him was a blur. A blur of vision; blood and sweat stung his eyes and he had a tough time focusing. A blur of consciousness; he fought instinctively, blocking the incoming savagery of his attacker. A blur of feeling; his body numbed. The fire in his side a dull pulse. His arms and legs heavy with pins and needles. The torn fabric of his mask fluttered on his lips with every labored exhalation of breath. A blur of sound, muddled noises, screams and shouts and the *smack smack* of every landing punch Edward Salazar threw at him. Hodge's own arms, bruised and sore and weakening, grew heavy. His body felt like lead, and he was not sure how much longer he could hold on.

But through this blur of sensations, three words arrived as if they were whispered in his ear.

"Get up, Scrapper."

Hodge knew it had to be his imagination, but he thought the words came from Thomas. That was impossible because the kid was safe with Jimmy in Brooklyn.

With Thomas, Hodge was going to change his life around. He had a purpose to keep going, but now he knew he had failed the kid. But Hodge took solace knowing that even if he died here and now, Edward Salazar would go down for the rest of his life. Even if none of these men watching his execution spoke up, the cops would have enough with the assault on Jimmy's home. Thomas would be safe. Hodge's arms began to falter, and so did his thoughts.

"GET UP SCRAPPER!"

Motion to the side caused Hodge's attention to drift, and the quick shift of his body caused Salazar to miss a punch aimed at Hodge's face. The punch went into the pier and Salazar screamed wildly. He grabbed his wrist and looked down at his hand as if it were a foreign object.

Hodge caught sight of what had distracted him, and he knew he had to be hallucinating. Thomas, pursued by a large man with a newsboy cap, was running toward him.

Salazar's weight shifted and Hodge managed to dislodge him from his body. He shook his head and squeezed his eyes shut, sure that Thomas was just a figure of his imagination, but when he opened his eyes again, the kid was still there.

Hodge didn't know where Salazar had gone, but Thomas was now by his side. The big man in the cap didn't take him away, but he stood protectively over the kid. Hodge lifted his leaden arm and touched the kid's face.

"You'll be alright, kid. You're strong," he said, the flutter of the mask tickling his lip.

"No. You've got to get up." Thomas took Hodge's hand from his cheek and stood. He tugged on Hodge's arm.

Hodge couldn't help but smile. His mind thought of the things that could have been. He knew that Thomas was the one who would save *him*. Not the other way around. And, in a way, the kid had saved him. He gave Hodge a purpose. He gave Hodge something to fight for again.

"Thank you, Thomas."

Thomas tugged harder and again the words came, "Get up, Scrapper!" This time Hodge knew they were real.

Hodge wanted to lie there and let the heaviness he felt take hold. He thought he'd be okay if that heaviness never let him go, never let him up; just pushed until there was nothing left.

"I'll take care of you, and then finish him off." Salazar stood where Thomas had been a moment ago.

The large man in the cap stepped in front of Salazar.

Salazar yelled, "Out of the way!"

"Can't do that." The man stood firm between Salazar and Thomas.

Hodge, without realizing he had moved, was on his feet. "Hey, one more round. What do you say, *Ready Eddie*?"

He brought his arms up, but his boxer's stance was not what it used to be. His arms hung halfway down his body, and it would be difficult to move them in position to block a head blow. Pain enveloped his body, but he had to protect the kid, and he *would* die trying. Of course, dying was not part of the plan.

He was in a weakened state, there was no denying that. He had taken some beatings over what felt like several days. Had it been several days since Thomas had showed up at the studio? He didn't know. Then there was the gun shot, the stab wound, and another vicious beating. Hodge was amazed he stood at all.

He wasn't sure how long that would last. He was sure of one thing though: he had to put Salazar down, fast and hard.

He had said one more round, but Hodge wasn't sure he could last even that long. He had to try though. The cops should be there any minute. If not Larry Cooper and his men, then someone from a local precinct. At least Hodge hoped so.

He stepped into Salazar's range and threw a jab. Hodge was happy to see that it staggered Salazar. He was hurting too.

Hodge threw a quick one, two. The jab landing squarely, but the cross a little off the mark. Still, it was enough to show Salazar that he still meant business, and Hodge could see that it frightened his opponent.

Salazar recovered, but not as quickly as before. He flew at Hodge, arms outstretched, wild, a manic look in his eyes. He clawed at Hodge's throat and growled like an animal. "Why won't you stay down." It was yelled; more of a statement than a question.

Hodge pulled Salazar into a clinch and began to work the body. A hook to the left, then the right and repeat. Every punch like a fistful of pain. There was a hollow crack, and Hodge, though not sure, thought he felt something shift in Salazar's ribs. A squeal escaped from Salazar and a wheeze, then a guttural growl, lower than before.

*I might just win this thing*, Hodge thought.

Salazar shoved his thumb into the knife wound on Hodge's side, then shoved him away. He grabbed at his ribs, the wheeze louder with every labored breath. It was time to end it.

Both men wore crimson masks, Salazar's made from blood, and Hodge's a mixture of blood and fabric. Both men stood on wobbly legs, but Hodge pulled whatever inner strength he could garner. He looked at Thomas, still on the wet cold pier, and he pulled in more. Though every muscle, joint, and inch of his body screamed in protest, Hodge stepped forward and smacked Salazar with another jab. From that jab, he launched into a combo. A second jab, a cross, a hook, a cross, a jab.

Then putting all his weight behind it, Hodge pivoted into an upper cut that managed to lift Salazar off his feet. His body seemed to levitate and hold before falling smack onto his back. Salazar started to get up on an elbow, but it slid out from under him, and he did not make another attempt. He let out a croaking, weak laugh, but said nothing else.

"Hey!"

The shout came from behind Hodge. He spun on his heel and lifted his arms in defense the best that he could. But he knew he would not live through another fight.

It took a moment for his eyes to register what he saw. The uniform, the badge glistening in the lamps from the cars, the pistol pointing at his chest. Hodge could no longer hold his hands up, and they fell to his sides like they had just given up the ghost. The patrolman was followed by other officers who spread out around the crowd trying to keep control.

Hodge didn't know if he was about to get shot, arrested or clapped on the back, but he hoped one would happen soon, because he needed to lie down. The uniform, a man in his thirties with a thick black mustache and coal black eyes to match, looked the scene over and settled on Hodge again before holstering his pistol.

"What are you supposed to be? Some kind of superhero?" The patrolman asked.

"No," Hodge felt a smile spread, but his swollen lips felt like they were about to burst, "but I play one on the radio."

The patrolman looked at him strangely. Hodge swayed. Before he knew it, he was already falling. His head bounced when it hit the ground. Feet approached him, there were shouts, but, like a burned-out lightbulb, Hodge went dark.

# 14

"Edward Salazar has been put in jail for so many charges that they might as well read all the ones possible right out of the law books. Chief among them is conspiracy to commit treason. Luckily for us, and for him, I suppose, we caught one of the spies. He willingly gave up the rest of the Germans." Larry Cooper stood by Hodge's hospital bed with his hands on his hips. He wore a self-satisfied smile as if he had done most of the work. Yet here Hodge was all the worse for wear.

A week later, his body still felt like it went through a meat grinder. Not only was he suffering from the pain of his injuries, but Hodge was also going a bit stir crazy. He didn't know how much longer he could take his stay at the hospital, and the doctors had not given him any estimate. Their response, *we'd like to keep you here for monitoring.* What more they could monitor, he did not know, but Mary told him to be a "patient patient." She had thought this was the cleverest thing in the world. Thomas seemed to agree with her, but Hodge had crossed his arms over his chest and, if he remembered correctly, let out a frustrated *harrumph.* But Mary and Thomas's visits were what kept him going; kept him sane.

Mary and Thomas were not his only visitors, though. Aside from the police asking him questions, the boys from the radio station stopped by. They excitedly told him how the show's popularity was skyrocketing. Jimmy told Hodge that fan mail had increased at the station by 200%, and that is in under a week of the story breaking. Hodge had a feeling this was a bit of hyperbole, but he took it with a grin.

When Billy Bradley, wearing the world's largest smile, slapped a newspaper onto Hodge's bed, the front-page headline read, "Radio Hero Plays the Part in Real Life." Hodge thought that maybe there was some truth to Jimmy's fan mail claims. The people loved a hero.

Hodge's most surprising visitor though, was Grace. She too had read the story in the paper, along with the one Mary wrote, which in Hodge's biased opinion was better than the one brought by Billy Bradley.

When she arrived, she stood at the door. Her hand rested on the jamb, and Grace had just one foot past the room's threshold. Hodge had been napping and did not know how long she had stood there watching him; he got the feeling it was for a long time. He didn't think his nap was the reason for her hesitancy.

"Hiya, Gracie," Hodge said.

She came into the room then.

"Oh Frank," was all she said.

She dabbed at her eyes with a lace handkerchief. Hodge recognized it as the one he had given her on one of their first dates. That night the rain came unexpectedly, and all he had to help clean herself up was that little handkerchief, when what she needed was a towel and a fresh set of clothes. They had stood under a tiny awning laughing and holding each other. Hodge had lifted Gracie's mascara-stained face and they kissed for the first time. He thought she would have gotten rid of it when she got rid of him.

"You should see the other guy... then again, I wouldn't. He is not in a place for a nice lady like you."

A silence grew then, and Hodge's feelings caused a stir of confusion in him. He hadn't expected to see Grace. In some ways, when he left Thomas with her, he had expected to never see her again, but then as the ordeal progressed, he hadn't expected to see anyone again. Ever.

Grace looked as beautiful as ever, but something changed. He knew what it was, of course, he was no longer in love with her. He knew he hadn't been for a while, but there was always something pulling him back to her. And, apparently, her to him.

"How are you?" Gracie finally stepped into the room.

"I'm good, Gracie. I think for the first time in a long time I am good." And Hodge felt it.

Despite the physical pain, the turmoil, and the struggle he had gone through, he came out the other side feeling stronger, feeling… better.

Grace watched him closely. She stepped up to the bed and continued to watch in silence. There was a certain comfort in their silence. Something that he didn't think they had ever truly felt in their relationship before. Grace placed a warm hand to Hodge's cheek. She laughed.

"What?" Hodge asked.

"Your stubble. I was just remembering when…" Her words trailed off, but she didn't have to finish them. They used to lay in bed some mornings and Hodge would take her delicate hand and rub it on his stubble. She'd pull away in mock outrage, pretending to be hurt, but loving the rough scratching. "I'm glad you're okay, Frank."

"I am." Grace turned to leave, and Hodge said in a whisper, "I loved you, Gracie."

She turned back, "I know, and I loved you. Don't mess it up with this one. She is a special lady."

As if Grace had invoked her, Mary appeared. Seeing Grace, Mary stopped at the door. Grace touched Mary's arm. "Take care of him. He's an idiot sometimes, but his heart is in the right place."

Mary returned the gesture, placing her hand over Grace's. Hodge recognized something in the gesture between the two women. Something passed silently between them, something he was sure he would never understand. Hodge just hoped he wasn't a shared burden for the only two women he had ever loved. And that thought led to a realization. Hodge loved Mary. He knew it was probably crazy, but he felt it within him. He felt it with his entire being. He barely knew the woman, but he knew that he loved her. With that came a sort of freedom. She had seen him in his worst, weakest state, even before the fight for his life. And then she had seen him at his best.

"How are you holding up, Frank?" Mary asked when they were alone.

"I'm better."

# 15

Thomas walked through the hospital with Frank when he was finally released. Thomas had been staying with Jimmy and his family. For the last week, he shared a room with James, and the two had grown close. James was a little older but did not try to make Thomas feel that way. Like he was a superior. He had welcomed Thomas into his room without fuss or "rules" to abide by. He and Agnes, who insisted that Thomas call her Aggie, just like Uncle Frank, also became attached to Thomas's hip. She was like a little sister to him, just like James felt like an older brother. He was welcomed in the household like he was their family, and Thomas was able to start healing.

Now, he and Frank were followed by the *clack clack* of Frank's cane on the tiled floor. Thomas was tired, but he held his head up for his hero. Since the distraction of running for his life was gone, he felt spent emotionally. Physically, he wasn't sure how he could still be awake, let alone standing. There were moments where he wished he wasn't; moments where he wished he was shot down with his mother and father. Thomas did not voice these thoughts, and no matter how sad and broken he felt, they were fleeting. He lost the two most important people in his life, and no one could ever replace them, but he knew he'd be okay. He had no idea what would happen to him, but he knew he'd be okay.

They stepped outside into the cold. The sun warmed their faces. In the middle of a line of cars, Jimmy sat waiting to pull up and retrieve them. Hodge took in a breath and looked down at Thomas.

"You okay, Mr. Hodge?" Thomas got ready to go and grab help from any passing nurse or orderly.

"Yeah, kid. I just- I wanted to ask you something. You don't have to answer right away, okay? You can take your time to think about it." Frank watched as the line of cars moved forward.

"What is it?"

"Well, you see, Mary says she knows a woman that works with the city, and…well, how would you like to come live with me?"

Thomas wasn't sure he had heard right. He stared up at Frank Hodge, his once fictional and now literal hero. The man who had donned the mask of the Scarlet Scrapper to bring justice to his parents. Before stepping out of that hospital, Thomas had no idea where his life would take him, and he knew, even now, that what the future held in store was a mystery, but he was not prepared for this. Of course he had hoped, but he never let himself believe…

Frank began to fidget, and Thomas got ready to run for help again, but when he looked up into Frank's eyes, he knew somebody on the hospital staff was not the type of help that Frank needed.

"Like I said," Frank's voice was strained, he wore a nervous smile. "You don't need to decide right now. You can take some time to think it over." Thomas shook his head, and Frank's shoulders slumped. He nodded solemnly. "It's okay, kid. We'll figure something else out."

"No!" Thomas hadn't meant to shout it. He threw his arms around Frank's waist without thinking. Frank winced in pain. Thomas apologized but didn't let go. "I mean I don't have to think it over, Mr. Hodge."

"I told you to call me Frank. The Scarlet Scrapper business was bad enough, but Mr. Hodge isn't much better."

"I want to stay with you," Thomas said.

Frank's body relaxed in Thomas's arms, but his breathing became labored. He patted Thomas's head. "That's good, kid. That's real good."

Jimmy pulled up in the car, and Thomas helped Frank in. He climbed in after so that Frank was sitting between Jimmy and Thomas. Jimmy adjusted his glasses and looked over the faces of both of his passengers.

"I take it you two fellas will be rooming together?" Jimmy asked, but Thomas and Frank did not have to answer. Their smiles said it all.

Jimmy pulled into traffic, and they drove away from the hospital.

# 16

Hodge sat at the bar, a seltzer water dripping condensation onto the bar top. He looked at his watch, and then at the reflection of the bar behind him. The stool was uncomfortable and spun at the slightest movement causing Hodge to twist back. This motion enraged his still tender sides. As the seconds ticked by, he began to feel more restless, and his body stiffened. He was moving better now, but he still felt the injuries. He guessed he would probably feel them for the rest of his life. Still, his healing had begun. And not just on a physical level.

While Hodge had not been back to work at the station yet, Jimmy had been delivering scripts for upcoming shows. Much to Hodge's surprise, he had started to enjoy reading them. He felt an excitement for the stories that had lacked since the thrill of being on the radio wore off. Hodge didn't know if Jimmy's recent experiences helped fuel the stories, but the writing had certainly improved.

They were getting closer to Thomas living with him. In the meantime, Thomas had been allowed to stay with Jimmy and his family so as not to stretch an already thin system for orphaned children. Once Hodge was well enough, he would take over care for the kid. In fact, that was one of the reasons he was at the bar.

The reason he was there that night was twofold though. He would be discussing his adoption of Thomas, but he would also be meeting with Mary. Hodge hoped that another discussion about the future could be had, as well. But Mary was late, and Hodge feared that she would not show up. She said she forgave him, she said she'd be foolish not to, but maybe she was still sore. Even as he thought this, he knew it wasn't true. And to use Mary's words, he would be foolish to think it were. Hodge looked at his watch again. Besides, Mary was not that late.

Hodge watched the bustle of activity the Rose Club had to offer through the mirror. It was a much classier place than the dive he spent all those years drinking in before he was set to go on air. Behind him people danced, and unlike Sally and Eddie from the dive he used to go to, these people danced to the tune of the playing jazz band. And it wasn't just one couple, but a floor of them. Instead of Harold stripping his layers of clothes as he walked to a table, Hodge saw gentlemen escorting their ladies to tables. And they were all dressed to the nines. The waitresses did not look like they'd rather club you in the head, like Alice, but they were pleasant when bringing a drink.

Not only was the clientele a higher class, but the club's aesthetic was on a whole different level of classy. The booths were bound in a rose red leather, with glass partitions etched with a rose design. The carpet on the floor, no signs of wear and tear, held the same tasteful rose design as the etched glass of the booths. The rose theme could easily be overdone, especially at a place called the Rose Club, but in this instance, it was not.

He spotted Mary at the far end of the bar. She hadn't seen him yet, and Hodge took the time to look her over. A line from *Romeo and Juliet* came to mind, *Did my heart love till now?*

*Forswear it sight/ For I ne'er saw true beauty till this night.* Mary looked radiant, all done up in a pastel plaid dress. Compared to the other women in the club, Mary was underdressed, but by far, more beautiful than anyone else. Hodge knew he may have been biased in his assessment, but more than a few heads turned her way as she spotted him and headed toward him.

Hodge began to stand, but Mary hurried over and told him to sit.

"Let's go to a booth," Hodge said. He offered her his arm and escorted her to a table in the corner.

When they were seated, he said, "You look stunning."

Mary looked around. She looked uncomfortable. "I have never been here, and when I suggested it, I didn't think all these people would be so dressed up."

She looked down at her outfit.

"Mary," He waited until she met his eye. "There is no one else here tonight, but you and me. And you look beautiful."

She blushed. When Hodge put his hand over hers on the table, she blushed an even deeper shade of red.

"You look good too, Frank," Mary said.

He didn't. While the swelling in his lips and eyes had gone down, it was still visible in his eyes. The skin around his face was a sickly purplish yellow, and the lacerations on his cheeks and forehead were healing, but still held crude scabs that made him look more like Frankenstein's monster than the doctor that created him. The bruised fruit look of his face extended down into his torso, disappearing under compression wraps to keep his cracked ribs from moving too much.

"I don't," Hodge said.

"You look better," Mary said, but it came out as more of a question.

"I'll take it." They both laughed.

Any tension, or nervousness that they had been feeling melted away. He squeezed her hand. And her own nervousness seemed to be replaced by something else. Tears began to fill her eyes and flowed down her cheeks.

"Oh, damn." Mary dabbed at the tears with a cloth napkin from the table.

"Mary, what is it?" Hodge shifted forward and pain racked through his ribs.

Mary didn't seem to notice his wince of pain. She looked at him squarely.

"Frank, I'm scared." She went on before he could say anything. "What if we're moving too fast? Everything was so quick and sudden. When we first met on the street, I didn't like you very much."

"I think it's safe to say we got off on the wrong foot," Hodge agreed.

"Then, I watched as you performed the show. I saw something else. There was passion there, Frank. You said you hated the show, hated the scripts, the character, but you were there. In the moment, you became the Scarlet Scrapper. I think- I think that was when I started falling. When you asked me to dinner that night, I felt your need. I saw that you needed a connection, and I felt it as much as you.

"But I'm scared. I thought I was in love before, but it wasn't right. He wasn't right. With him it took me a good while before I felt comfortable enough to even tell him I loved him. I don't think I ever truly did. So, I'm scared now, because I feel it now. And, this time, there is no doubt in me. How can that be when I hardly know you?"

"It's because you know everything you need to, Mary. Your heart is telling you. My heart is sending the same message. I don't know how it hit so fast, but it did. Maybe it's the life and death situation we found ourselves in. Maybe it will wear off, but I don't think it will." Hodge thought back to the line from Shakespeare

228

that had come to him when Mary had walked in. "Maybe it's like Romeo and Juliet. Love at first sight."

"It is too rash, too unadvised, too sudden; Too like the lightning," Mary said.

"A fan of our bard Billy?" Hodge said and paused. The room seemed to quiet down. "Mary, I want to see where this thing takes us. I admit, I unabashedly leered at you in a lascivious manner when I first saw you, but in the short time we've known each other I have seen *you*. Not just your beauty. I've seen how smart you are. How fierce and strong you can be. I know it is sudden, but I also know that I have never felt this way before."

"Not even with Grace?" There was a hint of jealousy in her voice.

"Never. I love you, Mary."

"I- I love you too."

Hodge, fighting through the pain in his body, stretched across the table, and Mary met him more than halfway. They kissed. When they were finished, they sat back and enjoyed the music. It was a song that felt timeless, a song that felt like it could last forever.

# EPILOGUE

# The Adventures of the
# Scarlet Scrapper Will Continue

Hodge never would have expected to feel that good walking under that red neon sign again. The electric hum of the letters spelling out *Radio*, once something he loathed, now felt somehow like a comfort. Hodge took a deep breath and paused outside the door. He looked up at those letters now. His livelihood. His life. His body felt stiff from pain and the cold, and his stomach felt aflutter from nerves. He let the breath out slowly and, with a sheaf of paper tucked under his arm, pulled the door open.

He walked the long hallway and trailed a hand along the walls. His fingertips caressing the smooth stone. It felt like a lifetime ago that he had been there. In certain ways it was a different life. A less desired one. In ways, Hodge's life had become more complicated since the kid came into it. Before Thomas, Hodge had more freedom, but it was the type of freedom that in its own way had come with a chain. He had little responsibility and a lot of time. With that freedom, Hodge had no real purpose. Now, he had Thomas. Now, he had Mary. Now, he had happiness, or at least the start of it.

Hodge no longer loathed the days, the nights, himself. He had done something selfless. He had helped someone in need. Sure, he couldn't say he was perfectly happy, but he could say that he was starting to get there.

He walked through the heavy door and into the studio. The room burst into applause. It was just seven men in there, but to his ears it sounded like a sold-out arena. Hanging from the ceiling, where the cloud of smoke always hung, was a sign that read: Welcome Back Scarlet Scrapper. It was, of course, written in the deep red letters of the Scrapper himself. Hodge felt hot tears stream down his cheeks. He was not afraid to let them fall.

Bob and Billy Bradley clapped him on the back. The younger of the brothers pulled Hodge into an awkward hug, and Hodge, surprising even himself, hugged back. Jake Thompson, the show's narrator, shook Hodge's hand with so much energy that Hodge had to clamp his teeth shut as to not show the discomfort that jolted through his body.

The sound men, a clique all unto their own, came up next. They were the most awkward of the greetings, but each man welcomed Hodge back, and any residual tension seemed to fade away. Hodge was given a hero's welcome like he had never received before, not even when he came back from the war.

Last came Jimmy, who embraced Hodge longer and harder than anyone else, despite seeing him nearly every day of Hodge's recovery. Hodge patted his friend on the back and laughed.

"Jimmy, still in a bit of pain here," Hodge said.

"Sorry, Frankie." Jimmy let go and his smile was as wide as it could get. He held Hodge at arm's length and let out a satisfied breath. Jimmy nodded, a pleased look on his face. "Now we can get back to work."

"Sure thing, pally."

"We've been working on some new stories. I think you'll be happy with them." Jimmy went to the table where the microphones were and lifted a pile of scripts.

"Actually, I've got something for you too." Hodge held the sheaf of paper he had carried all the way there out to Jimmy. He was surprised by the spike in his nerves. Hodge had faced a lot in his life: a drunken, abusive father; fighters in the ring; a battlefield with bombs and guns going off everywhere; a mob boss; his new life with a kid; and his own demons. But none of that made him as nervous as handing that pile of papers to Jimmy.

"Just read it, pally."

Jimmy flipped to the next page. He didn't look up, and Hodge felt bile rise in his stomach. He couldn't stand the wait. He couldn't stand someone reading his work while he stood there.

"It was just a first try," Hodge explained.

But Jimmy held up a hand to silence him. He flipped another page.

"My God, Frank…" Jimmy looked up from the script. Hodge could not read his friend's face.

"It's bad?"

"It's… It's me!"

Hodge let out a laugh that felt half forced and half relief. Good or bad, the story, his script was out there now. "Of course it is. The Scarlet Scrapper has always been you. We were just too blind to see it. If you still want me more involved with the show, I'd like that."

Jimmy looked down at the script in his hands and then back at Hodge. He said, "This is perfect. Just perfect." Jimmy wrapped Hodge in another tight hug and whispered in his ear, "Thank you."

"Sure thing, pally."

"Hey," Jake Thompson said. "We going to get this show on the road, or what?"

Jimmy let go of Hodge and handed him that night's script. Hodge took it and stepped up to the microphone. He took out a cigarette as the theme music flared up. He lit it as Jake Thompson began the intro.

"The adventures of the Scarlet Scrapper. He hunts and fights for a better tomorrow. Enemies of America beware."

Hodge couldn't help but grin as his newest adventure began.

From the episode "The Counterfeit Caper" in
*The Adventures of the Scarlet Scrapper*
– April 24, 1943

**ANNOUNCER:** The Adventures of the Scarlet Scrapper.

**F/X:** A WHOOSH OF AIR FOLLOWED BY A PUNCH

**ANNOUNCER:** He hunts and fights for a better tomorrow. Enemies of America beware.

**Organ MUSIC UP**

**ANNOUNCER:** The Scarlet Scrapper is here!

**F/X:** A GUNSHOT FOLLOWED BY TWO PUNCHES

Organ MUSIC UP and FADE under Announcer

**ANNOUNCER:** Ride with the mysterious Scarlet Scrapper, whose identity is a secret to everyone, even our listeners at home… At least a secret until now. That's right Little Scrappers, it is the moment you've all been waiting for. In tonight's special episode in the Adventures of the Scarlet Scrapper, the Scrapper's secret identity will finally be revealed. Stay tuned.

**MUSIC UP and FADE under Announcer**

**ANNOUNCER:** In just a moment we will delve into a special adventure of the Scarlet Scrapper, his very first. That's right, folks. This is the unknown adventure that started it all, but first, maybe you're tired of eating the same boring cereal day after day. Well, if that's the case, maybe you want something with a marvelous taste. Something crunchy, something different, something delicious. Ask your mother to let you have the cereal you'll really love the taste of. Ask her for the big puffy cereal, Noble's Sweet Puffs, a nourishing part of a complete breakfast. Remind your mother to always look for the seal of approval on each box of Noble's Sweet Puffs. That seal tells her that Sweet Puffs are a pure product honestly advertised, and another thing, remind your mother that lots of grocers are featuring Noble's Sweet Puffs and bananas now. Ask her to get some of each next time she goes to the store. Try that delicious breakfast combination tomorrow morning. You'll think it's swell.

### MUSIC UP and FADE

**DOCTOR:** I'm sorry, Mr. Harvin, but I cannot deem you fit for service.

**SCRAPPER:** But doctor, you've just got to. I should have the right to fight for my country, same as anyone. I'm strong and fast. I know how to fight. I can do this great country proud.

**DOCTOR:** I am sorry, Mr. Harvin, Shane. I'm sure there are other ways for you to contribute to the war effort.

**SCRAPPER:** Sure, whatever you say, doc.

**F/X:** DOOR SLAMS SHUT FOLLOWED BY FOOTSTEPS

**SCRAPPER:** That's the third time I've been rejected. I've written to the government do-dads begging to let me serve. I've appealed and fought, but they just won't let me do my part.

**F/X:** GLASS SHATTERING

**F/X:** CLOTH TEARING

**SCRAPPER:** There, now that I cut out eye holes I can see them, but they'll never know my true identity. Somebody must stop that robbery, and since I'm the only one here, that someone is me.

**F/X:** RUNNING FOOTSTEPS

**SCRAPPER:** You there! Stop where you are!

**ROBBER:** What are you supposed to be?

**SCRAPPER:** I'm the one who is giving you one last chance to get out of here.

**ROBBER:** There are four of us, and only one of you. So, why don't you just scram!

**SCRAPPER:** I warned you.

**F/X:** PUNCH. PUNCH

**ROBBER:** (Groans)

**THUG:** Quit dancing around, fella. Make this easier on all of us.

**SCRAPPER:** You should have stopped when I gave you the chance!

**F/X:** PUNCH

**ROBBER:** There's still more of us than there are of you.

**SCRAPPER:** And it still doesn't seem fair for you.

**F/X:** PUNCH. PUNCH

**ROBBER:** (Groans)

**SCRAPPER:** That's one down, now to deal with the rest of you.

**THUG:** Forget this. I'm out of here.

**F/X:** RUNNING FOOTSTEPS

**ROBBER:** Wait for me! I'm not scrapping with this guy no more!

**SCRAPPER:** That's right. You better run, and don't let me catch you at this again. (pauses) Now, let me make sure no one is around so I can take this mask off. This may just be the answer. I can't fight on the war front, but like the doc said, there is plenty to do on the home front, and I think I may have just found my calling. Now, what to name myself? Say, wait a minute. What did that crook say? He didn't want to get into a scrap with me. And this mask, a piece of red, no, scarlet fabric. From this day forth, I will put myself in harm's way for the country I love. I will fight those who would compromise our mission of freedom overseas. I will be known as the Scarlet Scrapper!

*End of Excerpt*

# ACKNOWLEDGMENTS

I have to start by thanking one of my favorite authors, David Morrell. His friendship and advice have helped me greatly over the years. Without him there might have never been a Scarlet Scrapper. Also, Tom Stevenson and Bill Peace for being with me every step of the way. Their suggestions helped shape the book you've just read. Thanks go out to my editor Rod Gilley, he made the editing process simple and fun. Thank you, Bre. You came later in this journey, but you helped remove my blinders when it came to editing. I am so happy you are with me, always.

I want to thank all my students who created artwork of the Scarlet Scrapper. Their art will always have a place on my wall.

Finally, I want to thank all those writers who helped me escape into other worlds; worlds of heroes and villains, capes and cosmic powers, gods and monsters. Without these stories throughout my childhood, I am not sure I would have made it. Without these stories, all the stories in my head would not exist. Thank you.

# About Running Wild Press

Running Wild Press publishes stories that cross genres with great stories and writing. RIZE publishes great genre stories written by people of color and by authors who identify with other marginalized groups. Our team consists of:

Lisa Diane Kastner, Founder and Executive Editor

Joelle Mitchell, Licensing and Strategy Lead

Cody Sisco, Acquisition Editor, RIZE

Benjamin White, Acquisition Editor, Running Wild

Peter A. Wright, Acquisition Editor, Running Wild

Resa Alboher, Editor

Angela Andrews, Editor

Sandra Bush, Editor

Ashley Crantas, Editor

Rebecca Dimyan, Editor

Abigail Efird, Editor

Aimee Hardy, Editor

Henry L. Herz, Editor

Cecilia Kennedy, Editor

Barbara Lockwood, Editor

AE Williams, Editor

Scott Schultz, Editor

Rod Gilley, Editor

Kelly Ottiano, Editor

Carolyn Banks, Editor

Evangeline Estropia, Product Manager

Kimberly Ligutan, Product Manager

Pulp Art Studios, Cover Design

Standout Books, Interior Design

Polgarus Studios, Interior Design

Learn more about us and our stories at www.
runningwildpublishing.com

Loved this story and want more? Follow us at www.
runningwildpublishing.com, www.facebook/runningwildpress, on
Twitter @lisadkastner @RunWildBooks